T0012698

There are realities other than the mundane one we perceive. Its places, people and occurrences are inexplicable to rational scientific thinking and antithetical to our existence. Ancient lore, monsters, forbidden tomes, and diabolical cults are just the forerunners of the unimaginable entities who dwell in the cosmic void. They are coming for us: our world and our very minds.

Exposure to such horrors can lead to madness, but some bold souls must make a stand against these seemingly insurmountable odds. Defeating them will save the world as we know it; failure will usher in the end times. Can you hear the Call of Cthulhu?

CALL of CTHULHU.

The SHADOW
on the GLASS

JONATHAN L HOWARD

ACONYTE

First published by Aconyte Books in 2024

ISBN 978 1 83908 299 3

Ebook ISBN 978 1 83908 300 6

Cover art by 3 Bit Studios & Nick Tyler

Distributed in North America by Simon & Schuster Inc, New York, USA

Printed in the United States of America

9 8 7 6 5 4 3 2 1

ACONYTE BOOKS

An imprint of Asmodee Entertainment Ltd

Mercury House, Shipstones Business Centre

North Gate, Nottingham NG7 7FN, UK

aconytebooks.com // twitter.com/aconytebooks

For Dave Lockley,
A good and long-suffering friend
who likely deserves better than to have a
supercilious doctor named for him,
but he'll take what he's damn
well given, the ingrate.
I made you a doctor.
What else do you want?

CHAPTER ONE

THE SPIRITIST

Ectoplasm was the tattletale of the amateur. That was the opinion of William Grant, and hadn't he made a detailed and considered study of the phenomenon? Ectoplasm was, his opinion continued, trite and workaday and – worst of all – a mark of desperation. How poorly conducted must a séance be to require strands of extra-mortal material be produced to convince the sitters that the spiritist involved was worth the candle or, more exactly, the fee for the session? No, no, no. A properly conducted séance (note the acute accent) was, at its heart, a performance, and it is a poor performer who relies on props. Effusions of ectoplasm, accompanied by the undignified cacophony of rattles, tambourines, and trumpets played by an unseen ensemble, those might impress the yokels in the sticks and even the *petite bourgeoisie* in their homogeneous villas clustered in suburban cantons, but these were not the rabbits for which William Grant cared to set his snares. He preferred bigger beasts possessed of more rarefied sensibilities and substantially larger financial resources.

For an example, take the household of Mrs Iris Donnelly, a new widow of six weeks standing, and likely longer had she but known it. Six weeks since the Lutine Bell struck dolefully on the floor of the Underwriter's Room at the Royal Exchange to mark the loss of Her Majesty's gunboat the *HMS Bellevue*, overdue at Cape Town, presumed devoured by a squall somewhere down Africa's western coast. Six weeks now, and for forty-six more shall the black crape hang upon the pictures and mantels of the house, the mirrors remain covered, and Mrs Donnelly wear the weeds. It was a large house and well appointed, for Captain Donnelly was, as an aside, independently wealthy thanks to the investments of his father, which – by dint of being an only child –he had inherited only a couple of years before. But now he was gone, and his poor widow was not so very poor. After a decent period, there were plenty of bachelors who would be laying their suits at her door. Before then, however, Mrs Donnelly's worth would be decreased by a useful sum if William Grant had anything to do with it.

It had taken satisfyingly little work to gain an invitation; the reputation of Grant's enterprise was good among the chattering class, and this privately amused him – so subtle was the manner of criminality that he practised nowadays that new victims lined up to be fleeced just as sheep follow the shepherd. It was all, he had long since concluded, a matter of managing expectations. That, and having the best partner a chap in his line could possibly wish for.

He had carried out his preliminary interview with the prospective client, Mrs Donnelly, and been pleased to note in passing how well appointed and tastefully the house was presented. He also noted a couple of items of Catholic iconography (on display but in shadowed corners, faith and society being slightly at odds). He didn't care; if people wanted to believe in God or gods it was all the same to him, a vulnerability to the occult. An exploitable vulnerability. The interview had, otherwise, not been especially helpful. Mrs Donnelly was distracted by her abiding grief, and that was good in and of itself because the capacity of the distracted to accept the objectively absurd is so much greater. From the perspective of a reconnoitre into the blasted moor of her grief, however, it was useless, and Grant determined to be doubly sure of his background research. Lizzie was a wonder it was true, but he couldn't send her in without at least some ammunition.

Except, now that they stood on the doorstep of the house some five days later, she was not Lizzie. No, "Lizzie Whittle" was not a suitable name, nor even "Elizabeth Whittle", not for a spiritist renowned within the whispered conversations of the middle class. No, standing with Grant on that doorstep was no less than the new darling of the metropolis' darkened parlours, Miss Cerulia Trent. In her mid-twenties, fashionably coiffed, elegantly but not fustily dressed, understated jet jewellery, every detail was intended to project a quiet, otherworldly focus, right down to the careful softening and pumicing of her palms and fingers to remove every trace of her East End youth.

The door was answered by a middle-aged man, definitely not the butler and Grant read the situation immediately from previous experience. The servants had either been given the evening off and told in no uncertain terms not to be back until ten, or they were confined to barracks for the duration. This man was a friend, and Grant saw only curiosity in his face, not scepticism. Good. It was trite and uncomfortable if they had to trot out "negative emanations" from "unsympathetic minds" in order to put the kibosh upon a session. Lizzie could use a good sympathetic friend as a fulcrum to turn an evening to their advantage with such grace that it took an effort for Grant not to applaud at the sheer chutzpah of it. It was like being savvy with how a conjurer does a trick and yet still in awe at the flawless spectacle of expertise in motion.

Lizzie had always been good with people. Grant had seen that right from the first day he clapped eyes on her not even two years before. He'd not been long in the great city himself, and had almost instantly got himself the nickname of "Manchester" among the crowd within which he moved, out in his first digs in Spitalfields. It was not a nickname he wanted to keep. He'd left that northern city under, if not a cloud, then certainly a light mist of suspicion. Manchester Police's detective division was starting to take an interest in his activities, and that was bad enough, but when he dabbled in quack medicines, he discovered too late that he had stumbled upon the personal *bête noire* of the great man himself, Detective Inspector Jerome Caminada. Caminada regarded quacks with a biblical loathing and, when Grant heard that he'd been asking around after his modest enterprise, Grant was off to Manchester London

Road Station the next morning with a hastily packed trunk to buy a one-way ticket to the capital. A Mancunian born and bred, he hated to leave, but if there was one corner of Manchester that he had never yet experienced it was Strangeways Prison, and he would forego the pleasure of its hospitality all his born days if he had any say on the matter.

It had taken time and elocution lessons, but he no longer sounded Mancunian except in extremes when he might forget himself. Now he possessed a generic sort of London accent at which no one in that city would raise an eyebrow. He hated it – the accent sat in his mouth, throat, and sinus like a fistful of gravel – but it was camouflage. He hoped for the day when he was wealthy enough to go elsewhere, drop the pretence, and start enjoying vowels again. He just hoped that he hadn't entirely forgotten how to sound like a normal human being by then, and would not be forced to spend the rest of his days as a Londoner.

Elizabeth Whittle, by contrast, had been born in the East End, and when he first met her he had called her a cat because she yowled and spat so much. She wasn't working the streets yet – a small miracle given her looks – but he could see that it was on the cards, and he decided on an impulse to take her under his wing. The act turned out to been more brotherlike than he had at first anticipated and, somewhat to his own surprise, he had never taken her to his bed. Soon enough, their relationship settled into those platonic lines, and he realised that he never would, a resolution that bemused him more than it disappointed.

For her part, Lizzie was an adroit pupil, shedding her

own accent for something more refined far more easily than he had abandoned his own. What especially engaged him, however, was her way with people. It went far beyond simply being affable or approachable; she showed a, sometimes disconcerting, aptitude for reading people as easily as if they had stuck a scrap of paper bearing their intentions and inner thoughts upon their foreheads in a particularly frank parlour game.

"Regular Sherlock Holmes, you are, girl," he had once said to her.

"Lay off!" she replied, laughing. She didn't laugh often, the metamorphosis from Lizzie Whittle to Cerulia Trent having made her more serious and self-contained, and so he valued that sound.

As they were led into the Donnelly manse, the silence of the house weighed upon Grant, the air of an endless wake afflicting his nerve and, not for the first time, making him wonder how doggedly the Metropolitan Police might pursue harmless purveyors of useless medicines. But that was him; Lizzie – *Cerulia* – bloomed in that atmosphere of enduring grief; her eyes brightened, and she looked around the gloomy hallway – darkly and dirtily panelled a century before and the walls disfigured with unremarkable prints of assorted naval vessels – and smiled slightly as if she could see friendly spirits upon the parquet and stairs. The family friend paused to look at her curiously, and she turned her smile upon him.

"This is not such an unhappy house, I think. The dead are not resentful." She closed her eyes and then opened them a moment later, focusing squarely upon the man's own. It was a simple tactic, pure stagecraft, yet subtly mesmeric in its effect. "I think we may well find Captain Donnelly tonight."

These latter words made the man blink and frown, and Grant instantly knew that all was not right. Lizzie must have, too, but she maintained her serenity because Lizzie was never aught but a marvel, and could show grace under pressures that would buckle a diving bell.

"But the intention... which is to say, the *purpose* of this evening's meeting is not to speak to the captain," said the man.

Grant raised an eyebrow. Inwardly, he stormed. He had spent days researching every publicly available fact about Captain Ernest Donnelly, late of the *HMS Bellevue*, late of this world. He knew his service career, his club, his family, his schooling, his interests. Ye gods and little fish, he knew Donnelly's shoe size thanks to a chatty cobbler. He had rendered every fact onto lists written in clear block capitals, and Lizzie had sat and read them through time and again until she could rattle off anything with which he tested her. All that effort, and all for naught.

That is what he felt. What he said was, "Oh?"

At that moment, Mrs Donnelly entered the hall with a brace of spinster friends in tow. "Mr Grant!" she said, a far more alert creature than the one he had interviewed a few days before. She looked at Lizzie. "And you must be Miss Trent? I am so glad that you've come. I have heard such wonderful things about you!"

"Mrs Donnelly," said Grant, "I think we must have been speaking at cross purposes when last I visited. I was given the impression that you wished to communicate with your husband?"

"Oh!" Mrs Donnelly considered this. "Did I say that?"

Grant thought back on it, and his heart froze. No, he didn't remember her being so specific now he turned his mind to it. He had assumed that was what she wanted based on her recent bereavement, and had taken every reference to "him" to mean the lost captain. Now it transpired that the séance was for some other random soul of which they had no prior intelligence. It could be her childhood puppy for all they knew.

"Ah," said Miss Cerulia Trent blandly, "then there has been an unfortunate misunderstanding. I have spent the last day or two attuning myself to find your husband."

Grant could have kissed her. She was buying time to arrange for another session during which the mistake could be repaired.

Except... no, that wasn't Cerulia Trent's plan at all.

"But," she continued, gifting Mrs Donnelly a strange, dreamlike smile, "paradoxically, James is closer still. I can offer no guarantees as to the clarity of communication, but..." the smile faded and Trent's eyes – it was impossible to think of her as Lizzie Whittle when she was like this – lost focus, seeking out a higher plain just beyond the veil, "... he is here."

Grant wracked his memory. James? That was the name of the Donnellys' older son. Their younger, Reginald, was currently away at boarding school. Yes, James had died, what? Two, three years ago?

"He will not enter into me," said Trent, her eyes closing, her forehead furrowing. "He is… diffident. Apologetic. I will speak as he speaks, an echo. I…" Her face slackened, and her eyes opened, exposing only whites. One of the spinsters behind Mrs Donnelly gasped at the sight. "*Mama.*" Her voice had become oddly toneless, the voice of a somniloquist. "*I am so sorry. Can you ever forgive me?*"

"James?" Mrs Donnelly said in a ghastly whisper. "Is that truly you?"

"*I should have said no to Papa. I would still be here for you now if I had.*"

"Your father always had to have his way," said Mrs Donnelly. Grant saw the tears start in her eyes and part of him curdled. He hated it when they cried, but he always forgot how much he hated it after their cheques cleared, only to be reminded the next time. "Now the sea has taken you both from me."

"*It was the yellow fever, Mama. I caught it when we went ashore at Maceio.*" A ruminative pause. "*I thought I was getting better.*"

"He took you from me!" She was crying freely now. The spinster who had not gasped stood by her and put her arm around her. "Stupid, stupid man! He always had to have the last word!"

"*Papa knows he was wrong.*"

Mrs Donnelly looked up suddenly at this.

"*He will not speak. He carries his own purgatory with him. I have forgiven him. Please, Mama, you must forgive him, too.*

He only ever wanted what he thought was best for me, and that was to be like him."

"I cannot," she said in a small voice. "He has taken too much from me."

"Then think of Reggie. He is blameless in all this. Think of his future. I shall watch over you both, always, and so shall Papa. What is done is done. Please allow for my hope that, one day, you will forgive him, too. I love you, Mama."

Miss Cerulia Trent blinked and, when she did, her eyes ceased to be so alarming. "He's gone," she said faintly. "May I sit down?"

William Grant didn't know whether to be delighted, angry, or terrified, so he settled for astonished. They were in a hansom on its way to the Kensington house where they both had rooms. Miss Trent had neither offered nor been pressed to repeat the experiment, and the next hour had been occupied by a gathering in repressed spirits while the little visitation had been discussed. Miss Trent had, he had noted, got in quickly with an explanation that the late James Donnelly had not communicated with her in words exactly, so she had interpreted his intentions into the clumsy mode of mortal speech, thus forestalling any pettifogging complaints as to "That is not how he used to speak". As it was, Mrs Donnelly said that was *exactly* the way James used to speak, and this was confirmed by those of her friends who had known the man in life.

"There weren't nowt in what I wrote about yellow fever, Lizzie. Where'd that come from?"

In the oblique light from the streetlights as the hansom rattled along, he could see her profile and that she was smiling. "You're talking like a northern barbarian again, Bill Grant," she said.

She was right, which didn't improve his temper. He realigned his speech into the hated mode, and tried again. "Don't change the subject. How'd you know about the yellow fever? And wherever he caught it?"

"Insurance. I went to the library and went through the newspaper archive. You read the captain's death announcement, didn't you? The one for James is *very* different. Chalk and cheese. The one for James is much more personal. Flowery, even. Losing him broke his mother's heart. Captain Donnelly's loss was presented as dry as sand in the Sahara."

"And it mentioned yellow fever?"

"Oh, no. Just a fatal sickness. So I dressed as a scullery maid looking for work and got chatting with their butler at the back door. He was *very* helpful." She laughed a half-laugh that emerged from her nostrils as a derisive snort. "Men are such awful gossips."

"You did *what*?"

"I got the job done, didn't I? Told me about the old man bullying his son into the service, and then what killed James in Brazil." She reached into her reticule and produced a small bag that chinked pleasingly when she shook it. "No idea how much is in here, seemed rude to ask at the time, but it's gold. Certainly worth the effort we expended to get it."

"Lizzie bloody Whittle." He shook his head. "You're a prodigy at this game."

"The name's Miss Cerulia bloody Trent," she replied and there was a smirk in her voice as she said it.

The house in Kensington was cosmopolitan enough that smelling salts were not required at the sight of a single woman entering the apartments of a gentleman, or vice versa. Grant preferred to visit Miss Cerulia Trent than have her visit him, as he felt his rooms were, at best, utilitarian and, at worst, boring. He had never quite got the hang of decoration. There were some bits and pieces of exotica that he had bought off market barrows with the hope that he might seem travelled and worldly-wise, but there was no coherence in his choices and the effect was of somebody who'd just randomly bought a lot of things off market barrows. He had also bought a collection of eighty year-old hunting scenes and hung them around the place, having thought they might lend it some old world gravitas. The first time Lizzie, which is to say *Cerulia*, had clapped eyes upon them, she had said nothing but only given him a sideways glance that he did not like at all. Now, the ludicrous men in their hunting pink, jumping over hedgerows on anatomically unlikely horses embarrassed him, and it was only the spectre of blank walls that prevented him selling them again. He needed something better, but what constituted "better" evaded him in his wounded aesthetic.

The rooms of Miss Cerulia Trent, in comparison, were lavishly appointed and perfect as a consultancy space for those clients that wished to come to her. Gewgaws and bric-a-brac from Rome to Tokyo clustered the surfaces and the walls, silken embroideries draped the furniture which itself was tastefully outré and more than enough to satisfy any visitor that they were in the den of an impressive intellect out of the norm. That it had all been selected by a former market girl out of the East End with no formal education but yet possessed of a quick, resourceful, and hungry mind may have amused Lizzie. It certainly amused Grant, who had appreciated from an early age that the greatest asset of the upper echelons lay in their inherited wealth and the opportunities it offered, not in their breeding such as it was.

Grant liked those rooms. Sitting there amidst the artefacts of a dozen other cultures, he felt somehow transported himself, and that beyond the heavy velvet curtains upon the windows lay something greater and more unfathomably exotic than a grimy city full of coppers who would have him up before the beak in a heartbeat if they should even once get an inkling of what he was up to.

Lizzie was standing before the guarded fireplace, looking at the brass Buddha that sat there on the mantelpiece beside a quietly ticking French carriage clock. "Do you believe in God?" she asked suddenly.

Inured to her odd little moments of philosophical inquiry, he replied, "Yes", instantly.

"Why?"

That stumped Grant, for the honest answer would have been, "Because everybody else does", but that didn't strike him as very satisfying even to himself.

Lizzie watched him struggle in unfamiliar territory for a few seconds before saying, "What sort of kind, benevolent god would have killed James Donnelly like that, and driven a wedge between his father and mother such that she could hardly give a tuppenny damn when her husband died?" She touched the cheek of the Buddha with her fingertip. "I sometimes think the Buddhists might be onto something, you know. What goes around comes around."

"Is that what they believe?" said Grant, who had no idea what Buddhists might think, or even where on the globe he might find Buddhaland.

"It's a little more complicated than that, but in essence, yes."

"Well," said Grant, rising and helping himself to a sweet sherry from the unlocked tantalus as it was becoming evident that Lizzie wasn't going to offer him one, "given what we're up to, it's probably just as well that they're wrong."

She looked at him. "So, you prefer Hell?" He had no answer to that, either, so she added, "To the Buddhists, life is a treadmill to become divine. To them, we're already living in Hell."

Grant busied himself with his glass; there was no talking with Lizzie when she was being so very Cerulia. "They may be onto something, there. Drink, Lizzie?"

She shook her head. "Divvy up the take, Bill, there's a love. I'm tired."

He took the bag from her reticule and emptied it onto the table. He whistled at the sight of so many gold sovereigns before starting to separate them into two equal mounds. There was an uneven number, and he slid the spare to Lizzie's stack without hesitation. The evening had gone from near disaster to unexpected triumph thanks to her after all, and William Grant was the fairest of criminals. "How are we going to move next with Mrs Donnelly? Have you got anything in mind?"

Lizzie shook her head. "For her, nothing. If she invites us again, I shall regretfully tell her 'no'. Her son has moved on to a better place and her husband is too ashamed to ever speak to her again. She still has Reginald and should concentrate her efforts on raising him properly. At some point, her anger with her husband will fade and then her grief will open like a wound. Her suffering isn't over yet. We won't add to it."

Grant scooped up his share and put it in his pocket. "Is that a conscience you're getting, girl?"

She turned to face him, crossing her arms. "I've never lacked for one, Bill Grant. And nor have you. I saw your face tonight. Next time, let's stick to people what have got it coming, eh?" She considered her words. "I mean, let's stick to people that have it coming. Bloody hell, I'm sounding like I've just walked off selling oranges in the halls. I truly am tired. Go on, Bill, sling your hook. I need some sleep before I forget how to be Cerulia Trent altogether."

Grant laughed, but accepted the cue gracefully. He drained his glass, gathered up his overcoat and hat and went to the door. "Not you, girl. You're a natural. But I know what you mean. Let's make our pile and go and do something that won't get the boys in blue excitable, eh? Mayhap we should leave London, hmmm? Try our luck in France."

Lizzie smiled and shook her head. "You and bloody France. You don't even speak the lingo."

"I speak a bit of the *parlez-vous*," he said, stung.

"You'll need more than a bit if we're going to be the wolves over there and not the sheep." She looked off into the middle distance. "Maybe I could learn it."

"Maybe you could," said Grant, confident that she probably could and would certainly have a better accent than him, but mainly pleased that she was at least accepting the possibility of falling upon the monied French. He'd heard stories of Gallic wealth that he wished to test and, in any case, it felt more patriotic to rob foreigners.

She read him as easily then as she read any of the other books she had amassed in the adjoining room it pleased her to call her library. "No promises, Bill Grant, but maybe a change of scenery wouldn't be so awful. Now clear off. Madam Cerulia Trent requires her beauty sleep."

CHAPTER TWO

TWO VISITORS

And so this was the nature of the business of Miss Cerulia Trent and Mr William Grant: immoral, certainly; lucrative, definitely; criminal... well, perhaps not. For they never asked for money, trusting to the strictures of social nicety to bind their clients as tightly as a leather stock. The middle class was famously obsessed with money and, equally, very keen not to talk about it. The citizens of Kensal and Finchley were not vulgarians who bragged about their wealth. They were not buccaneers or Americans. Wealth was to be assiduously garnered at well-nigh any cost and, once acquired, it was to be a source of mild embarrassment. Only the nouveau riche might be expected to make a song and dance about it, but who wanted to be the nouveau riche? Nobody, least of all the nouveau riche. So, there was form to observe, and one such was that a service should always be paid for, even something as extraordinary as speaking for the dead. Thus, bags of sovereigns, hastily scribbled and uncrossed cheques, even jewellery found itself in the hands of Miss Trent and Mr Grant. They, for their part, only acknowledged these offerings with a pained little nod that seemed to say, "But that we could eschew this earthly lucre, but alas! We needs must keep a roof above our heads and food in the larder. Oh, gross world of materiality, that we are reduced thus!" And then they went home and drank champagne.

That these were offerings freely given without importuning was an important point, the kind of important point that makes the counsel for the defence very happy. Even a barrister wet behind the ears and possessed of a pristine wig could easily make the argument that a gift freely given can in no way be regarded as having been extorted by foul means. Is there a world of spirits with which Miss Trent might communicate? Prove that there isn't. Is Miss Trent "possessed" during these sessions? She claims not, only that she hears voices and repeats what they say. Who can say that she is lying? Plus, all those vulgar drums and bugles, and effusions of ectoplasm that prove to be only bleached muslin, she has no truck with such flummery. She and her reputation are reliant only upon what she says, and what she says carries weight with her listeners. This is why they reward her, and if there is a crime being committed here, it is as intangible as the spirits that may or may not attend Miss Trent. Is it a séance, or only a performance of a séance? So many uncertainties, all too feathery to convince the stout English yeomen who make up juries. In any case, so delicately whispered was the business of Trent and Grant among the comfortably well-to-do of London, that it seemed very unlikely to ever make its way to the indelicate shell-like ears of the rozzers, and that was to the good.

The only people who might report them were their clients and, as their clients were apparently as pleased as anyone communing with the souls of the recently dead might be, that seemed an unlikely direction from which to be chirped, which is to say, informed upon to the police.

This then, was the state of affairs, as Trent and Grant gently absorbed money from people who could afford it, in return for a little performative grief counselling. Everyone was happy, or at least, as happy as the tragedy of bereavement ever allows. They might have carried on slowly and patiently turning tears into gold indefinitely, or at least until they grew weary of it and decamped to the Riviera to practise some new wheeze upon the French, but for events that began with Grant meeting a troubling man upon the doorstep of the house in Kensington as he was about to leave for his lunch one day.

He opened the door to find this man studying the plate on the gatepost. His first impression was mixed, but little of it was good. The fellow was not tall, perhaps an inch or two over five feet, and as muscular as a boxer; Grant could see how his build wrestled unhappily with the serge suit he wore like an imposition, his wardrobe completed with a pair of brown boots and a bowler upon his head, its brim curled to the degree that the unfashionable found fashionable. The man himself was home to a full beard, the signs of a fading tan, a disturbingly intense stare, and – "Are you Mr William Grant?" – an interesting accent.

He didn't look like any sort of police officer Grant had ever seen before, so he replied, "Yes, I am he. How may I help you?"

The man didn't answer at first but looked up and down the street. It was not an unpleasant street, nor even a thoroughfare, but the man did not like it, and the street did not seem fond of the man either. He struck Grant as a creature of the wide, open spaces, and the encroaching stone and brick of the metropolis imposed upon and contained him. "I was just going out," said Grant, "but I can spare you a few minutes. Would you like to come in?" The man nodded and entered out of the day, visibly relieved to do so. Grant led the way up the stairs, and did not enjoy a single step of it. He had seen men like this often enough in his life, quiet men for whom violence was only a chore, but a chore diligently performed even unto the sticking point. If a bookie had appeared on the landing and offered Grant evens that the man was carrying a blade that was something more than a pocketknife, he would have accepted the bet instantly. The walk up to his rooms had never seemed so long as it did with his back exposed to such an individual.

Yet when they reached Grant's rooms and he showed the man into the one he used as his office, the man was diffident, taking off his bowler in a spasm and wringing the rim in his hands as he spoke. "Thing is, it's like this, Mr Grant. You represent that medium, don't you? Miss Trent?"

Grant smiled. "She wouldn't like it if she heard you call her that. She prefers *spiritist*."

"But she can talk to the dead, can't she? That's what my governor heard."

On the doorstep, Grant would have been hard pushed to definitively identify the man's accent from those few words. South African, perhaps. But now he had more to work with, he was confident that the fellow was Australian. The Australians were a race distilled from boated criminals back in the day, so perhaps he had been unfair to identify this man as one. A man can't help his forebears, after all, and some apples do drop far from the tree. Australia, he was told, had been transfigured from a midden heap upon which the Empire emptied its gaols into a bountiful land fecund with opportunity, natural resources, and a variety of venomous creatures. A wise, hardworking man who made the most of the former while avoiding the latter might do very well for himself. This train of thought also led Grant to recall newspaper stories that he had read in recent months and drew him to the conclusion that he might well know who the man's "governor" actually was.

"She hears voices, that's true, and the evidence indicates that they are likely to be the voices of the dead. Beyond that, she won't make any claims." Somewhere, a hypothetical counsel for the defence applauded such equivocalness.

"The governor's heard good things about her, that's all. Y'see, he lost his missus a couple of years ago and… well, he ain't never really got over it." He ranged that disturbing stare upon Grant once more and Grant suddenly started wondering again if the man was armed. "He just wants some comfort. To know she's all right in the other place. Your Miss Trent, could she do that for him?"

"She could try, but you must tell your master that there are no guarantees in experiments such as this."

"He knows that. Oh, and he asked me to ask you what the fee would be."

"There's no fee – Miss Trent does what she does to help people. That's not to say there are no expenses to cover and everyday bills to meet, but we depend on gifts for those. If your master wishes to contribute, it would be gratefully received, but it's not mandatory. There'll be no invoices or receipts."

(*No physical evidence of fraud,* added the hypothetical counsel in Grant's imagination, nodding his approval.)

"Well, then, will she visit?"

"Visit who and where?"

The man reached into his breast pocket and produced a card. Grant read it and was in no way surprised to find it belonged to Sir Donovan Clay.

It could hardly have been anyone else, given the manner of herald he sent before him. Donovan Clay had gone to Australia as a youth and made the most of those opportunities, meandering from trade to trade until he had enough capital to start his own mining company. This company had prospered, and Clay had become prodigiously rich. Finally, in his fifties, he had returned to the old country to enjoy the fruits of his labours, leaving the company in safe hands to continue to enrich him from afar. On his return, he had duly been knighted for his contributions to the economy of the Empire, but his horizons were not without their clouds. Shortly before leaving Australia for, in all probability, the last time, his adored wife of some ten years, Sophia, had been stricken by a sudden illness and shortly thereafter died. The tragedy had tickled the jaded palates of London society, and he had been in receipt of a blizzard of invitations on his arrival, a blizzard that only grew denser after his knighthood. The vast majority, however, were graciously declined. The great knight's heart was broken and might never be repaired. It was all too desperately romantic, and the gossip columns speculated gently upon it for some weeks until there was nothing left to say. Now Sir Donovan sat in endless mourning in his house in (Grant read from the card) Barking.

"It's usual for me to go over first for an interview, you understand, to tell Sir Donovan what to expect, to settle the time, to make sure that there's nothing that might upset Miss Trent. She's very sensitive, of course, and the oddest things can cause her psychic distress."

The man nodded. "I'll tell the governor. We can settle all that by telegram, right?"

Grant nodded. The man's diffidence had slowly evaporated as they had spoken, and the sense that Grant was sharing a room with a dangerous animal had returned to him. He wanted to be done with the man as soon as he could. "I daresay."

"That's settled then." He stuck out his hand. "Good to meet you, Mr Grant."

Grant shook it. "You didn't mention your name?"

"Me?" The man seemed bemused that anyone would want to know it. "My name's Lynch. Good day to you, Mr Grant."

Grant dined at the Plantagenet Rooms that afternoon, alone but for his thoughts and a steak and kidney pie. He knew he should have been delighted. He avoided all but the periphery of London's spiritualist community, eager not to be associated too closely with that covey of table-rappers and speakers-in-tongues, but even from that limited exposure, it was no secret that Sir Donovan was a promiscuous and generous patron of spirit media the Home Counties over. There was hardly a one of them who hadn't been invited out to the house in the fields of Barking to spew ectoplasm and intone unearthly verities in what they fondly hoped was something approximating the voice of the late Mrs Clay. Whatever Sir Donovan hoped to gain from these séances, however, he didn't seem to be finding it; lucrative though these events were, they were also singular. Grant had not heard of a single spiritualist being invited back. Not that those so blessed were so very unhappy about that; they were delighted by the size of the cheques they received for their troubles, and equally delighted that they did not have to trek out to the wilds east of the city again to a house that was generally agreed to be "off-putting". Considering most of them had, in Grant's estimation, the spiritual sensitivity of a leg of mutton, it was striking how many described the atmosphere of the house as unpleasant.

Perhaps, Grant thought, indulging in a sip from his half pint of brown ale, it really was haunted.

Later, he was to have reason to think the house in Kensington was haunted, if only by strange men intently reading the plaque on the door post. *Another client,* he thought and, assuming the friendly if slightly distant mien that he had developed for the role of a spiritist's agent, sometimes amanuensis, he made to greet the stranger. But the man turned to face him, and Grant had the very strong sense that the man wasn't nearly enough of a stranger at all.

"Mr William Grant?" said the man in a no-nonsense "Let's get the pleasantries out of the way" tone that Grant knew all too well.

It took a huge effort of will for him to only say, "That's me. How can I help you?" rather than the reflexive "Yes, officer" that lurked in the back of his throat. He knew the man, he felt sure, and the great deal of Lancastrian accent that had been squeezed into six syllables made it seem very likely he was from the streets of Manchester. This, Grant felt, did not bode well.

"Might I have a word, Mr Grant? Not here. Indoors, maybe."

"What's this about?"

The man sighed and showed Grant the palm of his gloved hand and there, cupped within it to avoid it being seen by passersby, was a Metropolitan Police warrant card. Grant's heart sank, though he did his best to hide his dismay. "Well, you'd better come in, I suppose. You can tell me there."

For the second time in a couple of hours he walked up to his rooms followed by a man he dearly wished wasn't there. As before, he led the officer to his office, and offered him a chair, which he declined.

"That's all right, sir. I wasn't planning on staying long."

"May I see your *bona fides* again, please?" said Grant, trying to sound extra southern via the deployment of Latin.

It seemed to work. "You what?" said the police officer, then, "Oh, me card. Of course."

Detective Sergeant N Bradley Grant read from it. "Thank you."

The name was all too familiar. Grant remembered walking across Albert Square in Manchester one day three years before with an acquaintance of dubious honesty, who suddenly stopped him and drew him to one side to avoid another brace of men walking by from the town hall. "That's Detective Jerome himself," whispered his companion, watching the pair as they went by, deep in conversation. "With another of his lot. Bradley, that one is. All as keen as mustard to fill 'is boots when the time comes. Word to the wise… you remember those faces and you avoid 'em, all right?"

Grant had moved all the way to London to do so, and a fat lot of good it seemed to have done him.

"So, what's this about, detective sergeant?"

Bradley looked at a phrenology bust sitting on a side table with obvious disapproval before replying. "You're in the ghost game, I understand, Mr Grant. You and Miss Cerulia Trent."

"Ghost game? If you mean we experiment in spiritualism, yes, that's true."

Bradley was looking around the room, and Grant began to wish that he hadn't lavished quite so much on its discordant decoration. The initial intention was that it should overawe visitors, but it was plainly provoking Bradley in quite another way. "Does very well for you, obviously." He looked Grant in the eye. "Must be very lucrative, these *experiments*."

"All contributions are voluntary. We have never asked for money."

"Don't need to, though." Bradley went off to glare at a framed chakra chart. "Do you?"

Grant began to understand what was actually happening; Bradley had no solid evidence of anything. His intention was purely to intimidate and leave Grant with no doubt he and Lizzie were now very much under the microscope. Bradley didn't especially care if he would ever be able to put them in the dock; he would be perfectly happy just to be shot of them out of his parish. This was starting to sound appealing to Grant, too.

"I am not sure I quite understand what it is to which you're alluding, officer," said Grant carefully, sure that if he tried to speak any more southernly, he would dissolve into a cloud of pure grammar.

"Yes, you do, sir. You understand very well." He walked over to Grant and studied his face carefully. "I feel sure I've seen you somewhere before, sir."

"Perhaps on the street?"

"I don't think so, sir. I've only recently joined the Metropolitan force. Previously I was in Manchester."

"Well, that can't be it. I haven't been in Manchester for a good many years," said Grant, "and even then it was only for a couple of days. Perhaps you're thinking of somebody else. I don't have a very distinctive face."

Bradley was silent for several seconds, and Grant knew with sickening certainty that Bradley was no longer trying to identify him, but committing his face to memory.

"I wouldn't say that, sir," Bradley said finally. "I wouldn't say that at all."

He hardly waited for Lizzie to open the door before he pushed inside and paced furiously up and down the floor. "It's over," he said distractedly, "they're onto us."

Lizzie closed the door and looked at him, worried. "Who? What are you talking about?"

"I just had a bluebottle I know from Manchester turn up right on the bloody doorstep and all but tell me to get out of town unless I want my collar felt."

"So, they've got no case. He's just fishing, Bill."

He stopped and glared at her. "And he'll keep on fishing until he has something that'll stand up. This feller, he has a chip on his shoulder, I'm telling you. Wants to make his mark, and he won't do that without arrests."

"And you know him?"

"To look at. He didn't know me, but he does now. This whole game, Lizzie, we could only play it when folk were being discreet. This Bradley feller, somebody's talked to him. How else would he know about us?"

"A brass plate saying, *Miss Cerulia Trent, Spiritist,* maybe?"

He thought about that. "No. It can't be that easy. Can it? He just read the plate and decided to run a stick along the railings on the strength of it?"

"You tell me. He's a detective with something to prove, strolls into town from some backwater–"

"Manchester's not exactly a backwater…"

"–and spots a chance to make a bit of noise. So, you tell me, does that sound like the kind of thing he'd do?"

Grant nodded. "Aye. It is that. Fact remains, he's got something to prove, and I don't fancy being the poor beggar he proves it on, and nor should you."

Lizzie sat down. "That much is true. He'll stick to our heels like fresh tar now. Sit down, Bill, you're making me feel tired."

Grant pulled up a chair and sat opposite her. "What are we going to do? I hadn't really thought what to do in such a happenstance. I always thought we'd be able to just pull the wool over everyone's eyes and make ourselves scarce if any sort of trouble blew along. But this geezer's going to make the whole town uncomfortable for us."

She shrugged. "Find a silver lining, I suppose."

"How'd you mean?"

She smiled a little wanly. "Maybe this is the world telling us it's time to go and trouble the French after all."

He could hardly hide his surprise. "You really want to?"

"It's not a terrible idea, 'though I would have preferred to be doing it a year or two down the road. I've been thinking about it. We need some bedding in time, and some flash to ginger up the plants, but I'm not sure we have enough gilt to do a bang-up job of it. Maybe we do, but it'd be tight. Not really the way I wanted it."

"Silver linings, eh? I might have one for you," and he told her about the visit from Sir Donovan Clay's man, Lynch. She was duly impressed.

"Clay's meant to be swimming in it, isn't he? Lights his cigars with ten bob notes?"

"*That* might be putting it strongly, but, yes, this place of his out in the east is supposed to be a big old house full of staff, spark pin in his silk cravat big enough to make a Dutchman stare, and more money in the bank than he knows what to do with."

"I have a few ideas what to do with it."

"Aye, me too. Lizzie, if we're going to go after Sir Donovan, we're going to have to make a bloody good fist of it, especially if he's going to part with any of his pile, never mind the sort of grab we're going to need for France."

"Don't worry about that. I had a feeling he'd come knocking. He's bothered every other table-rapper in town. He even had Mr Tolliver in, and you'd have to be born touched to believe a word Tolliver says. Paid him, though, and paid him well. Tolliver was strolling around like the cock of the walk afterwards."

"But Tolliver's an idiot."

"Exactly, and if the likes of him can do well with Sir Donovan, how do you think we might fare, eh?"

Grant considered this. He smiled. "Bonjour, France!" he said, employing the hardest pronunciation of "j".

Lizzie smiled to see him smile. Then she sobered. "But

we can't beat around the bush. This detective will be looking to make life difficult as quick as ever he can. You get a telegram sent for an appointment and get over to Barking. Find the lay of the land. I'll start finding out what I can about Sir Donovan. We'll give him a séance he won't soon forget. Then we're off and away, sharp as you like."

"Travel to Calais and then down to the Mediterranean, eh, girl?"

She nodded. "Supposed to be warm down there, isn't it?"

"Warm as toast, and full of old, rich folk, I'm told."

"Good enough. One thing, though, Bill. I don't want to do the spiritist game anymore, all right? Let's think of something different, eh?"

Grant was momentarily dumbfounded. "Change the game? But you're so good at it."

"Well, I'll get good at something else. I'm tired of dabbling with the dead, Bill. I've got me limits. I don't want to do it anymore."

He wanted to argue, but he couldn't find it in himself to do so. She really was so very good at easing the ghosts out from between people's words, it scared him sometimes, honestly and truly.

But there was much about their plan that lacked logic if he had cared to examine it carefully. It would make much more sense for them to share out their reserves and head in opposite directions, for example, but that thought had occurred to neither of them. The very fact that it hadn't, of course, was also the explanation for why it hadn't, but they couldn't see that, either.

And so, tied together by more than money and circumstance, they made their plans for the morrow.

Chapter Three

BARKING

The house of Sir Donovan Clay lay one train ticket and a mile's worth of shoe leather away. Grant didn't mind the trouble of a stroll, and he appreciated the chance to be out of town proper. Manchester was smoke and cobbles in its heart, but if you set your cap at any cardinal point and started walking, you would be out in fields within an hour. Much the same held true for London if you gave yourself closer to two hours, and Barking was the perfect demonstration of that. Close by the drop in the land that took one down to Barking Level, the marshlands by the Thames, Barking Town itself felt like any number of fishing villages that had unexpectedly swollen into something a bit grander by the flow of day visitors eager to see something other than bricks and chimneys that you might find anywhere around the coastline. That little warren of streets gave out quickly into open land, however; fields, and commons, their corners peppered with clusters of cottages, a few small farms, the occasional larger house, and even a windmill or two. One day, the hungry city would cover all of this. Grant knew, because it had already happened elsewhere around London in living memory. For now, however, you could look at the trees and the hedgerows and fool yourself into thinking it might last forever.

Sir Donovan's house was tucked away on a triangle of land cut from the corner of one of the great fields, bounded on two sides by less travelled roads on the northwestern and southern sides and to the rear by a deep copse of trees that was part of the house's estate with a dirt track to complete the triangle beyond. The roadsides and boundaries were hedged off with high box trees, penetrated here and there with garden doors, and on the south by two broad gates leading into a short avenue that led directly to the house.

William Grant did not regard himself as an overly sensitive soul, but despite that, his first sight of the house's upper floor glowering above the green of the hedge brought an unpleasant prickle to the back of his neck. It was a decently-sized stack, built – he guessed –no more than fifteen or twenty years before as a comfortable villa for somebody who likely worked in the City and who wanted a station decently close to hand while still buying himself some privacy. It was this latter aspect that troubled Grant, the way the house seemed resentful of everything, of every passerby, of even a passing glance. It crouched behind some additional half-hearted topiary like a wounded lion, and everyone who has ever indulged themselves in a penny dreadful knows that is the most dangerous sort.

On the other hand, he admitted to himself when the scope of his fancy brought itself home to him a moment or two later, suburban mansions were rarely known to tear apart strangers. Not around London, anyway. There were probably byelaws against it.

Grant read the name of the house on the gatepost – "Elmwood" – and noted as he approached the front door that there were several examples of those trees in the copse beyond the house. He did not need to draw the bellpull; the door opened as he reached the small portico and there stood Clay's man, waiting for him. "Mr Lynch," said Grant. "I'm a little early. I hope that's not an inconvenience?"

"No," said Lynch, ushering him into the hallway. "Early's good."

In truth, Grant had organised his arrival to be slightly earlier than was considered polite. Debrett's etiquette guide suggested ten minutes was ideal, and Grant had arrived almost a quarter of an hour early specifically to catch the household just that fraction unprepared. That Lynch seemed entirely untroubled suggested that the stratagem had failed. To the contrary, it was Grant who felt slightly rattled. Now he had received the impression that the house waited silently, its inmates in stasis, until such moment as anyone set foot beyond the gate, only at which point did they become animated. It was a silly fancy, but as he was led into the morning room, it was one that grew upon him. Elmwood did not feel nearly so much a home as an exhibit. He received no sense of it being a living place, but only a setting.

"Sir Donovan will be with you soon," said Lynch, and retired. A butler might have offered refreshment, and the oversight made Grant wonder if the house contained any staff in the usual sense, or did Sir Donovan surround himself only with people he had brought back from Australia? That would certainly align with the public perception of the industrialist as a "diamond in the rough". The phrase struck Grant as slightly ludicrous in this case; diamonds in the rough were usually in line to be cut and polished. Any social jeweller who tried that with Sir Donovan could only look forward to failure and, in all likelihood, a stay in the hospital – the great man being, by all accounts, as formidable in frame as he was shy of patience.

And here he was now. Lynch opened the door and stood aside to let through his employer. Sir Donovan Clay was, in person, rather more imposing than even his reputation had suggested. He was a big man, fair-haired and possessed of glacial blue eyes that studied Grant keenly as soon as he brought them to bear. Full-bearded, he had the air of some ancient chieftain about him, and the suit he wore seemed almost to creak with internal tensions as it sought to present at least a civilised layer of varnish upon a man who looked like he should be dressed in furs.

"This is Mr Grant, boss," said Lynch. "Feller who represents Miss Cerulia Trent."

"Mr Grant!" Sir Donovan smiled broadly. It was possibly the most threatening thing Grant had ever seen in his life, for it was not a friendly smile, but the rapacious grimace of a man who is pleased with what fate has brought him. "I am delighted you have come to visit us. You had no trouble finding the place, then? No? No! It's not so difficult if you pick up the right road from the station." He grasped Grant's hand to shake it, and Grant felt his bones protest under the pressure of that grip. "I have heard the most wonderful things about your Miss Trent. I am very keen to bring her here." The smile faded and Sir Donovan became serious. "My poor wife, you understand. I miss her terribly. I put great store by your Miss Trent to talk to her."

"Miss Trent does have a remarkable talent, Sir Donovan, but I must emphasise that there are no guarantees. She will do her utmost, of course, but if the conditions are not right... well, that's a great part of why I make these visits before time. Sometimes it's the simplest and seemingly least consequential things that can spell the difference between success and failure."

"As in life, so in death, eh? Yes, yes, I understand. Well, I am at your disposal for the next half an hour, Mr Grant. What do you need to know?"

Grant looked around the room. "Well, in the first instance, where is the experiment to take place? In here?"

"Experiment?"

"We avoid the term *séance*, sir. It has connotations that do not sit well with Miss Trent. We prefer *session* or especially *experiment*, as we work towards a more scientific understanding of what occurs."

"Science, eh? Well, that's good. I applaud your pragmatism."

"Of course, the most solid principle of practical science is the repeatable experiment, and even at this early hurdle, we stumble. There are subtleties at play that, in all candidness, elude us. We are blundering in the dark until such time as we start to discern the shape of the truth. Then we shall begin to make real progress. Perhaps one day we shall be able to talk to the departed as easily as we talk to one another, but until then, everything is experimentation."

Sir Donovan nodded with enthusiasm. "I like that. I like that! I am a very practical man, you see, Mr Grant. Everything I have, I have gathered by taking action, by bending my back, by taking it in my own two hands. You will understand, then, how difficult I find the field of spiritualism. I have heard so many talk to me about 'vibrations' and 'vital frequencies' and so forth, and it has driven me to distraction. Not that I disbelieve the sincerity of those using such terms, but by my own lack of comprehension of what they mean by that! Do you see? Science offers the promise of understanding, and I want to understand so very much. Why, I said as much just the other day to Lynch, here. Didn't I say as much just the other day, eh, Lynch?"

Lynch, standing quietly by the door, nodded. "Yes, boss."

Sir Donovan's fascination with science didn't come as a surprise given his background, but to hear it evinced in such energetic terms from a man large in body and personality was like witnessing a bear enthusing about the telegraph. It was amusing, and yet still somehow threatening.

"The room?" said Sir Donovan suddenly, snapping Grant back to the present with alacrity. "*This* room? Good Lord, no! Come along, my good fellow, I'll show you where I've chosen."

Lynch opened the door to allow Sir Donovan and Grant through, and then followed them to another door across the hall. Sir Donovan opened this one himself and swept in first. "The old dining room. I don't like it much, myself. Prefer to take my meals in my study, and we don't get many visitors out here to dine, do we, Lynch?"

Lynch agreed that they did not.

"My club's better for that. So, I just come in here to read now and then. I do like that sofa by the French windows, mind you. Sometimes a fellow just wants to slouch and read the paper, eh?"

Grant could see why the dining room wasn't often used. It was an odd, deep room, badly proportioned, with only the French windows to give it natural light. Away from the windows was a round table that looked like walnut to Grant's eye, with six chairs surrounding it. He walked around the table, noting candle sconces on the walls as well as gas mantles, but no chandeliers or similar descending from the ceiling. "Do you have any other sitters in mind, sir?" asked Grant.

"Sitters? Well, no. Just myself, Miss Trent, yourself, and perhaps Lynch here."

Grant shook his head. "I never sit at the table. I observe."

Sir Donovan looked at him strangely for a moment, then a light of understanding bloomed in his eyes and he smiled, wagging a finger at Grant. "Of course you do! The scientific method, eh? Somebody has to observe, to make observations and notes. Excellent! Excellent! Well, just me, Lynch, and your Miss Trent, then. Is that enough? Do we need more?"

"We generally get better results with more people, especially if they knew the sadly departed." He neglected to add that such people also acted as a well of trivial but telling details about the *sadly departed* that Lizzie was adept at drawing upon without them even noticing.

"Well, there's the household, I suppose. Brought all my own people over from Australia. All of 'em knew poor Sophie. How about that?"

"No family?"

"Hers? Few enough, and all in the Antipodes. For me, none to speak of." Then he paused and he smiled a quiet little smile that seemed very wrong on his face. "But for Great-Uncle Mathias. He's quite ancient and infirm, but I think he would want to be here for this." He crossed his arms and regarded Grant as if posing for a heroic portrait, only requiring a freshly slain tiger beneath his foot to complete the image. "Well, Mr Grant? Is all to your satisfaction?"

In truth, the dining room's ill-wrought form and the dimness around the table suited Grant very nicely; people were inclined to be very open – not to say gullible – to the possibilities of a shadowed world of the dead in the properly concocted atmosphere and the room could only aid in that. Still, he ummed and ahhed for a few moments. It never does to be seen to be too keen. "It should suffice, sir. The final arbiter must, of course, be Miss Trent or, more exactly, the spirits with which she attempts to communicate. I feel optimistic about this, though. Yes, I think so. You mentioned tomorrow evening?"

"No time like the present, or as near the present as is practical. Shall we say eight o'clock?"

With the time and venue agreed, Grant was prepared to leave, but instead Sir Donovan asked him to his study. There, he unlocked a drawer in a great mahogany desk, took out a chequebook, and wrote out a cheque to more than Grant was used to for any five "experiments".

"This is remarkably generous, sir," he said, eyeing the sum that, breathtakingly, was made out to cash. "Are you sure? We ask for no fee, nor even expenses, in most circumstances."

"Your dedication to science is admirable, Mr Grant, but it won't put food on your plate or a coat on your back. This endeavour is worth a great deal to me, and money is only money. Be assured that there is another cheque of equal size awaiting you after the session, perhaps more if all goes well."

Presently, Grant was once more beneath the small portico, rendered somewhat lightheaded by the figurative weight of gold embodied as a slip of paper in his breast pocket.

"See you tomorrow evening, Mr Grant," said Lynch, having accompanied him to the door. "Should be an interesting time, eh?" Grant had a momentary impression of the usually impassive Lynch smirking before the door closed with a final and dismissive click.

•••

Travelling back into London proper, Grant was already planning what his immediate actions should be with regard to realising the value of the cheque. By itself it would allow them to get onto the continent a few hours after they'd concluded their business the following evening. He was troubled with what to do with the promised second cheque, but that could be cashed possibly in Dover or in France. That said, he didn't like the idea of leaving quite such an obvious paper trail across the English Channel. Perhaps it would be better to leave more decorously the following day rather than haring out of the city like thieves in the night. He didn't relish those extra hours of vulnerability, but they really did need every shilling if they were to make a decent fist of it on the Mediterranean. Besides, it was quite possible that he was giving Detective Sergeant Bradley more credit than he deserved. Bradley might want to be a new Jerome Caminada, but the very reasons that Caminada was a legend were because he was so very clever, tenacious, and possessed of a terrifying memory. It seemed very unfair to inflict two Caminadas upon the criminal classes in a single generation. No, even Caminada himself was not omniscient, and Bradley was no Caminada. Grant was exaggerating the danger he represented, he felt sure. Another few hours, particularly hours spent away from their rooms, would present no threat.

So, what to do in the short term? Grant made up his mind to travel to Seven Dials, buy a money belt from Whittakers' the leatherwork shop, then visit the bank Sir Donovan had drawn the cheque upon, wait while they confirmed its authenticity (which he trusted wouldn't take long, having noted the presence of a telephone receiver in Sir Donovan's study), receive the money in lower denominations (hence the need for a money belt), and then finally go to Kensington to brief Lizzie on his day, suggest his plans for leaving the country, and check preparations for the session. A full day, but a profitable one that promised much for the future.

As is often the way with full days, however, matters started to go awry almost immediately. On leaving Whittakers', he noted a fellow across the way nonchalantly standing in a doorway and smoking a cigarette. The man wore a brown suit and a Homburg to match, but black boots, which Grant had considered a brave choice when he had first espied the man upon the platform at Barking. Now here he was, trying to look inconspicuous in the heart of the West End. Grant was decently sure it was the same man, but determined to test the proposition. Thus, he sauntered along the road, glancing in the windows as he went and finally managed to catch a clear glance of the man reflected in the glass, walking slowly up the opposite pavement, intently watching Grant. Grant continued a little further, directed his sauntering into the entry of a yard and, as soon as he was out of sight, galloped through the yard's opposite exit, down to the hub of the seven lanes, and back around.

He discovered his shadow looking gloomily into the now empty yard, scratching the back of his head in wonderment at this miraculous disappearance. Sidling quietly up behind the man, he said loudly in his ear, "Tell Mr Bradley he has to do better," causing the man to jump a few inches into the air. Grant gave the startled man the evil eye and walked away, watching his erstwhile pursuer over his shoulder. The man diminished as the distance grew, but made no further attempt to follow. Once he was out of sight, Grant doubled this way and that for some twenty minutes, watching the crowds carefully for recurring faces, for it wouldn't be the first time a wily copper had put some hopeless tyro of a plainclothes constable out as a stalking horse to draw attention away from more seasoned officers. If that was the case here, however, they were beyond his power to spot and finally, now running much later than planned, he made his way to Sir Donovan's bank to transact his business there.

Here, at least, he managed to make up some lost time as the bank had been forewarned by Sir Donovan to expect Grant and the money was rendered up with pleasing promptness. They didn't even raise an eyebrow when he asked for a room to borrow while he stowed it away into his new belt. Then he headed straight back to Kensington. It seemed pointless to employ a more roundabout route given that Bradley already knew where he roomed and would have the place under observation in all likelihood.

That was Grant's logic, but he could see no obvious watchers lurking around the street before the house. That meant nothing, of course; there was every chance that, if they really were the subject of determined police surveillance, it would be easy enough to rent or commandeer a room across the way to act as an observation post. Well, let them fritter away their precept on the endeavour; there were ways and means of getting a couple of steamer trunks out of a house unseen, and then he and Lizzie would be off and away, and damn Detective Sergeant Bradley for his impertinence.

Grant went straight up to Lizzie's rooms and was admitted smartly. She'd just brewed a pot of tea, and the two of them sat down to drink it while Grant laid out what he had learned in Barking, as well as his encounter with one of the Metropolitan Police's lesser heroes in Seven Dials.

"I don't tell you that to worry you, Liz," he said, "only to say that it's plain we can't stay in London, in case you were in any doubt."

Lizzie shook her head at the news. "The city's rotten with footpads and garroters and they waste their time with the likes of us? The world's a mess, Bill Grant. There's no goodness in it at all."

"Oh, I wouldn't say that," he said, and rose to remove the money belt. Her eyes bulged when he unbuttoned its pockets and showed the wealth within.

"What? He paid us up front? Oh, Bill, let's not bother going. Let's leave tonight. He's given us more than enough!"

"Oh, Lizzie, he's given us half of enough. This is just a down payment. We get the same again even if you say you can't find his wife to talk to. Imagine what we'll get for a good showing, eh?"

She looked at the notes and gold coins. "The same again? It's an awful lot. Oh, Bill, I don't like this. He's up to something. I can feel it."

"Up to something?" Grant scoffed. "Oh, come on, girl, it's not like you to get the morbs. He's a knight, after all.

He's got a long way to fall if he's not on the square. I'll be there, too, you know. There'll be other sitters, and even Sir Donovan's great-uncle. You'll be as safe as the Bank of England."

"It just seems different from anything we've done before. How did he strike you?"

"Who?" asked Grant, still thinking about Sir Donovan's great-uncle.

"Sir Donovan! What was he like?"

"Well, you've seen the pictures. Big feller. Bluff. Bit full of himself, if truth be told. But very keen to have the session! Properly enthusiastic."

"So, he loves his wife, Sophia?"

"He does. Called her 'Sophie', by the way."

"Talked about her a lot, did he? Still full of grief after four years of mourning? House full of black crape and pictures of her?"

Grant thought about it, and as he did, his own enthusiasm waned. "He hardly mentioned her."

Lizzie said nothing, but only regarded him as she sat with her teacup cradled in her hands.

"No black crape, neither. No obvious signs of mourning in the house. He weren't even wearing black."

"Fancy that," said Lizzie, and indulged herself with a sip of tea. "Sounds proper heartbroken, don't he?"

"Means nothing, Lizzie. Different folk mourn in different ways. He might be past the trappings. He just wants to speak to her, to say goodbye."

"Did he say that?"

Grant shook his head. He tried a different tack. "That money could be really handy, Liz."

She nodded at the open money belt lying on the table. "I thought what we have here was enough?"

"It is, but every bob extra makes life easier over the Channel. It's not like we're changing the plan. We're just getting on with it."

Lizzie sighed and looked into her cup as if the tea leaves showing shyly on the China might supply a definitive answer. "I know how daft it sounds, Bill, but I just don't think this gull is a right 'un. I asked around. Since he arrived in London, he's attended more spirit sessions than you or I have, and we conduct the bloody things! Leaves a trail of gold behind him that'd wipe the Queen's eye, but never, ever has a second session with the same medium. Don't you think that's proper odd? He pays so well, they're all as happy as sand boys, but never a return performance."

"Maybe they didn't give him what he wants?"

Lizzie shook her head dismissively. "Oh, come along! You know the kind of people he's had in! It's been nothing but tables rapping like a military tattoo, his wife speaking in as many accents as mediums... oh, and did you hear that Madame Petrovsky misheard when she was told the departed was Australian and put on an Austrian accent throughout? Mr Petrovsky looked like he would have welcomed death himself at that moment, and half of the other sitters could hardly keep themselves from laughing."

"My God!" Grant had not heard this tale. "How did Sir Donovan take it?"

"He thanked them for a very interesting evening and paid them in full! I don't understand it at all. He has a reputation of brooking no nonsense, of having no tolerance at all for fools, yet he laughs off a music hall act like the Petrovskys?" She looked earnestly at Grant. "He can't be such a great dunce, can he? He's up to something. He *must* be."

Grant rubbed his ear lobe while he thought it through. "The important bit of that story, Liz, is that he paid them. Look, just give me a minute…" He rose and went out. Three minutes later he was back. "Here, look at this," he said, and produced a small pistol of a hammerless design from his jacket pocket.

Lizzie looked at it dubiously. "You told me that you don't like barkers."

"I don't. That's why I usually leave it in its box. Hasn't been out since I bought it, except for cleaning. I just keep the thing for if there's trouble. I'll take it along tomorrow. I don't think there'll be any need for it, but if there is, well, I've got it to hand."

Lizzie was still staring at the gun. "I've seen more threatening nutcrackers." She looked him in the eye and smiled. "If Sir Donovan's such a big man as you say, you should take an elephant gun or the like."

"Don't be daft, Lizzie," he said, slipping the pistol back into his pocket. "An elephant gun would ruin the line of my jacket."

CHAPTER FOUR

THE SHADOW ON THE GLASS

Lizzie's habitual insouciance was less evident the following day and dimmed still further as the time to leave for Sir Donovan's house grew close. Grant hailed a hansom cab and held the door while Lizzie, now in the character of Miss Cerulia Trent, stepped aboard. Joining her, he directed the cabby to take them out to Barking and settled to watch the thoroughfares of early evening London go by in the deepening gloom. There was little conversation. Grant couldn't remember ever seeing Lizzie like this, as dour as an aristocrat in a tumbrel going off for a brief interview with Madame La Guillotine. He'd gauged the journey would likely take around ninety minutes and could see that it was likely to be a very long hour and a half for both of them.

Grant's apprehensions grew until he finally asked her, "Are you going to be all right, Lizzie?" as the cab rattled along the Whitechapel Road approaching Bow.

"I'm not Lizzie now," she said, watching an old soldier begging for beer money on the pavement. "I'm Miss Cerulia

Trent." She closed her eyes as if remembering a painful memory. "It's so difficult. Making myself forget who Lizzie Whittle is for hours at a time. I hate it Mr Grant. I hate it."

Grant noted the formality of her address. This was how she prepared for sessions, he knew, by not simply dressing the part, but by putting on the personage like a mask. He had never really considered how wearing that must be, but now it was impossible to ignore. "It's just the job, Miss Trent," he said, playing along so easily that it made him wonder if he, too, didn't so much assume the persona of Miss Trent's manager as have it possess him. Considered in that light, he could feel part of Lizzie's discomfort.

The road was busy, and the hansom stopped for a minute while a dray waggon manoeuvred into a side street, its path impeded by a trench opened by roadworks. Outside, guarding the works, was a night watchman standing by an iron brazier, warming his hands while he kept a weatherly eye on the dray. The cab's glass was grimy with smuts and dust and the watchman's shadow was plainly visible on it, rimed with the pale orange light of the fire. Miss Trent leaned back into her seat and nodded towards it. "Have you ever seen a shadow puppet show?" she asked Grant.

He thought back, and found a distant memory coated in the dust of inattention. "When I were but a lad," he said. Some hall or another, a show for the kiddies. A great white sheet of muslin hung up upon which appeared the silhouettes of angels and devils. A child being led out in fits of tears. He wondered if the child had been him. "Long while back."

"My papa took me to see one just off Piccadilly Circus when I was a girl," said Miss Cerulia Trent. "They had a big pane of frosted glass with limelight behind it. It was the story of Saint George and the dragon, I remember that. I remember the dragon. And I remember the shadows. Not just the ones you were meant to see, the puppets right up against the glass, sharp as anything. I mean the shadows that were blurred and could have been anything. The shadows of the puppeteers, of the sticks they mount the puppets on. All soft. Just hints of what might be casting them. I think of that puppet show when I do a session. That's how Miss Trent does what she does, I think. I think of the land of the living split from the afterlife by a great piece of frosted glass that no one else can see. That's how she's blessed. That's how she's cursed. And, when she looks at it, all she can see, all *I* can see are shadows on it, all smudged." She looked intently at the shadow of the watchman on the dirty pane as she spoke, touched the window with the fingertips of one gloved hand. "But they never come right to the glass so that I can see their silhouettes as clearly as I might. I'm glad about that, mind you. That's a mercy. If they ever reached it, why... why it's only glass, after all."

The dray had finally shouldered its way around the roadworks and was vanishing up the side street. The hansom moved on. Miss Trent sighed and returned her hand to the fox fur muff on her lap, a gift from Grant after their first successful foray into spiritualism. "This is the last time," he said. "The last time. I promise."

"I know." She looked forward past the horse, past Whitechapel Road, past Bow and the far horizon. "I know."

The roads approaching the house bore no lampposts and the hansom progressed by the light of its oil reflectors. They pulled up before the gate, and the cabman helped Miss Trent step down. "You'll have trouble finding another hansom out here, sir," he said to Grant. "Do you want me to wait?"

Grant thought on it. "We're likely to be in there a couple of hours," he said finally. "It's a long time to wait out here in the sticks."

"Oh, don't you worry about that, sir. If it's a couple of hours, I'll drive back to Barking Town, find a saloon bar for an hour or so, and then come out again to be here for you at, what? Ten o'clock? How does that suit?"

That suited very well for Grant and he thanked the cabby. He and Miss Trent watched the hansom rattle off down the rough, unadopted road. As it vanished from view, they were left in silence but for the soughing of the wind over the hedge tops and through the nearby trees.

"It's going to rain," said Miss Trent.

"Rain?" Grant looked at the bleak, empty sky and the stars that winked knowingly in the firmament. He adjusted his hat. "No, surely not."

The wind gusted and she drew her travelling shawl more closely around her shoulders. "There's a storm coming. I can feel it." She looked at him, and in the gloom, her wan face was ghostly. "Let's get on and do this, Bill. Last one, and we're done."

He didn't like the look of her, or the catch in her voice, but he just said, "Yes, that's a promise. If we're not in France by this time tomorrow, or at least well on the way, I'll want to know why. A new life."

"A new life." She echoed his words so quietly that he almost missed them. She drew a deep breath, visibly steeled herself, and said, "Then let's cut on, eh? Let's be done with this."

Grant opened the gate and allowed Miss Trent through, and further escorted her to the portico. He'd barely laid hand upon the bell pull when the door swept open and there was Sir Donovan Clay. "There you are! There you are! Capital! Please, Miss Trent, Mr Grant, please come in!"

There was a self-satisfied ebullience in Sir Donovan's manner that Grant did not like at all. In his experience, people stepping to the edge of that most final of mysteries did so quietly and with deference to their own mortality. Their host, in contrast, had the manner of the doorman to a particularly indecorous dance hall, and it did not sit well with Grant. He thought of how weighty that first cheque had been, however, and the prospect of one at least as lucrative, and used that future to steady his nerves. If push came to shove, he reminded himself, he had a pistol in his pocket and more than enough will to use it. But, of course, it would not come to that. It was all just nerves, after all.

Besides, the house was busier than he had anticipated. When Sir Donovan had suggested the circle would be small, Grant had taken him at his word, but the hallway and sitting room seemed to be full of men dressed in suits that were much more expensive than their wearers. Sir Donovan looked to have reversed the policy of transportation and shipped a good part of Australia's criminal class back to the Old Country. Grant had grown up on hard streets and knew thugs when he saw them, and he saw them now in proliferation. There had to be eight or nine of them. A small pistol now seemed markedly insufficient to Grant's needs; he would have preferred a Maxim gun.

"Our cab is due back at ten," he said suddenly, offering a wafer-thin assurance that they were known to be there and a fellow human being would be back to collect them from the house of Sir Donovan Clay. Grant was not sure why he felt so much on the back heel. After all, Sir Donovan was a knight of the realm. He certainly wouldn't stoop to any criminality, surely? An absurd sort of straw to grasp at, but Grant's nerves were on edge. It was impossible that they were in any danger. What could a man like Sir Donovan possibly have to gain? No, it was ridiculous. He had simply allowed himself to be influenced by Lizzie's misgivings. All would be well. Of course it would.

"Ten? Oh, we'll be done long before that, I expect," said Sir Donovan with disquieting certainty and a fierce grin that seemed very much out of place at a séance. "This way! This way!" And so saying, he led the party into the long, deep dining room. Grant tried to catch Miss Trent's eye, that he might somehow speechlessly communicate to her that, if she could perhaps affect the appearance of a case of the vapours and spend the next two hours upon a chaise longue having smelling salts wafted under her nose, this would be the ideal time, but she looked around the room and at the other sitters as they processed into the dining room, and never once at him.

Grant's state of mind was not improved at all by the discovery that this room was not as it had been during his interview with Sir Donovan the previous day. The small, homely dining table was gone and in its place was an oval monster of dark mahogany, around which there were twelve chairs. The chair placed at the head of the table, furthest from the window, was a prodigious high-backed thing, more suitable for a cardinal than a spiritist. Despite that, Miss Trent was shepherded into it, and now, rather too late in proceedings, she sought out Grant with her gaze. The helplessness in her face broke his heart, but events were plainly too far advanced for an outbreak of procrastinatory histrionics. All he could do was try to will her to manage no great feat that evening, simply to say that the ethers were disturbed and any experiment was doomed to failure.

Even as he thought it, thunder boomed, and he jumped slightly, amusing a couple of the hirelings. He didn't care – there was a storm coming on, and rapidly, too. He could hardly believe it, but the wind was rising, and he could hear the trees whispering agitatedly amongst themselves beyond the French windows. Miss Trent – *Lizzie* – had been right after all, although he'd never seen a storm develop like that before and it troubled him.

Sir Donovan had absented himself from the room, but

now he returned, escorting a curious figure, an ancient swathed in bed robes and blankets. The figure was almost doubled over, and moved slowly and with difficulty, Sir Donovan chivvying it along with the gentle imprecations one reserves for an elder family member. "Here we are, uncle," he said, and he had that devilish grin upon his face the whole time, "we're all gathered together for a lovely séance. Isn't that capital, hmmm? We shall see what we shall see, hmmm?" He looked sideways at Grant. "My Great-Uncle Mathias, sir. He may not be as nimble as he once was, but his mind remains sharp, and he does hate so very much to be left out of proceedings."

Grant noticed that the hirelings uniformly grew more sober at the appearance of Sir Donovan's great-uncle, and those who were closest moved away. Not, he thought, entirely out of deference.

The ancient, obscured but for a peep of nose and chin beneath a voluminous nightcap, was duly installed in the chair to the right of Sir Donovan's own seat, directly opposite where Miss Trent sat so that his back was to the French windows. Sir Donovan drew back that chair but addressed Grant before sitting. "You may sit over there, Mr Grant, in my reading chair." He gestured to the armchair close by the windows. "Is that all right?"

Grant forced himself back into his role. "Perfectly so, Sir Donovan. My part is to observe, after all. That, and to assist Miss Trent should she suffer any form of distress. It's rare, but we must be prepared."

"Indeed so, indeed so," said Sir Donovan, taking his seat

beside the silent uncle. He waited until all his men had also sat down – there were indeed nine of them – and then, remarkably, rubbed his hands together as if addressing a directors' meeting in a year of record profits. "Well, then. No time like the present, eh? Miss Trent, would you please be so kind as to begin proceedings?"

Thunder rolled again, much closer, but Grant did not startle this time.

Grant went around the room, turning down the gas mantles so that they barely produced a glow. He let the candles be; they provided little light and he felt that they added to the ambiance. Atmosphere was everything, after all. Just enough darkness to limit the faculties and allow blessed credulity to enter the room. Satisfied, he returned to the armchair, nodded to Miss Trent, and sat down. He did not like the look of the table at all. It beggared belief that Sir Donovan had suddenly found eight playmates for Lynch and spontaneously decided to refurbish the dining room in the day since Grant had visited. This had been his intention all along, but to what purpose? The deception itself was transparent enough; he had not wanted to worry Grant by mentioning this brutish little *grex venalium* would be in attendance, and that had been wise (or at least cunning) because the prospect of eight more Lynches would have warned off many a soul less sensitive to danger than William Grant. What concerned Grant was why Sir Donovan felt that they were necessary at all. As for the great table, that was an extraordinary thing. Beyond the practical aspect that its predecessor would never have held twelve sitters without a great deal of crowding, it would surely have been easier just to invite fewer guests, if he could dignify obvious employees as such. Nothing about the sitting served to calm Grant's nerves so much as an iota. Thunder rolled again, and Grant wondered why its suddenness was now perhaps the only thing that did not disturb him.

"Sophia Clay." Miss Trent's voice rang clearly through the room, her excellent projection the result of several lessons with a theatrical coach. The sound of her voice gave Grant something to focus on apart from his misgivings, and he did so, checking the weight of the pistol in his pocket. "I am looking for Sophia Clay. Are you present? Are you near, Sophia?"

"She always preferred to be called 'Sophie,'" rumbled the bulk of Sir Donovan Clay, the largest dark mountain in a dismal range arrayed around Miss Trent. He said it as if it was an affectation of his late wife that he invited the company to mock, not a thread connecting him to a loved and missed wife. Grant's distrust of Sir Donovan mellowed into dislike in that moment.

"Sophie," said Miss Trent to the air. "Sophie Clay. Are you here tonight? Your husband Donovan wants to speak with you. Please, you have nothing to fear. There is only love here tonight."

Grant doubted that. He dearly wished that she would just spend five minutes plaintively calling for Sophie for good form and then admit defeat. Sir Donovan could even keep his cheque. Grant just wanted to get Lizzie and himself far, far away, back into town and the safety of the house in Kensington. It was absurd that they could be so isolated so close to the city proper. They might as well be on the moon.

Lightning flashed, sharply illuminating the room through a gap in the curtains, and thunder shook the glass in the windows only a moment later, causing several of Sir Donovan's men to flinch. A moment later, rain lashed against the window. Lizzie had been so very right. A storm had curdled into that empty sky and was already almost overhead.

"Sophie…" Miss Trent's voice was tremulous, and Grant – a veteran of every single one of her previous sessions and their rehearsals – knew that something was wrong. She would give those five minutes to offer at least some value for money and then call a halt, he was sure of it. She wanted to be out of that house as much as he did, even if it meant walking to Barking Town in a storm. A few more plaintive cries for the lost soul of Sophie Clay and then…

"Who's there?" The tone was not that of a vague question, but of a specific challenge and it made Grant's hackles rise. They had decided early in their practice that they would avoid their sessions being visited by random wandering souls. That way led to too many complications and an inevitable encounter with some noble savage in the role of spirit guide from a conveniently distant land like the Americas or Egypt or Norway or suchlike, just like every other medium in Britain. Further, while Lizzie was a very convincing actor, he had never heard her assay the emotion of fear before, and that was undeniably present in her tone now.

"Who are you?"

The candle flames flickered in a sudden errant draft, strong enough to make some gutter, and the mantles glowed as their flames burned blue.

Grant rose from his chair. "Miss Trent…" He had never interrupted a session before, but he had had more than enough of this one.

"Sit down, man," growled Sir Donovan Clay, the voice rising from the great dark mound closest to him at the table. "Don't interfere."

In that moment, Grant realised that he had never been in control of the session, never been its stage manager. His presence was being tolerated and no more. Now the inclusion of Lynch and his covey of men at the table made a horrible, sickening sense. He reached into his pocket and gripped the handgun there.

All grew quiet, the wind falling away, the rain abating, the thunder and lightning pausing in their fury.

There was an awful electricity in the room, a dreadful static that made the hairs on Grant's arms and the back of his neck prickle and rise, and he could not tell if its cause was emotional or external, only that he felt locked in place as if an element in a *tableaux vivant*. The world, the universe, seemed to turn with that poorly-dimensioned dining room as its fulcrum, a sense of process beyond human comprehension in train, a moment of terrible implacability that bore away all that might be regarded as purely rational as easily as a pickaxe through a plate-glass window. Something different, something greater, something unknowable, something alien to everything Grant had ever experienced or felt or imagined in his life was present in that room. All he wanted to do was grab Lizzie's hand and drag her out of there before creation shattered around them, but he could not move from the spot, and could only watch as Miss Trent – as Lizzie – threw back her head and, framed by that absurd throne upon which she had been installed, screamed, "Who are you?"

Lightning struck then, such that the concussion of its thunder threw open the French windows and the rain descended like a curtain. Every candle guttered on the instant and the mantles flickered out. There should have been no light, but there was: a queasy opalescent glow that grew with the rapidity of a catching fire, and it was emanating from the eyes and mouth of Miss Cerulia Trent as she rose slowly to her feet, shuddering and her scream never-ending and rising in violence even as it ceased to be anything any human throat could ever have issued.

Months before when they had started upon their path, they had agreed that they would attempt no effects for the bafflement of the other sitters. They were difficult to carry off and too easily detected by any sceptics at the table. Thus, the momentary hope that rose in Grant's breast that this was all stagecraft, that Lizzie had consulted with some conjuror and developed a more convincing ectoplasmic manifestation, died almost immediately. This awful, almost physical light that bulged from her open mouth and staring eyes was no mummery. It was some interloper universe, virulent in its energies, pushing through her and indifferent to her fate. He knew then that he was watching Lizzie Whittle die, and there was not a thing that he could do to prevent it.

Then, amidst the howling and booming of the sodden gale rolling in from the estuary, he heard Sir Donovan say to himself in that distinctive baritone growl, "Magnificent! Magnificent!" Grant hated him so much in that moment that he forgot to be terrified and so movement returned to him.

The light suddenly attenuated and a moment later winked out, plunging the room into gloom, now lit only fitfully by the lightning. Miss Cerulia Trent, a spiritist whose only powers Grant had long believed lay in her wit and thespian abilities, wilted and collapsed across the head of the table. Grant was by her in a moment, helping her to her feet with difficulty for she seemed so devoid of animation that she felt as boneless as a bolster. Lightning flashed, and he was caught there, rimed in the glare.

"What's that? What are you about, sir?" demanded Sir Donovan.

"We're leaving. Miss Trent has had a very nasty turn." Even as he said it, it struck him as an absurd understatement to describe somebody's head lighting up like a lighthouse as a "nasty turn".

"She's going nowhere, Grant," said Sir Donovan, no trace of bonhomie remaining.

The room plunged into darkness then, a darkness so

deep as to deny all illumination, as if all the company had been struck blind. Gauging roughly where the windows must be, Grant half pulled, but mainly carried Miss Trent in that direction. Somebody barged into him with a muffled oath and a gasp of whisky-smelling breath, but then they were gone, and he heard the sound of a body falling heavily a couple of yards away. He yelped as he was grabbed by the upper arm in a grip that seemed to be just short of breaking the bone. "Let me go!" he cried out, but the room was in uproar by then and his voice was lost in the tumult of shouts, curses, and toppling furniture. Whoever held him had a grip like iron upon his bicep and brooked no resistance, dragging him and, with him, Miss Trent across the room. Suddenly, he had rain and the wind in his face, and the darkness swirled away from them like smoke. He tried to turn to face his persecutor, but a rasping voice close to his ear barked, "Run, you fool!" and he was given a powerful shove that sent him reeling out into the sodden turf of the house's formal lawn.

He fell to one knee, and Miss Trent fell half across him, barely conscious herself. Marshalling his scattered wits, Grant grasped her around the shoulders and drew her back to her feet. "C'mon, Lizzie!" he said urgently, close by her ear, although he doubted she could hear him given the violence of the storm. "Let's get out of this bedlam, eh?"

She made no reply. He steered her staggering steps to one of the doors in the hedge, unbolted it, and half carried her through into the lane beyond. He kicked the door shut with his heel – no point giving Sir Donovan and his men any clues as to which way they had gone – and looked around frantically, trying to re-orientate himself. A neigh and a stamp drew his attention and he saw, wonders of all wonders, a hansom cab standing unattended in the road. *Had two hours passed already?* he thought dazedly. *Had the cabby come early?* And where was the cabby, anyway? Had he gone up to the house, abandoning his cab in the middle of the way, untethered in a storm? Not that it mattered in the slightest, because – sympathetic to the travails of the stolid British worker as he might be in the usual run of things – in the present circumstance, it was every man for himself. Grant got the doors behind the traces open and managed to get Lizzie lying along the seat reasonably securely. He closed the doors, climbed up, found the cabby's whip, took the reins, and drove the horse to a sprightly trot and then a canter, however unwise that might have been in the murk and rain. All that mattered was that they escape, and the knowledge that Lizzie might be dying all the while tormented him every yard of the way.

CHAPTER FIVE

THE UNTURNED MIND

Later, Grant would remember little but impressions of the drive back into town on the stolen hansom. He remembered how the rain fell away behind them like a veil as they approached Barking Town proper, of how somebody there glanced curiously at him as he drove by and he was suddenly very conscious of how he must have looked, soaked to the skin and hatless. He worried about being stopped all the way through town, but the roads were gratifyingly clear by that hour and, if any coppers thought his appearance curious, they still did not trouble themselves to try and halt him. The journey was interminable, and by the time he reached Kensington, he was sure he had travelled far enough to arrive at Land's End. Now he was faced with the problem of what to do with the horse and cab, so he abandoned them around the corner from a nearby cab rank and hoped somebody would assume the horse had not been properly tethered and had wandered off a little way.

Lizzie was as slack as a rag doll against his side as

he dragged her the couple of hundred yards to their apartments and then lifted her over his shoulder and carried her up the stairs, hoping against hope that none of the other residents would come out to see what was heralded by his slow, heavy, uncertain steps. Damning propriety and the prospect of ascending another flight of stairs, he took her to his rooms and placed her on the long, comfortable couch he favoured for smoking and reading the newspaper. Then he went off to fetch a pillow and a blanket. Only then, when she was safely embedded in Scottish wool, albeit still dressed but for her shoes, he sat down opposite in a despairing funk and wondered what he should do. A doctor was the obvious recourse, but any respectable doctor would ask a lot of questions that Grant would either be unable or unwilling to answer. Fortunately, the circles in which he moved meant that he had the acquaintance of at least one doctor who was somewhere well short of respectable. The man was struck off, of course, but he still had his little bag of medicaments and instruments, and if he should prove to be drunk at the moment, why, Grant was more than prepared to hold his head in a basin of icy water until he wasn't.

After making sure that Lizzie was breathing steadily, he took his second favourite hat from the rack, and went out to seek something roughly equating to medical help. Doctor Quince had spent two years in Wormwood Scrubs for performing what the prosecution had identified as an abortion, but which Quince had sworn on oath had been a desperate intervention that came to naught. It seemed the judge had been at least vaguely sympathetic with that explanation, as the terms of the Offences Against the Person Act of 1861 would have permitted him to throw the book at the hapless Quince with a great deal more violence than equated to two years. In any event, Quince was struck from the medical register and, shunned by his former circle, had entered into a state of near penury. A lesser man might have found solace only in a gin bottle and finished his days coughing blood in a Shoreditch slum, but Quince preferred to continue to practice medicine, albeit illegally and with a small sideline in medicines that were not entirely as efficacious as he sometimes made out.

Grant went at a quick dogtrot to Paddington, and there hammered on Quince's door in an unloved tenement hard by the station. Quince came to the door blessedly sober, if irked. "Good God, Bill Grant, what's the to-do?" He was dishevelled, but judging by the loose collar buttoned only at the rear and the open book clasped in his hand, he had fallen asleep while reading and not while entertaining himself with a bottle of cheap sherry.

"It's Lizzie, Doc. She's had some sort of fit. I can't wake her up. You must come quickly!"

"Lizzie?" Quince was fond of Lizzie Whittle in an avuncular fashion, and was immediately spurred to gather his things, make himself presentable for the street, and follow Grant back at a fast walk.

They found her much as Grant had left her. Quince pulled a chair over by the sofa, threw off his hat and jacket, opened his medical bag, and withdrew his stethoscope. "I shall have to open her blouse to hear her heart, Bill. Kindly don't lay me out."

"Do whatever you need to, Doc. Just help her."

And so Quince did. He listened to her heart, checked her pulse, depressed her tongue, set up a little acetylene burner and reflected the light via a handheld mirror into her eyes when he drew the lids up, all this and more, all the while muttering to himself as he worked. Finally, some fifteen minutes later he settled back in his chair and regarded Lizzie Whittle with a thoughtful frown.

"Well?" asked Grant.

"Well. She is, as far as I can make out, in splendid health. Her heartbeat is strong and regular without the hint of a murmur, her reflexes are perfect, her temperature is exactly what it should be, and indications are that her blood pressure is acceptable."

"Indications? Can't you measure it?"

Quince favoured him with a withering glance. "Do I *look* like I can afford a sphygmomanometer?"

Grant presumed not and held his silence. Quince continued, "But she entirely ignores smelling salts and other attempts to rouse her. I've seen and attended to comatose patients in the past, however, and this seems different. More akin to an extraordinarily deep sleep. What happened to her?"

Grant thought back to the house of Sir Donovan Clay, the thunder, the lightning. And that horrible light, as pale as that from Doctor Quince's acetylene burner, glowing from Lizzie's eyes and mouth, making a jack o'lantern of her skull. "She just collapsed," he said finally. "Went down like she'd been coldcocked."

"Had she suffered some sort of trauma, either physical or mental? Some sort of shock?"

"You know what we do, Doc. There was a session."

"A séance?"

"If you must. It all got a little out of hand." He looked at Lizzie tucked up under the blanket. "It got very out of hand. It was supposed to be the last time, too."

Quince took off his pince-nez and rubbed his eyes. "I am not a religious man, or one to believe in the 'Great Unseen', but I do think you are wise to have decided to give this particular line of work up. I am not so vain as to think Hamlet may not have been very correct when he told Horatio that there are more things in heaven and earth, certainly than one might find in my own poor philosophy. But brave heart, Bill. Lizzie seems healthy, but perhaps she suffered a mental shock at this wretched séance of yours, became overwrought and simply fainted."

Grant scoffed. "Lizzie? She's hardly of a nervous disposition."

Quince stood to put on his jacket. "I've seen men I'd put money on in a fight with a bear reduced to weeping and a-trembling almost literally at the drop of a hat. Speaking of which, where did I put mine? Ah." He recovered his bowler from the table. "My point being that we're only recently starting to grasp what a curious box of tricks the human mind is. London and its surrounds are riddled with asylums, but they cure nothing in them; they're just spoil heaps of discarded people. The received wisdom is that madness is a sign of moral degradation or of intrinsic structural faults in the brain. But consider, what if we are all a great deal more fragile between the ears than we might like to believe? The twentieth century shall be the century of the alienist, I feel sure. Perhaps I should reinvent myself for that time, hmm? In any event…" He opened his bag to put away his instruments, and then counted out a few small pastilles into a small, flat tin. "A dilute preparation of valerian. When she awakens – and I feel sure that she will within the next day – give her one every eight hours until they give out. They have a gentle sedative effect, my hope being that it will help her face whatever caused the trauma with some equanimity. I'm sorry, Bill, but that's all I can do."

Grant held the tin dubiously. "What if she doesn't wake?"

"Then you will you need a doctor who *hasn't* been struck off, because she will have to go into hospital to be kept under medical observation. But…" he shook Grant's hand as he prepared to leave, "I truly don't believe it will come to that. Lizzie might look a frail creature when she's dressed like a funeral lily like that, but we both know she has the constitution of an ox. Whatever is wrong with her, her own body is dealing with it at the moment. She will awaken presently, and likely demand a plate of bacon and eggs. You shouldn't worry, although I know that's a vain hope. Just keep an eye on her. If she hasn't woken by, let's say, midday tomorrow…"

"Call a doctor."

"Call a *real* doctor, yes. She'll be all right, and you should get a little sleep yourself, hmm? You look as wrung out as a cloth. Goodnight, Bill."

Grant didn't believe he would sleep well that night half-turned into the armchair across the floor from Lizzie, who was now resting – still clothed – in his bed. And yet midnight found him sunk into a deep sleep occasioned by exertion and reaction. Deep it may have been, but it was not untroubled. His dreams, as a rule, were simple things, and his nightmares generally involved his luck finally running out and suffering his arrest. He especially disliked the ones that turned Dartmoor Prison into a school, the screws walked around with canes while the inmates painfully scrawled meaningless phrases on slates. This one, however, was very different, but no less unpleasant for all that.

He dreamt he was in that terrible house of recent memory in the wilds of East Barking, but now it was daytime, and the sunlight cut into the dining room through the French windows. It was now much as he had first seen it, with the smaller, less imposing table. At the head of it, however, there was still that great high-backed chair, now grown greater still and atop a dais, fit for an emperor. Lizzie sat upon it and looked at him with an expression of such heartrending terror that he couldn't help but laugh, though he knew not why. Suddenly, she was dragged from the chair and out of the door into the hallway, although Grant couldn't quite make out who was doing the pulling. She screamed all the way, and he waved merrily at her until the door slammed shut and her cries instantly halted.

"We can do better than that, can't we, my boy?" Sir Donovan Clay was up on the dais by the throne. Now sitting upon it was a very convincing wax effigy of Lizzie, wearing that slightly imperious expression she employed whilst being Miss Cerulia Trent. Sir Donovan had a burning spill in his hand and used it to light a wick in the centre of the waxwork's crown. Once he was satisfied that it was properly alight, he stepped down to join Grant. More quickly than he would have believed possible, the light burnt its way down inside the head. Lizzie's eyes liquefied and ran from her eye sockets, to reappear a moment later when dark wax vomited from her mouth. The flickering light of the wick shone through her eyes and her mouth and Grant thought, *Ah, that is how she did it.*

There was a crash. Great-Uncle Mathias had accidentally knocked the clock from the mantelpiece and was now on all fours, gathering up the pieces and, remarkably, repairing the clock perfectly as he went. "Dear great-nuncle!" cried Sir Donovan. "I have no idea what we would do without him." He drew Grant to the French windows, which swung silently open as they approached, admitting a terrible light that hurt Grant's eyes. "Play time!" said Sir Donovan. "Out you go! Run around!"

Grant was unclear whether he should go without taking one or other of the Lizzies with him. "Run, you fool," said a thin voice in his ear.

Outside, there was no lawn, no trees, no hedgerows, and – he realised when he looked back – no house. He was in some awful red desert, the only vegetation in sight being low scrub and clusters of little flowers, beaming bravely in the hellish sand. There was a sound behind him, and he found the waxwork of Lizzie standing there, the top of its head missing, the hair burnt away, and the fierce glow of the desert sun emanating from its eyes and mouth.

"You bloody idiot, Bill Grant," it said, in Lizzie's voice.

He was awoken by the sound of porcelain careening off the wainscoting, a sharp metallic sound that pulled him from the well of sleep with impolite alacrity. He blinked wildly to find the room in the subdued light of full day beyond the curtains. Lizzie was awake and up. She appeared to have kicked the chamber pot in passing, hence the commotion. Grant had a vague memory of arranging it by the bed in case she was taken ill in the early hours.

"Lizzie! You're awake! Oh, girl! You had me worried!"

She had been standing, looking at the still spinning chamber pot as if it were an unexpected animal of some description. Now she looked upon him in much the same way. His jubilation cooled. She looked at her hands, as if expecting to find herself clutching the answers to some questions that she did not care to ask. "Lizzie…" she said.

"That's you," he said carefully. He'd heard of sudden shocks scattering wits and sometimes memories. He prayed that this was not the case here. "Elizabeth Whittle. I call you 'Lizzie'. Don't you know me, Lizzie?"

She glanced sideways at him, but did not answer. Instead, she looked around Grant's bedroom. "Where am I?"

It suddenly struck him how inappropriate it was for her

to find herself in a man's bedroom. Perhaps he should have carried her up another flight of stairs to her own bed after all. That couldn't be helped now. "You're in my bedroom. You were flaked out last night. I couldn't rouse you at all. I had Doc Quince come over to have a look at you, but he wasn't much help neither. Oh." He fumbled in his waistcoat pocket and found the tiny tin of pastilles Quince had given him. He opened it and offered her one. "He said you should have one of these every few hours until you were more yourself."

She accepted it and studied the pastille, rolling it between her fingers. "More myself…" she echoed. He thought she was going to take the medicine but instead she just sniffed it, an act from which she seemed to derive some quiet satisfaction. Then she said "No," and handed the pastille back to him.

"Lizzie, please, you're not well."

"I am well," she said. She looked around, paused to study the print of an engraving of the Admiralty Arch he'd hung over the fireplace. "This is not my room."

"No."

"Take me to my room." Her gaze dropped, as if she was remembering something. She looked him in the eye once more. "*Please* take me to my room."

"I can't stay with you for very long if I do."

"Why not?"

"Well…" The house might be far more tolerant of its occupants' activities than other parts of the city, but even it had its limits. "People might talk."

She considered this. "What will they say?"

"Well... you know? That... well, that there's something going on between us."

She looked at him with slightly lowered brows, as if she suspected him of deliberate abstrusity. Then her brow cleared. "Oh. You mean sex."

He couldn't have been more shocked if she had produced a stiletto and stabbed him. "Bloody hell, Lizzie!"

"Take me to my room," she said, splendidly unconcerned by his wounded social mores.

They progressed up the stairs to Lizzie's room. At the landing, she paused, plainly unsure of which door to go to. As Grant crested the last riser, the door to the left opened and Mr Summerbee stepped out. "Good morning, Miss Trent! Mr Grant," he said, as he locked his door.

Lizzie looked at him curiously, then turned to her own door on the right. "This is my room, then," she said more in the nature of a statement than a question.

Summerbee was on the top step when she said it, and now it was his turn to pause and adopt a curious expression.

"She's had a bit of a knock," Grant told him in a whisper. "She's not quite all there at the moment."

She tried the handle and found it locked. Frustrated, she turned to the two men. Seeing them in quiet conversation, she said with the air of a pronouncement, "We are not having sex."

"Good Lord!" said Mr Summerbee while Grant sighed heavily in soul-deep exasperation.

"I don't know what to do," he said to Summerbee, still in a whisper. "She's not herself at all."

Summerbee, who had only ever seen Lizzie in the dour, taciturn persona of Miss Cerulia Trent, could very well see that. "It's all that table-rapping nonsense you indulge her in," he whispered back. "It's turned her mind. She needs to be put under the doctor immediately."

"I do not require a doctor," she said, cutting across their conversation, enunciating her words in a clear, precise way that Grant did not like at all. She looked at the door. "But a nurse would be useful. Just until I am all here at the moment, I am myself again, and my mind is unturned." She tapped the door. "It will not open."

Grant fumbled out the keys from his pocket that he had removed from her reticule in his rooms. "It's locked."

"Ah," said Lizzie, stepping away from the door as he approached, and canting her head to look more clearly at the keyhole beneath the handle, "it is locked."

"Good luck, Grant," said Summerbee, and louder for the benefit of Miss Trent, although it was plain that recent events had made no inroads upon her hearing, "I hope you feel better soon, Miss Trent."

He descended immediately and so was, fortunately, already out of earshot when Lizzie said to Grant, "Why does he call me 'Miss Trent' when you told me my name is Elizabeth Whittle?"

Somehow, in the depths of his concern for Lizzie, it had never occurred to him that in her current state she might well compromise them both. The realisation clenched his heart. Getting the door unlocked, Grant hustled her inside quickly before she said anything else in public that they both might have cause to regret.

"I live here," she said, as he closed the door behind them. She inhaled through her nose. "The smell is better than your room." She looked suddenly at him. "Why did you mislead me about my name?"

"I didn't," he said testily. "Sit down, Lizzie. We have to talk."

She didn't move for a moment, then sat heavily upon the floor.

"Damn it all, Lizzie! On a chair! On a bloody chair! What has got into you?"

Unperturbed, she rose and sat in an armchair. "Explain why I have so many names."

Controlling his frustration with difficulty, he sat down on the sofa opposite her. "You don't, not really. Your name *is* Elizabeth Whittle, Lizzie for short. Miss Cerulia Trent, well, that's like a stage name, really."

"I am an actor."

"No! No, not really, although you play a role." He could see beating around the bush was only going to result in endless misunderstanding, so he took a deep breath and prepared to tell her a truth he avoided most of the time himself. "Lizzie, what we do isn't quite kosher, if you get my drift." She plainly didn't. He tried again. "What we do, it's… I'm not saying it's against the law, but, well, it might not be completely moral."

She digested this. "Are we criminals?"

"Perhaps? We sort of… skirt around the law. It'd be a difficult case to prove in court."

"What do we do?"

And there was the crux of it. He summoned his mettle and said, "We let the bereaved think that you can talk to their loved ones, and if they give us money for that, well, we didn't exactly ask them to."

"I tell them that I can speak to the dead?"

"Yes."

"For money?"

"Yes. But we never ask! That's what's clever about it."

She thought longer on this. "Human grief is a powerful emotion," she said at last. "Always money. It is always money."

Even in the midst of everything else that had happened and was happening, it struck him as a peculiar comment. "Can't live without money, Lizzie."

"Humanity does not need money to function," she said. "That it does is a choice, not a necessity." Once more, she turned upon him that strange penetrating gaze that she had exhibited since waking. "Was I lying to someone about speaking to the dead when I fainted?"

"Look, we never choose anyone who can't afford to lose a few bob, girl–"

"Was I lying to someone about speaking to the dead when I fainted?"

Grant wasn't sure what it was about the repetition that he found so unnerving. Perhaps that it was a perfect echo in intonation, pitch, and timing. Or, perhaps, because he'd received the faintest intimation of inverted commas around the word "fainted" on both occasions.

"That was the idea," he conceded. "But we... you never actually got that far. Things went wrong straight away."

"Where did this happen?"

"At a session. A séance."

"In the east of London?"

"In Barking, yes. You remember that?"

She did not answer, but only grew silent for a long minute. Then she said, "Am I lucky?"

"What?"

"Do people like me?"

"Yes. Yes, of course people like you and, yes, back in the East End they used to call you 'Lucky Lizzie', as you always had the knack of falling on your feet. You always got your way, one way or another. Why are you asking me these things?"

Another silence. Then, "I am unwell. Until I am all here at the moment, I am myself again, and my mind is unturned, I shall require a nurse to look after me." She looked at her forearms in their sleeves, then down at her dress. "I shall require help dressing." A brief pause and then she added under her breath, "This costume is complicated." She looked up at him expectantly.

It took him a few moments to catch her meaning. "What... *now*? You want a nurse right now, this minute?"

"Yes." She continued to look at him steadily. She seemed to have largely fallen out of the habit of blinking. "Please."

Grant had never found it necessary to hire a nurse at his

leisure, never mind as a matter of urgency, but nevertheless he agreed to sally forth and find one. Leaving Lizzie with the admonition to stay there and not to experiment with the fireplace or the gas, he went out, vaguely hoping that there were such things as street corner nurse vendors.

On the way out of the building, however, Grant had the good fortune once again to run into Mr Summerbee, now returning with his newspaper and tobacco. "How's Miss Trent?" asked Summerbee.

"In need of supervision. I say, old man, you wouldn't know where I might hire a nurse, would you?"

"As a matter of fact, yes, I do." He gave Grant his shopping while he took out his notebook, scribbled a name, tore out the page and presented it to Grant in exchange for his things. "That's the agency where I hired a nurse to look after my mother when she was recovering from pneumonia. Excellent reputation, and the lady – impeccable references, by the way – doted on mother until she was back in good fettle. Very happy to recommend them. Can't remember the number, only the street, but they're in the big red building across the way from the music hall. You know the one?"

Grant did indeed know the one and, after thanking Mr Summerbee sincerely for his help, he set off with worry dogging his every step.

Chapter Six

MISS CHURCH

William Grant made his way to the big red building just across from the music hall with haste and found the agency on the second floor. The place was not bustling, but that was the way with agencies as a rule and Grant took that as no aspersion upon the company's success or standards. Indeed, it seemed that the entire permanent staff consisted of two women, one who sat at the reception desk in the small front office, and a second (a middle-aged woman whose manner betrayed extensive experience in service) who owned the agency and sat within the private office. He was ushered in this sanctum on declaring his business, and offered tea, which he declined.

"A nurse," said the owner, Mrs Sedge, settling into her chair after the niceties had been observed. "For children?"

"No, for… well, I suppose you'd call her an invalid, although she's not bedridden. She's had a shock recently and just needs someone to keep an eye on her until she's right again."

Mrs Sedge took in his mild dishevelment and unshaven chin and nodded. "So, some hospital experience would be useful? Ah, we have a handful of ladies who would fit the bill, but..." she busied herself with a ledger for a few moments, "I am very sorry to say that they are all currently placed. We might have one become free at the end of the month, if that would be convenient?"

Grant shook his head, considering inwardly that, by all rights, he and Lizzie should now be in France. It all seemed very unfair, all the more so because he could not quite quantify exactly what had gone wrong, only that something had gone truly *terribly* wrong. "That would be too long, I'm afraid. She needs to have a nurse as soon as is possible. I can't look after her myself, you understand? The patient, she's not my wife or family. She's a friend. It simply wouldn't be... well–"

"Proper," finished the manager. "No, I understand entirely. It would not be at all proper."

"I'm on tenterhooks just being away from her this long," said Grant. "I'm dreadfully worried."

"What has the doctor said?"

"The doctor? Oh, bed rest and a nurse. Hence..." He waved at the office.

"Quite, quite. Well, I'm very sorry, sir, but there's simply nobody suitable for the needs of your friend just now. Or, at least, not on our books." She took a blank card from a caddie, dipped her pen in the inkpot, and wrote quickly. "This is the address of another agency. We maintain a friendly rivalry with one another and send on clients as the need arises.

They may be able to help you." She pressed it to her desk blotter and handed it over. "I wish you the best of luck, sir."

Grant left clutching the card, nodding to the receptionist, and wishing her a good morning as he did so, noting in passing that there was another young woman waiting on one of guest chairs by the door. He was in the building's entry hall, nodding to the concierge when he was brought up short by a cry of, "Excuse me, sir!" to his rear.

The agency's other visitor, a young blonde woman, was hurrying down the steps behind him. "Sir!" she said on reaching him. "I know it's beastly to eavesdrop, but the door was open a crack and I couldn't help but hear some of your conversation with Mrs Sedge. You need a nurse? I do have testimonials, but I fear not enough to impress Mrs Sedge." She paused, very aware that she was committing all manner of social and professional faux pas in approaching him so directly.

Grant, for his part, was impressed by her courage in doing so. "Yes, I do need a nurse. Do you have any hospital experience? To be exact, have you ever dealt with anyone suffering from bad shock?"

The woman nodded decisively. "My previous employer, Mrs Wright, she was in a train crash and it made a proper mare's nest of her nerves, if you'll forgive the phrase. I stayed with her almost a year until she was all square. You'll understand I can't talk about it too much for privacy's sake, but I have seen it all, sir, truly I have. I'm sure I'm just who you're looking for and, if not, well, at least you'll have time to find somebody else."

"That is a convincing argument, I admit. What's your name and your terms?"

"Amelia Church, sir, and thirty shillings a month, plus maintenance, uniform, and lodging on top. I keep full accounts, sir."

That was eighteen pounds per annum (plus whatever maintenance, uniform, and lodging came to), more than he'd would have liked, but some bullets simply have to be bitten. "Very well then, Miss Church, you may consider yourself employed to at least the turn of the month. Please come with me. I shall introduce you to your charge."

Grant and Miss Church discovered Miss Trent standing at her dinner table studying a stack of newspapers and magazines she had gathered from around her rooms. She looked up as they entered.

"This," said Grant to Miss Church, indicating Lizzie, "Is Miss Cerulia Trent." As he said it, Lizzie turned on him that oddly dispassionate yet threatening gaze that she had developed in the last few hours. It had the quality of a battleship turning its guns upon a fishing smack, and he did not enjoy it at all. She said nothing, however. He continued, "You will be looking after her."

"Are you a nurse?" asked Miss Trent.

"I am," replied Miss Church.

"I feel an urgent requirement to urinate, but this clothing is incomprehensible to me."

Grant would have said something, but his first impulse was to cry, "Lizzie!" and while he was strangling that impulse down, Miss Church said, "Of course, dear," and then to Grant, "Where are the amenities?" He told her, and Miss Church took Miss Trent away, chattering amicably about the weather as they went.

Grant wanted to collapse into a chair, or help himself to a whisky and soda, but it was far too early in the day for that and instead he drifted over to the table and looked at the stack of publications Lizzie had left behind, assorted magazines and old newspapers waiting to go out in the rubbish. They were arranged either side of the open newspaper in the middle, and he realised that one pile was of periodicals yet to be studied and the other of discards. She couldn't have been studying them so very carefully, however, as the discard pile was quite high and he hadn't been out so very long. On an impulse, he checked the dates. They were in perfect chronological order. She had arranged them thus in one heap, studied them, and then placed them into the discard. The efficiency of it impressed him, and he wondered what she was looking for.

Presently Trent and Church returned. The former seemed intent on telling Grant exactly how her ablutions had proceeded, but Miss Church cut across her with, "I don't think Mr Grant needs all the details, my dear. In any case, that dress is hardly suitable for daywear. Let's see what you have in your wardrobe and I can explain the niceties of how clothing works while we're about it."

Miss Church guided her into her bedroom, and he heard Miss Trent say in a cool yet faintly injured tone, "The fastenings are unnecessarily convoluted," just as the door closed.

Miss Church's wages and expenses suddenly seemed a very great bargain to Grant. He also realised that he was thinking of his friend and colleague far more as "Miss Trent" than as "Lizzie". Miss Cerulia Trent had been created as an unworldly woman possessed of otherworldly talents, distant and unknowable. It *had* been a role and nothing more, but Grant wondered if that were still true. Even as a character created for their enrichment, however, he felt sure that Miss Trent should know full well how to dress herself. What to make of a precisely expressive savage who regarded hooks and eyelets as a grave imposition upon her dignity, he had no idea at all.

He looked down at himself and remembered how Mrs Sedge at the agency had taken in his sadly curled jacket lapels and burred chin. He really did need a wash, shave, and a change of clothes. He went to the bedroom door and tapped gently. "Miss Church? I'm going downstairs to my rooms… I'm at No.2, by the way… to tidy myself up a little. If you need anything, please don't hesitate to fetch me."

"Very good, Mr Grant," she replied through the wood of the door, "You take your time. If you'll forgive me for saying so, you seem exhausted. If you want to sleep, that might be wise."

She was right, of course. A few hours snatched sleep in an armchair hadn't served to refresh him a great deal, and the thought of even an hour or two in his own bed was quite compelling. "I may well do that. If I don't answer straight away, I'll probably be asleep, so knock harder if you need me."

"I shall, but I wouldn't worry, sir. Get some rest."

"Thank you. I shall."

And so saying, he took his leave of the rooms of Miss Cerulia Trent.

Grant was more grateful than he might have expected to be allowed some time to himself. He decided to shave before sleeping as he wanted a cup of tea and if he was boiling the kettle, then he might as well boil some extra water for the basin. As he waited by the gas ring, he considered one great element of the previous night's events that had until now waited in the shadow of Lizzie's – Miss Trent's – wellbeing, and that was how every bad feeling she had expressed about the session at Barking had come true, not least in Sir Donovan's distinctly ungentlemanly behaviour. Might he come after them in their Kensington fastness? Yes, he very well might, but not immediately and, Grant felt sure, not at the head of a pack of his hirelings. This was, after all, London, not New York. Grant sighed; if only he had not been so stubborn and, yes, greedy, they might have been well on the way to the Côte d'Azur by now. As things lay, it might be necessary to find a bolthole quickly in case Sir Donovan's interest in them had not waned.

He then stood by the window, enjoying his tea as well as the feeling of being rather more civilised after a wash and shave, when he was surprised to see Miss Trent and Miss Church on the pavement outside, walking along.

Miss Church was talking animatedly while Miss Trent only listened intently, it seemed to him. He also noticed something else that disturbed him greatly. Lizzie was a good actor for all her lack of formal training, and had always instinctively understood that different people move in different ways. When she was Elizabeth Whittle, she positively galumphed along. Not the most elegant mode of deportment by any means, but one that spoke eloquently of her vivacity and of her early life in the East End. As Miss Cerulia Trent, however, she withdrew into herself, all but gliding along in a procession of tiny steps and not a swing of her arms in evidence. The way she was walking now, however, was neither of these things, but rather a walk bland in its anonymity, a grand arithmetical mean of all strides. Lizzie was positively nondescript in that moment, and suddenly he truly couldn't think of her as "Lizzie" any longer. "Miss Trent" would have to do henceforth until such time as Lizzie Whittle was fully restored. Such thoughts rattled through his mind in the time it took him to button his shirt, throw on a tie, lace up his shoes, and grab his jacket and hat. Then he was out of his door and in pursuit.

At first he feared that the couple of minutes it had taken him to prepare for the street had robbed him of his mark. But no, there were Miss Church and Miss Trent by the roadside, awaiting the arrival of an omnibus at the stop. He ducked into the doorway of a general store, wondering as he did so why he was being so secretive and continuing to ponder the point for some minutes while pretending to be absorbed in a display of Sunlight soap. Soon enough he heard the rattle of the horse-drawn omnibus of the LGOC, and slipped back out of the entry as he watched the two women board it. He flagged down a hansom and, giving the cabman probably the most exciting order he'd had that month of "Follow that omnibus!" he settled into the seat, feeling faintly absurd as he did so. What in blazes did he think they were doing? Miss Church had never clapped eyes upon Miss Trent until a couple of hours before and was undoubtedly doing what she believed best by taking Miss Trent out into the city in an attempt to ease her back into the mundane and workaday. Streets, buses, people, chatter, and bustle. Of course, that's all she was doing, and here he was, making a damnable fool of himself purely because… why? Because Miss Church hadn't told him about it beforehand. That was all there was to it. He was childishly jealous that he hadn't been consulted.

He was on the point of rapping on the cab roof to tell the cabby that he'd changed his mind when the gentleman leaned down and cried *sotto voce* through the hatch, "Here, mister! It's stopping!"

Indeed it was and, more to the point, Miss Church and Miss Trent were disembarking. Grant instructed the cabby to drive by and drop him fifty yards beyond the bus stop. Leaving the hansom and the cabby gripping a fare that included a ridiculously generous tip to assuage Grant's sense of being absolutely ridiculous, he followed the women as they made their way along a thoroughfare marked by banks and other such worthy buildings of stone rather than brick. In amongst all the assorted rival temples to Mammon, however, nestled the public free library, and it was into this building that the pair went. Grant felt perplexity; Miss Trent had her little library at home, and he knew that she hadn't read every volume. Perhaps they sought a rarer knowledge there? Perhaps, he wondered, Miss Church might want to see if there was any literature on Miss Trent's current state. Libraries must contain medical books, after all. That must certainly be it.

Sensibly, he should have turned on his heel and gone back to his rooms to rest. Having gone to all this trouble, however, he felt a perverse desire to double down upon his actions, and so he followed them inside at a discreet distance. They did not, he noticed, head for the sections signposted to deal with science and medicine, and nor did they trouble to question any librarian. Instead, they went into the general reading room and thence, to his mild astonishment, into the newspaper archive. Pretending to find something entirely fascinating in the bound 1860 annual of *Punch* magazine, Grant found a shadowed corner, and from there observed Miss Trent and Miss Church as, largely under the direction of Miss Church, they sought out a volume of *The Times* and another of *The Standard*. These they placed on one of the reading tables and, side by side, they began to search the pages. It was baffling to watch the pair diligently work their way through the pages in their own ways – Miss Church's head darting back and forth as she briefly noted each story before continuing on to the next, while Miss Trent just stared at the page as a whole before moving on. Baffling, but not a wildly exciting spectacle, and as the clock marked out the quarters one after another and the women returned volumes and took out new ones, Grant's attention wandered to the extent that he started to find thirty year old political sketches in *Punch* involving people he'd hardly heard of strangely captivating. He turned a page and found a cartoon of a hansom cab driver calling to a passing gentleman, "Now then, sir! Jump in. Drive you out of your mind for eighteen pence!"

Grant did not care for the cartoon at all. The cabby was drawn in such a way that he found him sinister, and the horse – fractious and stamping – seemed thin and poorly cared for. It also made him feel belatedly guilty for stealing the hansom the previous night. Yes, his need had been great, but the cabby had never been paid and had then been left marooned in the barbaric wilds of Barking. It was a poor way to reward a working man, all the more so when he had done them the kindness of waiting to take them back. Although… he had said he would wait in Barking Town and return at ten. Why, then, had Grant found his abandoned cab in the lane not even an hour later?

He glanced around the side of the bookcase behind which he had taken refuge and saw that the women were still methodically working their way through what seemed like reams of newsprint. He guessed it was perhaps intended to stir Miss Trent's memory, but it seemed a laborious way to do it. In any event, he didn't especially want the awkward questions that might ensue if they returned to the house and found him absent from his rooms, having necessarily arrived ahead of him. Besides which, he really was feeling very ragged and his bed seemed a simply tremendous place to be at that immediate moment. He returned the *Punch* annual to its place and left the library.

On the far side of the road, he could see the omnibus already rattling away and decided not to wait for its successor. After all, he wasn't such a long way from home and, given the steadily increasing body of traffic, he felt confident that, even should they follow him out right that minute, he would still beat them back given they would have to wait at least quarter of an hour for the next service. Besides, he could shave time off by taking a more direct route down a couple of back alleys.

It was in the very first of these less travelled back alleys that he was attacked. He heard a tread behind him and, reflexes sharpened by youthful fights in the ginnels of Manchester, he was already ducking to one side when a blow that would certainly have rattled his teeth and stunned him into a losing proposition instead glanced from just over his ear, sending his hat flying and himself sprawling. He was up again in a moment, much to the dismayed astonishment of his attacker who, looking into Grant's eyes and seeing murder there, turned on his heel and hared off. Grant could see that pursuit was pointless and instead recovered his hat, simmering with provoked violence. He knew where to find that fellow when the time came; it had been Detective Sergeant Bradley's green plainclothes constable again, now apparently indulging in some rather more muscular policing. Either the lad had overstepped his orders, or Bradley had put him up to it with the intention of driving Grant off his patch. Either way, there would be raised voices at New Scotland Yard if Grant had anything to do with it. He hadn't actually broken any laws that he was aware of, and if Bradley thought he'd give in to that kind of strong-arm nonsense, Grant would be perfectly delighted to disabuse him of the notion.

He touched his scalp where the blow had landed and found a shallow graze that was bleeding a little. Promising himself that next time he saw that lad, he'd bounce him teeth first down a flight of stone steps, Grant continued to his rooms, a basin of clean water, a bottle of iodine, a comfortable bed, and a reclined seething while he considered exactly what he would say to Bradley when he saw him.

Two hours later, after a train journey and a short walk, Mr Lynch arrived back at his employer's mansion east of Barking Town. Pausing only to hang up his coat and hat in the hall, he went straight to the study to report. Finding it empty, he looked into the drawing room and there found Sir Donovan Clay and three of the boys sitting around, smoking and reading the papers in a companionable silence. Seeing Lynch by the door, Sir Donovan rose and beckoned to follow him into the study, where he sat himself behind the desk and said, "Well?"

"Miss Trent seems to have taken on a companion or a nurse or something, boss. Grant went out this morning to an agency and came out with her."

Sir Donovan opened a foolscap notebook, took up a pen and dipped its nib in the inkwell. "Name?"

"No idea yet, but I'll find out. Took Miss Trent out to the free library after lunch."

"The library? To do what?" asked Sir Donovan, writing notes as he went.

"They were going through the newspapers. The more recent ones. Y'know, last eighteen months or so. I didn't dare go close enough to see what they were looking at, mind you."

"I really don't think she'd recognise you just from seeing you last night, Lynch."

"It wasn't so much her that I was worried about. Grant. He'd followed them along."

"You should have said they all went along together." He started an addendum to his notes.

"They didn't."

Sir Donovan's pen halted. He looked up slowly, unsure if Lynch was playing the goat. "What d'you mean, they didn't?"

"The two ladies came out first. I crossed the road and followed them to the omnibus stop. While I'm watching from across the way, up turns friend Grant. And here's the thing, boss… he doesn't join 'em. Instead, he goes off and skulks in a shop entry. Along comes the 'bus, and he hails a cab and follows."

Sir Donovan gave him a very narrow look. "He was following them, too?"

"That's how it looked. This Grant feller seems very protective towards Miss Trent."

"Perhaps... perhaps..." Sir Donovan mused for a few seconds before making another note. "Continue. This is all very interesting."

"So, Grant follows them into the library, watches them, too. He's watching them, I'm watching all of 'em. After a while he gets fidgety and comes out. So, I think, I'll just see what he's up to."

"I told you to stay with Miss Trent," said Sir Donovan in the growl of somebody who doesn't take insubordination or incompetence calmly.

"I did, boss," said Lynch with the stolid complacency of somebody who knows his employer's wonts all too well. "I stepped out to watch where he went and to hang around until the ladies came out again. Thing is, I saw someone else, some young feller I hadn't never seen afore. He follows Grant down the alley. Minute later, he's out of there like the Devil's on his coattails. I think Grant must have caught sight of him and realised he was being followed."

Sir Donovan paused again from his diligent note-taking. "You're sure you don't know this young man who followed Grant?"

"Never clapped eyes on him before, boss. I'd swear it on a stack of Bibles. Bit wet behind the ears to get clocked that easy, whoever he is. Anyway, so I couldn't go after him because of Miss Trent, right? Ten minutes later, out they come. I reckoned I knew they'd be going back, so I walked ahead of them to the 'bus stop and boarded ahead of them." Sir Donovan nodded, satisfied. People don't tend to feel that they're being followed by people ahead of them.

"Just as expected, back to her lodgings. Berry was waiting around when I got there, so I handed the reins to him and came back to give you chapter and verse."

"Good, good." Sir Donovan took a few minutes to complete his notes and then sat back, pleased. "Miss Trent is very important to all of our endeavours. It would be too bad if we can't find her when the time comes. Do you think this companion of hers might complicate matters?"

Lynch shook his head and curled his lip. "Just a chit o' a girl, boss. I could break her with my off hand."

Sir Donovan nodded. "Thought as much. It's Grant who's the problem. This other feller, the one who went after Grant, could be anything from a creditor to a cuckolded husband as far as we know. Probably nothing, but I'd prefer to know for sure, if only for the removal of doubt. I don't care to be taken by the lee, you understand. Not now. We're so close." He noted the slightly sour expression on Lynch's face and laughed. "I know, I know. It's one thing not to look a gift horse in the mouth, but when the horse hasn't even turned up yet, I think we're permitted a little cynicism and caution. I don't trust them, either, Lynch. But, at the same time, I have an odd feeling that they can't actually lie. That it's beyond them. Not an iota of proof of that, mind you, but I've yet to catch them even in a white lie of convenience so far."

"That true of our guest, too?"

Now Sir Donovan seemed less assured. "That one, I don't know. We shall just have to trust our sponsors to have a better grasp of it than we do." He looked seriously at

Lynch. "We are taking a huge risk, that much I know for a certainty."

Lynch shrugged. "Worth it though, isn't it, boss? If we get it wrong… well, we won't have long to regret it, will we? But, if we get it right…"

And here he smiled. A moment later Sir Donovan smiled, too; these were the beatific smiles of men for whom the near future promises the realised fruits of their every dream, and may the devil take the hindmost.

CHAPTER SEVEN
WORSE THAN THE DEVIL

The offices of New Scotland Yard on Victoria Embankment, overlooking the slowly moving waters of the River Thames, still smelled faintly of new paint in its less travelled corners, having only opened the year before. Mostly, however, it smelled of humans: sweat; paper; tobacco smoke; fear. Within its detective division, Detective Sergeant Norman Bradley felt blessed to have been given, if not an office, at least a quiet corner close by the door to his "governor's" domain. Detective Inspector Craddock largely left Bradley to get on with it, which suited Bradley well. Occasionally, Craddock would wander out, have a word, drop off a file, wander back in. Also occasionally, he would call Bradley in to discuss this case or that. Bradley liked Craddock; he was a copper who was in it to set matters aright, not for politics or – heaven forfend – to line his own pocket. One thing he did not miss since leaving Manchester was the stench of Superintendent William Bannister, a man so toweringly corrupt that even the watch committee stood by in thrall and let him do very much as he liked. Not that they'd been bribed, of course. The very thought.

He was just finishing off a handwritten report before it was sent to the secretarial pool to be rendered readable and grammatically correct when he became aware of Mr William Grant wearing a furious expression and his second best hat being led by a uniform constable to Bradley's desk. Bradley, rising, dismissed the constable and gestured to Grant to take a seat. "This is unexpected, Mr Grant," he said, foregoing the hypocrisy of calling it an unexpected pleasure. "How may I help you?"

"I'll not be sitting down," snapped Grant, "and I'm not for staying long either. I just wanted to tell you that next time you send someone after me, they'll be coming back in a tea chest, d'you understand me?"

Bradley sat down and steepled his fingers. "No. I don't understand you at all. What on earth makes you think I sent someone after you?"

For his answer, Grant snatched off his hat and bent down to show Bradley the righthand side of his skull. Bradley saw a shallow wound there, obviously fairly fresh. "Been in the wars, Mr Grant?"

"Been in the...? Listen to me, you confounded bluebottle! You sent one of your little constables after me to scare me out of London. Well, it won't work, y'hear?"

The door to Craddock's office opened and the man himself emerged. "Trouble, Bradley?" he asked, drawing on his pipe.

"I'm not sure, sir. I'm at a loss. Mr Grant here seems to

think it's the business of the Metropolitan Police to dispatch assassins to confound and injure random citizens."

"I see," said Craddock with splendid languor. "I didn't realise we had a budget for assassinations."

Grant fumed. "Oh, have your fun–"

"Most considerate, sir," said Bradley.

"–but this wound is my proof!"

"With respect," said Craddock, coming over to study the cut himself, "it proves perhaps that you were attacked, but is hardly sufficient to prove who did it. We might have made a little sport at your expense, sir, but the point is a valid one. The Criminal Investigation Division is not large. We simply do not have spare constables lying around to shadow people on the whim of their superiors. Every minute of police time is logged and pored over by accountants. Why would Detective Sergeant Bradley have dispatched one of these hypothetical coppers after you in any case?"

Grant was starting to develop a distinct sense that, yes, he was being ridiculed, but that in all fairness he had made himself ridiculous in the first place. Suddenly, he looked like he simply wanted to leave. "He's got it in for me."

"Is this true, Bradley?" asked Craddock.

"Yes, sir, it is. I believe Mr Grant to be playing a spiritualism confidence game, and I am keeping an eye on his activities, his and Miss Cerulia Trent's. In that belief, I visited him a couple of days ago to talk to him."

"You logged this?"

"It's in my notebook and my daily report."

"And the point of the visit?"

Bradley spoke to Craddock, but his gaze never left Grant. "To make him understand that preying on the bereaved is vile behaviour and that, if I get even one iota of evidence to show he and his colleague had broken the law, I would pursue it to the utmost."

"Well," said Craddock to Grant. "There you have it, sir. DS Bradley thinks you're a wrong 'un. I concur. If we're incorrect in that, then you have nothing to fear. There is no evidence to discover. But if you are, well, perhaps you might wish to reconsider your situation." He smiled beneficently at Grant, who had gone very pale. "Was there anything else we could help you with?"

"Actually," said Bradley, consulting a file box from the stack on the floor by his desk, "perhaps there's something Mr Grant could help us with." He opened the box, sorted through the papers within, and then produced something that he tossed on the desk.

Even without picking it up to examine it, Grant could see what it was. A disc perhaps five inches across of enamelled white metal with a black number on its face, held in a black leather cover with a loop of cord attached to its top end where it might be hitched around a coat button or through and back a coat buttonhole. "A cabby's licence. What of it?" Even as he said it, he realised that he was on very shaky ground.

"Well, this licence is interesting for a couple of reasons. Firstly, because it's a fake." Bradley looked intently at Grant's face as he added, "Not bad work, but some way short of perfect. And secondly, because it was discovered in the pocket of a body found at the high tide mark out at Halfway Reach. Dressed much like a cabby, but nobody from the ranks seemed to recognise him. Those that could bear to look at him at all, that is." He tossed another set of files from the box on the desk. Photographs.

"It can be difficult to recognise someone who's been in the water, I'm told," said Grant, clearly fighting the urge to run, glancing at the pictures.

"Oh, he was barely in the water, from what can be ascertained. Whoever dropped him in the river didn't have much of an idea of how the tides work, and he floated no distance before washing up. No, he's not a pretty sight because he was mutilated. Head partially shaved and then he was stabbed through the skull and into the brain–"

"My God…"

"–repeatedly. Six incisions, our Doctor Andrews tells us. Whatever caused the wounds made an awful mess when they were extracted. Emptied the poor fellow's brain pan like a boiled egg. Doctor Andrews is of the opinion that the man was alive when all six incisions were made. How he knows that, I have no idea. Clever man our Doctor Andrews, isn't he, sir?"

"Indeed he is," said Craddock. His pipe had gone out and he went to the office's fireplace to light a spill. He returned, sucking on the stem and drawing heat into the recalcitrant tobacco. "Funny night for fake cabbies, wasn't it, Bradley?"

"Indeed it was, sir." Then to Grant, "That very same night, cabbies on a rank in Kensington – you must know it, it's barely two hundred yards from your house – reported an abandoned cab. And here's the curious thing…"

"Its license was fake," said Grant, barely recognising his own voice.

"Exactly that, Mr Grant. A fake cabby, a fake cab." He leaned forward and smiled a warm smile that was the most threatening expression Grant had ever seen on a human face in his life. "Aren't you going to ask how, if you two were of a pair, the cab made its way to Kensington while – as seems likely – its owner was being horribly murdered out in the distant wastes of Barking?" The smile faded a tiny fraction. "We have a witness that states that the cab was driven by a hatless man who abandoned it and helped away a fashionably dressed young lady who seemed, and I quote, 'indisposed.'" He tilted his head towards Craddock. "I would guess the witness meant 'blind drunk' by that, wouldn't you, sir?"

Craddock nodded, a wise judge. "That would be my feeling."

Bradley looked Grant in the eye, the smile quite gone. "How's your Miss Trent, Mr Grant?"

Grant escaped the confines of New Scotland Yard with neither his dignity nor his equilibrium intact. There was some bluster of the "How dare you!" variety, he remembered many pressing engagements, and then he left with the sensation of smug coppers' looks burning across the nape of his neck and his shoulder blades.

So, the cabby was dead, and the only clue that the police

apparently possessed pointed squarely in Grant's direction. It was pale stuff, but people had danced on thin air at dawn in the yard of Newgate Prison for less. He also dearly wished that Bradley had been less forthcoming about how the man had died. Stabbed was bad enough – he had seen flesh hanging in flaps and scalps dangling off after a thorough kicking after street fights – but in the skull? No knife could do a thing like that, could it? It would scrape along the skull, wouldn't it? Who would do such a thing? It was monstrous. Barbaric. Un-English.

The mental image of Sir Donovan Clay's covey of pet thugs illuminated his mind's eye, and an ugly vista it presented.

But, even so, six deep wounds to the head and the brain missing? Surely even such bully boys wouldn't stoop to that? Surely not. By the time he climbed down from the omnibus, he was convinced that, surely, yes.

He arrived back at the house and went straight up to Lizzie's rooms, hoping against hope that Miss Church hadn't taken her on another improving jaunt to the library or a museum or similar. She had not, and she opened the door to Grant's knock. "I need a quick word with... Miss Trent." Miss Church looked at him steadily. "It's urgent," he added, "and private."

"Please enter, Mr Grant," said a voice from within the parlour that was Lizzie's but in a cadence that was not.

He was ushered in, and the door closed behind him with Miss Church, alas, on the inner side. "It's private," he repeated.

"Miss Church may hear whatever it is that you need so urgently to impart," said Miss Trent, for it was utterly impossible to think of her as Lizzie Whittle at that moment.

"She may not," said Grant, and glowered at the nurse. "This is… confidential."

"We have no secrets, Miss Church and I," said Miss Trent blandly. She had not once looked up at Grant since he had entered, her attention consumed by the stacks of current newspapers and books she seemed to have accrued somehow in the couple of hours that he'd been away.

Grant felt his blood heat and did not know whether it was in response to the situation as it stood or a reaction to his recent fright. In either case, he took a count of five before he replied for fear of what he might say. "You might not – although I doubt that – but I do." He turned to the nurse. "Miss Church. Wait outside, if you'd be so kind."

Miss Church looked him in the eye and the lack of concern for anything he might have to say was shockingly evident. "I take my orders from Miss Trent," she said. And as she said it, her gaze slid to her charge and Grant was astonished and disturbed to see a light of admiration, perhaps even adoration, kindle there.

"You damn well take them from me!" he said, failing to count to five on this occasion. "I pay you, girl, and don't you forget it!"

"I shall pay Miss Church in future," said Miss Trent. She considered her words, and added, "I shall pay her in pounds, shillings, and pennies."

William Grant looked at her for a long moment then,

and understood at last that his Lizzie was utterly gone. The anger guttered in him, and he sighed out the smoke of its passing. "The police are definitely interested in us. They have no evidence of wrongdoing, but they're taking a strong interest."

"Why would the police be interested in you?" said Miss Church.

Grant bristled at the interruption. "With the best will in the world, miss, that would be none of your business."

Miss Church ignored him and said to Miss Trent, "Police interference will complicate matters."

Grant frowned at her. "What? What are you talking about?"

Instead of providing an answer, Miss Church offered another question. "Do the police know where you live? Do they know about these rooms?"

"I..." Grant had the distinct sense that the whole conversation was getting away from him. "Yes. Yes, they came here. Look, just what... No. No, you're dismissed. Just go. I'll send along a day's wages." She didn't go, but Grant ignored her as if she had in the hope and expectation that she would go away if he ignored her long enough. He turned to Miss Trent. "It's only a matter of time before Bradley turns up on the doorstep and starts asking difficult questions. We have to go. Now. Today."

Miss Trent was distracted by her books and papers once more. "No," she said.

Grant scoffed indignantly. "No? *No?* Do you realise how much trouble we could be in, Lizzie?" He used her real name because he disliked the artificiality of using her pseudonym at the best of times. As he said it, however, it struck him that "Lizzie" was just as irrelevant to the woman sitting before him. "Please, will you just trust me? We have to leave before Bradley starts building a case against us. France won't be far enough. Italy, perhaps? We could go to Italy!"

"You may go to Italy," said Miss Cerulia Trent as she balanced two books in her hands, comparing the text. "Our work is here."

"Your work…" He looked at her aghast. "Your *work*? Lizzie… Miss Trent, you have to trust me when I say that matters are becoming *very* serious. The police will come again and they may do so with warrants. You will not be safe here. Please, I beg of you, come with me, at least until this all blows over."

Miss Trent closed both books simultaneously with sharp percussions. "It will not blow over."

"Miss Trent…" said Miss Church, a warning in her tone.

Miss Trent ignored her and instead transfixed Grant with that cold gaze. "I am important to you, am I not?"

Grant was startled by the question, but then felt forced into a corner by it. He glanced at Miss Church and then at Miss Trent. "Lizzie…" he said, an appeal in his tone.

"You feel that I am necessary to your happiness. Is that true?"

He didn't know how to reply.

"Miss *Trent*…" said Miss Church with a strange tautness in her voice.

"It is his world as well," said Miss Trent.

"He isn't ready!"

Miss Trent put down her books, arose from her chair, and approached Grant. She stood before him as if studying a wondrous statue in a gallery, reached out and touched the side of his face. "You are home to such emotions. It is one of the reasons that I admire you. A fleeting existence, but one of such inner colours."

"Lizzie… please… come away with me…"

"Do you love Elizabeth Whittle?" she said it quietly, but he heard every word with pure clarity.

"Yes," he said. He wanted to weep. "Yes. With all my heart."

"Then you have a reason to stand and fight, William Grant," she said. She nodded then to Miss Church. Grant started to turn to look at the nurse, but then the room became dark and boundless and he knew no more.

Even within the well of sleep, one knows when one is sleeping well, and that knowledge runs easily into resentment should anyone or anything threaten its serenity. Grant bridled a little when he heard the voice in the darkness, but it was Lizzie's voice so the irritation lasted only as long as it took to make that realisation.

Do you hear me?

In the blackness of his dreamless sleep, the first sound of the sentence came heavily like a drop of oil falling into dark water and spreading in a refractive rainbow meniscus. But the darkness was all-encompassing, and existed in all dimensions, not merely two. There was height, and time, and another sort of time Grant had never noticed before and was reasonably sure his pocket watch ignored, and so many more besides. The oil of the sound itself split into colours and he did not recognise all of them with his eyes, nor even the extremes of a vision he had never before experienced, but now instinctively understood that he had always possessed. The colours of the oil drop spread in all possible cardinal directions and he knew them: this one was consequence; this was permanence; this vibrant shade was tangents; he did not care for the colour of space.

I regret this necessity, but it is your battle too, William Grant.

He wondered at those last sounds for a moment until he remembered that they constituted his name. It took him a moment longer still to recall what a name was, a ludicrous concept to be sure. How could leaden syllables define him? He was a collection of colours, a pulse of vibrations. He had not chosen his name, and it was no sort of description, either.

I am preserving your sanity by disrupting it. I am saving your mind by destroying it. You have no choice but to trust me, and since you have no choice, I have no need to lie to you. And I say to you, William Grant, you can trust me. We are allies.

He wished Lizzie would stop using his name. It distracted him every time. He could see every William who ever was and every William who would ever be, every Grant who ever was and every Grant who would ever be, and he could see their interactions like pinholes in two cards, lined up and held to the light, a sky of stars, and every one of them a William Grant. There he was, over there, the dim unimportant dot of disreputable light who finagled money out of the bereaved. It saddened him to let the constellations down like that.

My name is not Cerulia Trent. My name is not Elizabeth Whittle. My name is...

And there was her true name, a spattering of colours that were not colours, the pattern as important as the hues, a name to conjure with, a name of which to be proud. It was the name of one who was trusted, courageous, experienced, stalwart. It was the name of a hero.

Just not, William Grant observed in a state of Olympian detachment, the name of a human.

Or even, he observed equably, any creature that he had previously understood as a creature. This was all very interesting, and his curiosity coloured the cosmos.

He was understanding the colours so much better now and, indeed, it was so risibly simple that he wondered why he didn't usually communicate in such a manner (although a deeper knowledge cradled in his brain told him they were not truly colours any more than humming a passage of music constitutes a full orchestra. There was something greater still, but he was so taken by paddling in the shallows of this new ontological ocean that he was content to limit his perceptions to it).

If he let them, the colours would tell him stories. He liked stories, and besides, these seemed important, so he sat back and watched them unfurl like the Northern Lights that he'd only ever seen in a painting. Unlike the painting, they danced and trembled and told the tale of a people who had dispensed with their bodies long since and now lived by seeking out new bodies of races on the cusp of thought. Grant, who only knew that "evolution" was some nonsense about monkeys, was immediately and smoothly inculcated into an understanding of natural selection that would have staggered any professor of natural history by its erudite totality. Here he stood on Earth long, long before Moses, before Adam, and here was such a species, thrown together by natural processes in a form less lovely than some of the fish he'd seen on the market. He was not frightened by them, however, for life is as life does, and live and let live, and other homilies that he found comforting even if how they applied to great conical beasts that slid around seemed unimportant in that moment. The race that was without bodies found the cone creatures and occupied them and were happy to do so, for they could not survive otherwise. In any event, the cone things were an evolutionary squib and would die out shortly in any case, and the bodiless ones knew that because... because...

A new idea came to him, and its scale hurt his mind. He could not accept. He would not accept it. Better his mind shatter like a dropped stoneware pint mug than accept such...

A small pain in his arm. An expression of concern.

Where was he? Oh, yes. Cone things.

The bodiless knew that the cone things would die out because time was not a line to them, but something more like a field in which they roamed about. Well, then, it was child's play to understand that they would therefore be able to see the cone creatures' imminent extinction. Such things happen all the time, and that is good, because now the bodiless ones could take the cone creatures as their new bodies, secure in the knowledge that they would not take away the eventualities of a new race, because those eventualities were never to pass. It was very elegant. If Grant had been able to remember what cheering was, he would have cheered the bodiless ones. It was just like taking to the lifeboats, after all. And that was why they had never taken over humanity, because humanity was not destined for a short existence, a whole stalk of grass in the meadow of time, that was humanity's lot, and it was not so bad. Yes, the bodiless ones were perfectly capable of taking human bodies, but never permanently, only as explorers into other parts of the meadow.

After all, wasn't that what had befallen … ?

There was a necessary corollary, and it scrabbled at Grant's heightened awareness. It came laden with emotional debris from the base creature he had been before, like a ship's anchor brought up with all manner of fouling from the seabed. It stank, and he shied away from it. He should not be distracted by that. There was so much more to understand.

But these were not his own thoughts. Where were they coming from? There was warmness in their tone, and he thought of Lizzie, but Lizzie was in the next room, and the voice that was hers was not using her words.

He could see new colours, smell emotions, taste time on his tongue like salt. He could also see a flickering gas mantel, smell damp brickwork, taste his own blood in his mouth. When he realised the reality of it all, felt his bonds and knew that he was tied to a chair in some dank cellar somewhere, he could have screamed with the frustration of everything that he had lost and all he must now endure.

"What *are* you?" he cried at Miss Cerulia Trent. "What have you done to her?"

Miss Trent approached, and he scented the hues of trust, courage, experience, and determination. As she had done before, she placed her hand on his cheek and looked him in the eye. "Elizabeth Whittle is safe and healthy, and being well looked after. We do not do what we have done lightly. We are not cruel, but we are desperate. We face total extermination. Humanity faces decimation and slavery. We – you and I – face a mutual enemy. Will you help us?"

He had no words. The foreshortening of his senses back into the confines of his skull and skin was the most terrible loss he had ever endured. No, it was only almost the most terrible loss.

Behind him, he heard Miss Church say, "It's useless, master. He's just a tuppenny-ha'penny confidence man. He's never given a tinker's cuss about anyone but himself."

Miss Trent had never looked away from his eyes. "I do not believe that to be entirely true in this case," she said.

"Lizzie's all right?" he asked.

"I will never lie to you, Mr Grant. Elizabeth Whittle is alive and well."

"*Is*," he echoed. "But she's in the past." He thought of the immensity of the meadow of time. "She's long dead."

"Only if we do not transpose minds once more. If I succeed in my mission in this present, she will be reunited with this body, and I shall return to mine."

"And if you fail?"

"Then I shall die in this present, she shall die in the past. You will likely die, too."

"She's telling the truth, Mr Grant," said Miss Church.

"I know," he replied. "I know that." He looked down at his left arm, the sleeve rolled up, the tourniquet on his bicep, the needle marks on the inside of his elbow. He'd seen opium and laudanum fiends and listened to their experiences. Whatever he had been given was certainly not of that ilk, but he had nevertheless been drugged, his sanity disrupted to preserve it, his mind saved from being destroyed, if only temporarily. "I can't help you–" he began, and heard Miss Church sigh, but he ignored her and continued, "–tied to a chair. I will do anything within my power to restore Lizzie, even if I have to fight the Devil to do it."

Miss Trent's unblinking gaze continued a moment longer. Then a nod to Miss Church, who started to undo Grant's bonds.

"You have to fight worse than the Devil, Mr Grant," she said quietly to him as she worked. "You have to fight Sir Donovan Clay."

Chapter Eight
WORLDS ENOUGH AND TIME

Grant needed to stop thinking if he wanted to get anything done, but it was hard to avoid dwelling on Lizzie and the terrible trial she was currently undergoing uncountable millennia in the past. It was easier not to think of how he had stopped viewing time as a river one bobbed along like a cork, but now rather saw it as that limitless meadow, all simultaneous and perceivable, should one's eyes be opened sufficiently wide. Miss Church had assured him that the drug she had employed upon him ("I truly *am* a nurse") was not addictive and had hinted that it was neither a product of the present nor actually a drug in the sense that a pharmacologist might recognise. That might be true; indeed – given the enormity of what he was now expected to comprehend – it would be fatuous to lie on such a point, but he found he still craved the clarity it had brought to him. Now that his mind was a small place again, it was difficult to take such truths in.

But now he knew what sort of body the current occupant

of Elizabeth Whittle's *corpus vivant* owned back in the oh-so-distant past, and that was currently inhabited by Lizzie. The great cone, the clawed tentacles, the head like a scientific instrument made from the flesh of fish. He hoped that those who were looking after her were keeping her well sedated. He could hardly imagine what it might be like to realise oneself not only in the wrong body, but the body of a creature that would not look out of place in the deepest reaches of the oldest ocean.

The idea of the creature lay etched in cognitive mercury in his mind. If he tried to think about it too hard, it ran over the cobbles of his thoughts to reform elsewhere, refusing close scrutiny. He assumed this was an effect of the drug, and he was glad of it. The idea thus existed in the parts of his memory occupied by all that was mundane and acceptable, like pavement bollards and pub signs, known but generally unremarked. The same could be said of how the knowledge had been communicated to him in the first place; the memory of the creature was too vivacious to have been conveyed by speech, or even a good picture. It was more as if he had once encountered at least one example and strolled by it as if it were a horse or a dog. If he wondered too hard at how he knew such a strange form, how he was familiar with its odd gliding lumber and the serpentine coiling of those clawed, boneless arms, he would have been at a loss, and then the ramifications would have crowded in upon him and then…

But that never happened, for the recollection fell into beads of quicksilver, even as he tried to grasp it, and ran away to reform somewhere else. It was a relief to remain in such artful ignorance, and he could only hope that a similar kindness had been extended to Lizzie, whenever she was.

A lot of things made a great deal more sense now that they had been explained, even if many elements of those explanations had then been quietly filed away by his mind into secret corners under covers reading "To Be Accepted Without Question". Questioning them, after all, necessitated thinking about them, and that might well be unwise. Better to let them reside in the shadows at the back of his awareness. Better and safer.

One of the safer elements was the provenance of Miss Church. Emerging from the cellar in which he had undergone his ordeal of the eons, Grant had found himself in the servants' hall of a small villa that he subsequently learned was in a quiet cul-de-sac in Chiswick.

"Chiswick?"

"Chiswick. It's quiet here and people keep themselves to themselves," said Miss Church.

"How on Earth did you spirit me from Kensington to Chiswick?"

"In a furniture delivery van, wrapped in a carpet," said a new voice. Grant looked over to see a familiar young man hovering by the back door. "I am very sorry about the business in the alleyway, sir," he said, giving every indication that he was prepared to bolt like a skittish cat if Grant made a move towards him. "I thought you meant the master harm."

"He means me," said Miss Trent, coming through the

door from the body of the house. "Mr Grant, this is Mr Robert Castle."

"I see," said Grant, unconsciously reaching up to smooth back his hair and thereby touching the small wound Castle had bestowed upon him. "And who might Mr Robert Castle be?"

"One of us," said Miss Church. "A concerned party and member of our little society."

"And what sort of society is that?"

"The secret sort. The neighbours think we are some sort of friendly society, and we make some efforts to support that misapprehension. But actually we're sort of a…" she paused, considering, "a sort of…" her eyebrows went up to denote mild surprise, as if she had never thought in quite such terms before that moment, "a sort of a cult, I suppose."

"A nice sort of a cult," added Mr Castle.

"Oh, yes. Nothing frightful or sordid. Certainly a nice cult."

The drug had, Grant realised, not preserved his sanity so much as selectively broken it in such a way that they might have been discussing the best damson jam recipe rather than a cult hidden in the borough of Hounslow. If there was anything that might have sent him raving into the night – and he could see that night had fallen through the high windows of the servants' hall – it was that this nest of occult conspiracy was in a leafy suburb of Chiswick. At some level, he had always known that Chiswick was up to something.

"I think," he said, "that I very much need a cup of tea."

•••

Tea was forthcoming, and the party withdrew to a more salubrious sitting room in the body of the house. Here Grant was invited to ask his questions, and – after taking a minute to sort the mountain of his curiosity into a more tractable prospect – he began.

"Sir Donovan Clay. Rich; yes, he's that. Eccentric; undoubtedly. A self-absorbed ass; assuredly. But these are charges that might be laid at the doors of many hundreds of Londoners. How is he the match or worse of the Devil?"

"Sir Donovan Clay is a traitor," said Castle.

"To the entire human race," added Miss Trent. "He has... made discoveries that it would be better that no human ever had, but – in the immensity of time and given the curiosity of humans – it was almost inevitable that it would occur again and again. Historically, this has always been the case up to this point. People discovered this thing, they were killed by it, and equilibrium was restored."

"But, Sir Donovan lives," said Grant.

"Indeed, he thrives, and that is because he has parleyed with those that would exterminate us. Mr Castle, the map, please."

Castle took a rolled up map from a cluster of others atop a bureau and spread it out upon the table, weighting its corners with bric-a-brac. Grant read the legend "Western Extents of Australasia".

Miss Trent pointed at part of the great yellow extent that covered much of the land. "This is the Great Sandy Desert, and approximately *here* is where Sir Donovan's mining concern is based." She tapped the paper with one gloved fingertip. She hesitated, looking at her hand for a moment, and Grant thought of Lizzie. "It is also the location of a city, a city we sealed in antiquity. A city containing a baleful threat."

"You have to understand," said Castle, "that Miss Whittle's… tenant…"

"Good God," said Miss Church under her breath.

"…is not of this Earth. Space is vast and more populated than even the most optimistic astronomers might guess. They came here a long time ago. A staggeringly long time ago."

"I think Mr Grant has enough to absorb without dragging cosmology into matters," said Miss Church.

"That depends on Mr Grant," said Miss Trent, looking up from the map to regard him intently. "You already know more than almost anyone on Earth does of this matter," she said directly to Grant. "Some absorb such knowledge easily. Others… less so. You do not need to know every detail to be of assistance to me and thereby hasten the return of the Elizabeth Whittle you know. At the same time, I will not withhold anything that you *do* need to know. You have a phrase, 'Ignorance is bliss'. Do you wish to remain in such blissful, if now partial, ignorance? Or do you wish me to tell you everything?"

Grant drew a deep breath, held it for a long moment, and then gave it slow, fatalistic vent.

"I suppose I am quite mad now, anyway, 'though I've always been told the mad don't think themselves mad. That is probably true now. I don't *feel* mad, only that I am taking part in some grand and absurd practical joke, and the masks will come off soon enough. But, then again, I don't really believe that, either." He smiled ruefully. "Perhaps I am mad, after all. For example, I now think of you as Miss Cerulia Trent, even though Lizzie and I created Miss Cerulia Trent out of whole cloth over a pot of tea. Please don't take offence, but I would like nothing more than for Miss Cerulia Trent to become merely a fictional character played by Lizzie Whittle once again, and I shall learn everything I need to learn to hasten that event and to help me understand what she's been through when she's restored."

"I take no offence at that, because it is what I desire too, William Grant," said Miss Trent. "As do all my race, and as would your race, too, if they only knew what awaited them should we fail. Very well, then. This is the nub of the matter."

"As Mr Castle has intimated," began Miss Cerulia Trent, "my people are not of Earth. Our original home is lost to us in the eons, long since left, long since forgotten. We are nomads of space, and of time."

"The Great Race of Yith", they called themselves without obvious irony, even if who or what or where "Yith" had been was a datum obscure even to them. Perhaps it was the name of the world upon which they had first evolved, but perhaps it was not. Shorn of definitive meaning, they were simply coming to call themselves "the Yith" or "the Yithians" because names are only labels, and those were as good as any. Certainly a racial name is of lower importance than a personal name, and here Grant was reminded of the shower of colours he'd experienced, the most glorious firework display that was the true name of Cerulia Trent, of the personality and history it carried. The Yith she was, was a hero, and the best chance of the Yith to survive the foreshadowed apocalypse in their future.

In the distant past, then, the Yith – intelligences without form – had abandoned some other world and come to primordial Earth, there to occupy the bodies of creatures that were as terrestrial as the dinosaurs or man, that were blessed to be on the cusp of true intelligence, yet doomed to suffer an early extinction because they never quite got that chance. It was a moment ripe for the Yith and they took it with alacrity, taking on new forms as a human might adopt a hat. Illumined with the ancient intelligence of the Yith, the fated extinction never occurred, and the Yith prospered in their new bodies, great conical creatures of thin chitin and dense hydrostatic skeletons.

They raised cities, and continued their cultural and scientific evolution, untroubled yet mindful of the other creatures of the Earth, and always careful to avoid imposing their presence too strongly for fear of pushing the engine of Nature from its ordained path. For they were cognisant of the future in the same way that a man upon a hilltop is cognisant of the land ahead, and while every detail was not easy to make out, it allowed them to see most major events that lay in the offing.

But they did not anticipate the Enemy, a race that had

never troubled to give itself a name. The Enemy tumbled around the cosmos like rambunctious, wicked children in a bone China shop, fuelled by boiled sweets and their own spite. They left destruction, chaos, and the ruination of whole worlds in their wake. Great bulks of what any other species would call tumorous growths but that it pleased them to regard as their bodies, the Enemy looked with greedy eyes upon the Earth and determined to take it from the Yith. They swept down, and passages through which they travelled gaped open in the skies like diseased stomata, disgorging the Enemy in their thousands.

The ensuing war was fought without quarter on both sides once it became apparent that the concepts of both mercy and taking prisoners were alien to the Enemy. The Yith lost city after city to the invaders, including the great capital of Pnakotus. Finally, they developed new weapons, terrifying devices that threw gouts of directed lightning, against which the Enemy were helpless. The tide of war changed definitively, and the Enemy ceded gain after gain until they were driven back to Pnakotus, and then down into the labyrinth of caves beneath it. There, the triumphant Yith sealed the entrances, containing the Enemy and leaving them to die miserably in the darkness.

But the Enemy did not draw their sustenance from food and drink, and so they did not die, but only lay in the great shadowed caverns and festered in their hatred of the Great Race of Yith."

"This city... Knackotters–"

"Pnakotus. Yes?"

"This wouldn't be the one in Australia you mentioned, would it?"

"What do you think?" said Mr Castle in an undertone, unnecessarily insolent.

Miss Trent nodded while Miss Church shot Mr Castle a glance every bit as withering as a bolt from a Yithian lightning gun. "It is. But our interest in it and Sir Donovan were the result of other developments. Might I continue?" Grant indicated that she might do so, and so she did.

The Yith could see the future, the past and even a hint of what might have been to either side of them in the great meadow of time. Perhaps in no crystalline detail, but well enough to know when major events might threaten them. Even the arrival of the Enemy had been foreseen, although their exact nature and their resistance to those weapons the Yith had immediately available came as unwelcome surprises.

With the remnants of the Enemy force entombed beneath Pnakotus, the Yith looked forward to a future that they believed they understood well. At some moment around sixty million years in Grant's past, but still millennia into the future of the Yith, a new and long-awaited threat would emerge and this one they would not be able to defeat. Consequently, they had not even tried, but had instead evolved a new plan.

"After humanity's extinction–" began Miss Trent.

"I beg your pardon?" said Grant, startled out of the slightly dreamlike state his mind had adopted as a safe way to absorb disturbing new data without turning to stewed cheese.

"You surely don't expect us to last forever, do you, old man?" said Mr Castle.

While Grant was grateful to the idea that Mr Castle, at least, would not last forever, he had never really questioned that people would remain as the dominant species, in all likelihood with the British Empire proving an equally immortal entity. That humanity could go the same way as the dodo was a new, unpleasant, and very personal concept.

"It is the way of the universe, Mr Grant," Miss Trent said. "Everything must change, sooner or later."

"Not your lot, though," he said more hotly than intended. "First sign of trouble and you can gallivant off to grab somebody else's body. You'll live forever."

She shook her head. "No. Even in our visions of the future, there is a darkness far ahead. Perhaps it is the limit of our sight, or perhaps there is nothing for us to see beyond that point. Our existence as a race may be long, but it is by no means infinite. Why, even the..." She paused and Grant thought he saw a glimmer of fear in her, flickering momentarily beneath the human face that concealed it. She rallied, and instead said, "But, I digress. After the extinction of humanity – which was a substantial period into the future, I assure you..." He found the use of the past tense less reassuring but said nothing. "...a new race reached the cusp of intelligence, but suffered a catastrophe that prevented its full flowering."

"Again? Just like your old... your current forms?"

"It happens frequently. The opportunity to reach full sapience is the rarity."

"And as a matter of interest, what creatures are these? The monkeys?"

Mr Castle laughed. "*We're* the monkeys, old chap."

"Sort of cockroaches, I've been given to understand," supplied Miss Church. "Rather big ones." She saw Grant's consternation. "Sorry."

"That has long been the anticipated next great exodus of my race. We also saw that the containment of the Enemy could not last forever, but that they would only escape long after we had escaped to the future and long, *long* before our arrival. Cheated of their chance at revenge and the definitive knowledge that they had been defeated for all time, they would sink into a state of racial ennui and finally become extinct themselves. This was all to the good."

Grant gave up trying to think of time as a meadow and returned to thinking of it more like a river, an easier concept for him to absorb. "But something changed, didn't it?"

Miss Trent nodded slowly. "That black horizon I told you of? It abruptly came much closer."

"How much so?"

"It is here."

It was as if, overnight, the Yith view of the meadow had suddenly become encroached upon by a black fog, the furthest edge of which was marked as the year 1891 Anno Domini. The great exodus of which Miss Trent had spoken was corrupted, forestalled, and foreshortened. The Yith, at the moment of the exodus, would find themselves unable to travel further than 1891 and be forced to occupy human bodies en masse. And then...

"We immediately suspected this might have something to do with the Enemy and so we asked our agents to investigate any possible resurgence."

"Agents?" said Grant.

"Hello," chorused Miss Church and Mr Castle.

"I did say that we are a sort of cult," added Miss Church. "The Yith are explorers of time, which they manage by temporarily possessing a human host body while the human mind occupies the Yith body in the past. They potter around for a while, gathering data while the human mind in the past is gently questioned about their everyday life, and the current state of art, science, politics, and so on. Over the centuries, a sort of... well, I suppose you might call it a mutual aid society has developed across the world to help the Yith in their pottering around, and to aid them to return when they're done. In return, they give us a bit of scientific help and help us dodge the occasional catastrophe. It's all very equitable. It's not like we're worshipping them or anything barbaric like that." She frowned and looked at Miss Trent. "You *don't* want to be worshipped, do you?"

"Absolutely not," said Miss Trent.

"Jolly good," said Mr Castle.

"So, as agents, what did you discover?" asked Grant, keener to understand the imminent threat to humanity than the niceties of running a cult that might or might not worship otherworldly entities.

Miss Church glanced at Miss Trent again, this time for tacit permission to take up the tale. "Well, the first thing to do was to check on the state of Pnakotus and, to our horror, we discovered a mining operation had been built on the site. We thought we'd forestalled anything like that by using our influence to make the area off-limits as a government reserve, but apparently Donovan Clay – as he was then – greased a few palms and worked his way past the restriction. We did what we could, but he had found high-alumina bauxite deposits and, what with the Bayer Process being perfected a few years ago… well, you can imagine."

Grant had little concept of what bauxite was, regardless of its alumina content, and he was sure that he'd never heard of the "Bayer Process", but it all seemed very clever and the sort of thing likely to involve large sums of money, so he nodded shrewdly and hoped that no one would ask him to explain any of this.

"So, we stood by," said Mr Castle, "or at least our counterparts in Perth did. The Australian Perth, that is. They waited for the inevitable moment when Pnakotus would be discovered or, worse yet, the Enemy released. But it never seemed to happen. We thought it might have when operations were suspended for a week, and we stood by, sure that reports of strange flying monsters and mass casualties would soon be coming out of the desert. But… nothing.

"We were beginning to believe that we must have entirely misunderstood the situation, when we received a report that there *had* been an accident at the mine at the beginning of the quietus. Fifteen men dead, and their bodies apparently irrecoverable for examination, or at least that's what the coroner was told. In hindsight, it seems that

Pnakotus is discovered, the Enemy is released, they killed the first people they encountered and then... well, we believe Sir Donovan somehow negotiated with them."

"I thought these things didn't understand negotiation?"

Miss Church said, "You have to bear in mind how long they have been trapped. Millions upon millions of years. They are *not* the Enemy of old. They may still hate the Great Race of Yith – indeed, by this time, our extermination is probably a point of faith for them and beyond disputation – but we do not truly know what Sir Donovan encountered in those tunnels, or how he communicated with them. What we do know, however, is what he offered them. The trapping and slaughter of the Great Race in this year. You may imagine what he will want in return."

"And that's the whole of what you know?" asked Grant.

"The majority of it, yes," admitted Castle. "So... any questions?"

"Dozens," said Grant. To Miss Trent, he said, "Firstly, how does he intend to stop you travelling onwards to the future you were expecting would be yours? These... cockroaches of yours."

"We do not know. We have never encountered a barrier thrown up in time before. It is a remarkable feat. The Enemy we fought in the past were possessed of a certain cunning, but they were not clever exactly. How they could have devised such an effect is confusing."

"Sir Donovan couldn't have come up with it? He's supposed to be pretty clever, isn't he?"

Mr Castle shook his head. "He's a smart 'un, no doubt,

but apart from being pretty lively with dynamite and blasting gelignite, he's not what you'd call the Newton of the age. As I say, the chemistry of explosives, he's your feller, but messing around with time itself? No, not him."

"So, it must be these Enemy creatures themselves? But then I wonder, why do they need him?"

"It's a knotty old puzzle, isn't it?" said Mr Castle, looking inside the teapot and being disappointed to find insufficient remaining for a cup.

"It is a puzzle we have very little time left to solve," said Miss Trent.

"You know," said Grant, "all through this, I've been wondering, 'Why, Lizzie? Why drop into her when nearly anyone else in that house would have been a better prospect?' You've never explained that."

"You have to understand, Mr Grant, that the transposition is not a perfectly accurate operation. The best we can hope for is a rough locale. We misread matters and assumed that you and Miss Whittle were members of his inner circle, that Sir Donovan had something planned for the evening. We hoped that performing the operation then would allow whatever these other activities were to obfuscate the transposition."

"You knew about the session? But how?" Grant thought for a moment, and answered himself. "The cabman. He was one of yours, wasn't he?" He looked at Miss Church. "You and your *cult* are very good at barging your way into the lives of others without so much as an excuse me, aren't you? So, this happening to Lizzie was just rotten luck, then?"

"No, not entirely," said Miss Trent. "There is a quality that all living creatures possess, a sort of potentiality if you will. When we settled upon one mind out of all those there that night, it was the one with the greatest such puissance. We did so in the belief that this must be one of the leaders of the conspiracy, perhaps even Sir Donovan himself."

"But it was Lizzie?"

"Alas, it was, and I apologise again at all that has befallen her and you as a result. Her mind was an incandescent light upon our instruments, Mr Grant. Elizabeth Whittle is a remarkable woman."

"I already knew that," said William Grant.

CHAPTER NINE

SIX WOUNDS

The situation, then, was dire. There is little in life so bad, however, that it may not deteriorate further.

Grant was much happier to return to Kensington, smugly middle class though it was. He did not like the environs of the Yith cult's discreet little house and, indeed, given the choice of wandering the reputedly doom-haunted tunnels beneath Pnakotus in the distant antipodes, or Chiswick, he would have needed a minute to think about it. He had started to brew a pot of tea, thought better of it, broke out a bottle of whisky, and now stood nursing a glass of a halfway decent single malt with a splash of water as he looked out of the window of Miss Trent's rooms into which the quartet had repaired. Perhaps he was growing overly on edge given recent revelations, but he had noted a man who reminded him of one of Sir Donovan's people behaving with mannered nonchalance in a doorway across the street. Now, twenty minutes later, there he remained.

"I think the house is under observation," he said to the others.

"I guarantee it," said Mr Castle. "Feller across the street? Looks like somebody poured a concoction of muscle and vinegar into a good suit and forgot to say 'when'? Him? One of Donovan's creatures. We should have stayed in Chiswick."

Though loath to admit it, Grant felt that was probably true. "I'm sorry about your colleague. The cabman, that is."

"Poor old Georgie Handforth." For once Castle didn't seem nearly so amused by life. "He was a good egg. Rotten luck that they caught him."

"He may still be alive," said Miss Church.

"No," said Grant. "I'm sorry. He isn't. I spoke to the police, and they told me about his death and implied with impertinent gall that they thought I was involved."

"Well, that's definite, then," said Castle. "Ugly way to go, beaten to death by a bunch of convict-spawned thugs."

"No," said Grant, "that's not what happened to him. It was awful, far worse than being beaten to death." He hesitated. "I don't wish to shock anyone…"

"Oh, don't be absurd," said Miss Church. "I think that we're all rather beyond that at this point, don't you?"

Quickly then, he gave a brief description of what he had learned in New Scotland Yard – the six brutal skull injuries and the removal of the brain. Despite her admonition, both Miss Church and Mr Castle seemed nevertheless shocked.

"Six wounds?" said Miss Trent with a sudden intensity

that perplexed and troubled Grant. "Equally spaced around the vault of the skull?"

"Yes." Grant found himself thinking of the mortuary photographs despite his best efforts not to. "Is that significant?"

"It is. There is an excellent chance that Mr Handforth is not dead."

"I assure you, I saw the pictures. I didn't want to, but that swine Bradley put them before me. Your man Handforth was the most deceased I have ever seen any man this side of an urn of ashes in Woking Crematorium. There was no chance of survival."

"Of his body, I agree, but you are not your body, Mr Grant. You are your brain, and your body is merely a convenient way of conveying it around. The same is… was true of Mr Handforth. His brain may still live, and therefore so does he."

There was an awful silence from the three entirely human occupants of the room. "Are you saying," said Castle with care, "that Georgie Handforth may still be alive right this moment as… a *brain* in – I don't know – a *jar* somewhere?"

"Not somewhere. In the house of Sir Donovan Clay. It is a convenient form for interrogation, I would guess, depending on how much control one has of the senses and assuming communication is possible."

"How do you know this?" said Grant with equal care. "What is the significance of the six incisions?"

"We have considered such a form of surgery. Hypothetically. For certain circumstances." Miss Church looked at her companions. "Hypothetically," she repeated.

"Oh, God," said Miss Church in a terrible whisper. "Poor Georgie."

"Poor us, too," said Castle. "If they know what he knows, then they know everything. The retreat in Chiswick isn't safe."

Grant shook his head. "There was no one watching it. There's the cul-de-sac road itself and the path to the rear, so that means they'd need at least two people. Just before we left, I scouted down the path to check the end wasn't observed, and then when we did leave via the front, there was nobody dawdling at the junction, certainly no one who looked like one of Sir Donovan's men. We only came under observation on returning here."

"Then I don't understand why they did… *that* to Georgie. If they can't get information out of him, what use is he to them? They might as well have just stuck a chiv in his back and dumped him in the Thames like any good, honest Englishman would instead of all this baroque how-do-you-do messing around with a feller's tuppenny." Miss Church looked blankly at him, so he added, "A knife. Stuck a knife in him."

"I was actually wondering what a 'tuppenny' might be."

"Head," supplied Grant. "It's rhyming slang." Leaving Miss Church very much at sea as to how "tuppenny" might possibly rhyme with "head", he continued, "I don't suppose there's any chance that it was done for the pure brutality of the act?"

"No," said Miss Trent. "At the very least, it was performed as an experiment. At the worst, they may be able to extract some information from him. That possibility means that we have no choice but to act swiftly. Sir Donovan must be stopped before he is able to complete whatever the Enemy's plan entails."

"This business with the session—"

"The séance, you mean?" asked Castle.

"We never liked that term. But what was it for? Surely Sir Donovan wouldn't take a rest from betraying humanity to these… *creatures* to mourn his wife, would he? I've seen enough grieving husbands to know he didn't give a tuppenny damn about losing his wife. In fact, in light of what you've told me, the coincidence of his wife dying just before he left Australia seems to grow less and less likely."

"Oh," said Miss Church, "I hadn't considered that. Surely even he…?" She shook her head. "But of course, he would. No crime is beyond him."

Castle frowned. "I don't like the man either, but we can't go accusing him of every possible crime just—"

"He is a traitor to the entire human race," she said firmly, and that was the end of that particular caveat.

The phrase had resonance, and the room was silent for a minute or two. Grant had heard similar a few times before in his life, usually employed by the yellow press over somebody who had criticised some raw-headed and bloody-boned policy or other to which the newspaper proprietors cleaved closely. This, however, was literal and without an ounce of hyperbole upon its frame, and that realisation solidified a horror upon Grant that thus far he had held at arm's length. He had met the Devil, and the Devil had a house out in Barking. "I'm truly sorry for the loss of your friend," he said at last. "He must have got lost in that wretched storm. It was coming down in stair rods that night. We could barely see where we were going."

"It was not a natural storm," said Miss Trent. "It hovered over that house and that house only. Something happened that night that had an effect upon the weather. I do not know what."

"The lightning was fierce," admitted Grant.

"Lightning," said Castle suddenly. "Oh, in all the fuss, I quite forgot to mention, Georgie took the lightning weapon with him that night. I suppose that's lost now, too."

Grant thought of the mighty stroke of lightning that had apparently struck the house or close nearby, the concussion of it throwing open the French windows into that dismal dining room.

"If they have it, then the Enemy know that we are close to them." Miss Trent's brow gathered in deep thought for a few seconds. "Everything must be expedited. We must move against them before they can move against us."

"You have more of these things?" asked Grant. "These weapons?"

"No," said Castle. "Well, not working examples, but in any case…" There was an awkward pause. "We're supposed to be jolly careful with them."

"I should hope so."

"No, old man, I mean we should be jolly careful that they don't fall into the wrong hands."

"Well, it's too late for that. If you're right then Sir Donovan already has one."

"Sir Donovan?" Castle looked at Grant without understanding for a long moment before comprehension dawned. "Oh, *him*? Oh, he might well do something frightful with it, I've no doubt, but I wasn't really talking about Sir Donovan. I meant the British Government. If the War Office wallahs were able to lay hands upon one of those blunderbusses, well... that would be very, very bad."

Grant, whose belief in the ruling powers – with the exception of the Home Office's attachment to maintaining police forces around the country – was touchingly uncritical, said "Why?"

"Because they might throw some scientists at it and possibly, just possibly, understand how they work, and if they manage that, it's a short step to making their own, and if they manage *that*... well. Stick a lightning gun into the hands of every feller in a red tunic and bigger examples aboard every ship in the fleet, and it would be carnage. You can see that, can't you?"

"No. I'd trust the British with them before I would anyone else."

"That's as may be, but you shouldn't trust them either. Think of all the scores to settle. How long before France is a scorched cinder? How long before the United States is part of the Empire again, whether it likes the idea or not, eh?"

"That wouldn't be so!"

"Wouldn't it? Can you guarantee that?"

Grant opened his mouth, and then shut it again. He could not.

"We have seen your future, Mr Grant," said Miss Trent. "There will be weapons to rival the lightning guns soon enough. Do not be in a hurry to risk your tomorrows."

"If we have any," said Miss Church. "What are we going to do about Sir Donovan and his allies? They might do anything, and if they do it before we're ready, the future may be a very terrible place."

Grant rose and returned to the window. Twitching back the half-height net curtain with a fingertip, he looked down into the street and at their lone observer, currently to be found pretending to read a newspaper. "Well," he said, "we could always just ask them."

It is traditional upon introducing a minor player in a drama to then spend some paragraphs detailing a brief biography of the debutant. In the case of "Jibsy" McMahon, this would be a wasted effort beyond taking a moment to explain that "Jibsy" was an epithet bestowed upon him indirectly by a prison warder who observed that in a more civilised age, McMahon would have ended up swinging in a gibbet and thereby saved everyone a lot of trouble. After a brief period of being called "Gibbet" by his associates, the nickname metamorphosed into the handier form of "Jibsy", and he was glad enough to adopt this and claim it for his own in preference to his given name, which was "Horace".

"Jibsy" McMahon had been told to keep an eye on the house in Kensington and particularly on the comings and goings of Madam Trent, whom he was set to follow should she show her face. The last sentinel of the house had been met with opprobrium and harsh commentary on his return to Barking for failing to see her leave the previous day and Jibsy had no desire to provoke the ire of his employer in a similar manner, especially given the high promises of what success would bring to those who proved trustworthy. After all, the boss had a rough temper on him when provoked, or even when unprovoked; it was too easy to lose his favour and very hard to reacquire it. Jibsy had managed to stay in Sir Donovan's good graces to date by the simple expedient of total, unquestioning obedience. It was a simple, effective strategy and it seemed to work, and so Jibsy – who was fond of simple, effective strategies –was diligent in his submission to the boss and his whims.

And so, we find Jibsy, lurking behind his unread newspaper, observing the windows he knew to belong to the rooms of Madam Trent and, below them, those of William Grant, as well as the door. He thought he had seen the net curtains of one of the upper storey windows twitch some twenty minutes previous, but otherwise there had been little excitement that day, and he was looking forward to being relieved in just over an hour. That prospect abruptly diminished when he saw Madam Trent, in the company of another young lady whose identity was unknown to him, leave the house, cross the road to his side, and then walk away from him. Nonchalantly tucking his newspaper under his arm and lighting a cigarette as a small compensation for the unlooked-for likely lengthening of his shift, he sauntered after them in lukewarm pursuit.

The two women were behaving in a manner he characterised as "shifty", and this added flavour to the hunt. Why else would two young ladies be projecting an aura of the clandestine unless they were up to no good? And why would he, a criminal even unto the third generation, not find himself inflamed by professional curiosity to discover what that might be? Thus, he was positively agog when the women made a sudden turn down a back alley.

He followed them for some twenty yards down the alleyway when, after a brief discussion, his prey halted and turned to face him. This was a surprising and unhappy development for Jibsy, although not nearly as surprising and unwelcome as the distinct feeling of a gun barrel pressing into the small of his back and the words, whispered in a male voice and in a tone that did not betoken the prospect of negotiations, "Make any trouble and I'll shoot you clean through the backbone."

Jibsy very slowly raised his hands and said, "No trouble from me, mate."

The man simply appeared at Bradley's desk. Only the moment before Bradley had cast a wary eye across the office and seen nothing of interest, looked down at the report he was writing, and – in the time it took him to finagle the spelling of "necessarily" into something more likely to please the staff of the Oxford English Dictionary's editorial board – the man somehow coalesced before him. He was more an urban than an urbane gentleman, possessed of an open, somewhat bland countenance and a pleasant mien, dressed in a decently tailored albeit off-the-rack suit and an inoffensive hat, which he held in his hand. He smiled at Bradley as if about to ask him for a charitable donation.

Bradley rose. "I'm sorry, sir, you caught me in a brown study. Detective Sergeant Bradley. How might I help you?"

"My name is Jowett, Geoffrey Jowett. I explained my business to the sergeant at the front desk, and he sent me to you."

Bradley absorbed this information and, given that many of his tasks to date for the Metropolitan force and therefore the reputation by which the sergeant would know him were to do with personation and fraud, he theorised that the man was here with a story of deception and chicanery. He invited Mr Jowett to sit and to tell him his woes.

"I am the secretary of a small society; small, but – I like to think – possessed of a membership of unusual intelligence and perceptiveness. The society is called the Metaphysical Investigation Conference, and it is our business to investigate the nature and limits of reality."

Bradley blinked. He'd rather been hoping for a tale of misappropriated Christmas club savings or similar. "How so?" he asked for lack of anything more intelligent or insightful to say.

Mr Jowett smiled beatifically. "There is a belief in some quarters that all the corners of our existence are well-enough understood in the modern age. We beg to disagree. While science has indeed made remarkable strides in recent years, we hold that there is still so much more than is even guessed at. To that end we have recruited everyone from philosophers to physicists, conjurers to chemists, and even a couple of members who regard themselves as true magicians. Decent fellows, though they do insist on spelling *magick* with a *k*, mind you."

"Quite a catholic gathering," said Bradley.

"We prefer to think of it as *eclectic*, but, yes, there are many schools of thought within our number. We meet once a month in the private dining room over *The Wine Press* in Soho, and such gatherings can get quite rambunctious, I may tell you." He paled, aware that he may be giving the wrong impression. "Intellectually, you understand. Voices are rarely raised."

Bradley nodded. "I understand, sir. So, how may I help you?"

"Well, you see, we are not just a talking shop. When we placed the word 'Investigation' in the middle of our society's name, it was no empty promise. One of our main activities is to send our members out into the world to investigate and report back upon instances of phenomena that fall outside the usual. It is there, you see, we are most likely to find the actual ragged edges of our true reality."

Finally, Bradley understood why the sergeant had sent the inoffensive Mr Jowett to him. "When you say 'outside the usual', how exactly do you mean, sir?"

"Oh, well, I'm sure that you can guess. Incidences of the sort that have been noted historically ever since anyone decided to note anything. Ghosts, curious manifestations, strange and unique creatures, communing with the dead, and so on. Things that are not at all fashionable in our scientific age, detective sergeant. And yet, such reports continue to accumulate. We send our people out with open minds and clear eyes, no expectations one way or the other. Almost invariably they return with disappointing news. Although, in the true spirit of the scientific method, no failure is ever disappointing in and of itself – only a realisation that perhaps the shadows of our knowledge are not as deep as we might wish."

"But, something has emerged during one of these investigations?" asked Bradley, hoping to prod Mr Jowett towards specifics.

"No, not exactly. Let me assure you, detective sergeant, we are not naive in our endeavours. We know full well that the vast majority of such reported phenomena shall turn out to have the most humdrum explanations. On the subject of communing with the dead, for example, we tend to rely on the conjurers in our number. They are adept at stagecraft and illusion, after all, and whenever we send them off to report upon this medium or that, they come back to tell us of fraud or, even more distressingly, delusion far more often than not. But not consistently. There have been a handful of cases where they have been unable to explain what they witnessed. This, of course, does not preclude any number of mundane explanations, but it has certainly justified further investigation. Over the last eight years since our formation, we have winnowed out a handful of truly remarkable individuals. If we could have but proved to a scientific certainty that their abilities were empirically sound, imagine what that would have meant!" Some colour appeared in Mr Jowett's cheeks as emotion lit in his breast. "A great re-ordering of everything we know, and everything that we thought we knew! A vast leap forward for science as a whole, a whole new field to investigate!" He subsided. "That was our hope, a culmination of our little society's entire raison d'être."

Bradley noted Jowett's use of the past tense. "What happened?"

Mr Jowett shrugged a little hopelessly. "They vanished. All of them. The absolute cream of England's finest mediumistic talents has vanished to a man and a woman."

Bradley took a sharp pencil from the old cigar box in which he kept them, flicked open his notebook, and started writing a short summation of what he had just heard. "Tell me, sir," he said as he wrote, "has your society conducted any business with a woman calling herself Miss Cerulia Trent and her manager, a Mr William Grant?"

Mr Jowett seemed mildly startled. "You know of Miss Trent?"

"I deal with fraud and confidence trickery, sir, and you'll therefore understand that bogus mediums fall very much under my purview. I've just recently been looking at Miss Trent and Mr Grant, but haven't yet arrived at any conclusions worthy of the name. I would be very interested in your view of them."

"Well, of course, anything to help the police in their enquiries. Easy enough to remember specifics, as I maintain the society's records and it was an investigation with its interesting points. To wit, it was the finding of the gentleman we sent along to one of Miss Trent's séances some months ago that she is not a true medium, although she is a remarkable performer for all that. There is a technique stage magicians use during so-called 'mentalist' acts wherein they elicit information from their volunteers without seeming to do so, a technique called 'cold reading' a subject. Miss Trent is an absolute master of it, able to piece together whole biographies from very few clues with a very high degree of accuracy. Indeed, our man was so impressed that he declined to call her a fraud, saying instead that she may still be of interest to the society, albeit not in the category that we had at first assumed given her profession."

"What then?"

"Well, a mind reader. A literal mind reader. If not that, then she has the very luck of the Devil, for many of her intuitive leaps were based upon markedly thin foreknowledge and yet were of remarkable accuracy."

"She couldn't have researched her sitters beforehand?"

"Of course, and every fraud does, but we make a point of trying to introduce changes to the attendant sitters, and our man himself is unknown to the medium until the first time he or she claps eyes upon them at the sitting. If there is foreknowledge being gained by some unknown method, that method itself is extraordinary and deserving of investigation."

Bradley studied his notes and then looked seriously at Mr Jowett. "To return to your reason for coming here today, you are in effect reporting multiple missing persons?"

"Oh, no. Not really. I'm sure most, if not all, have already been reported. But, you see, not all are in London or even the Home Counties. It was the feeling of the society's committee that we are probably the only people aware that there is a clear pattern here, that the missing are all of a feather. In which case, we could not possibly fail to pass on that knowledge to the authorities. Something is afoot, and it seems unlikely that whatever it is bodes well for the missing people. Indeed, it may already be too late for them."

"Too late? What makes you say that?"

"Because we found one of them." Mr Jowett grimaced like a concerned pug. "A remarkable young man by the name of Winston Barnaby, twenty-two years of age, the son of a North Finchley butcher. I shan't go into his bona fides beyond saying he'd undergone two rounds of tacit investigation from first one and then the other of our resident stage magicians and, on the second occasion, one of our 'magick with a k' magicians also attended. Both of the former gentlemen reported that they could find no trace of the mountebank in Mr Barnaby's conduct, while the latter declared Barnaby emanated 'arcane energies', whatever that means."

"And Mr Barnaby was later discovered dead?"

Jowett shook his head. "No. We found him a resident – likely a permanent resident I am told – of Colney Hatch. Which is to say, the lunatic asylum."

CHAPTER TEN

POET & ARTIST

By divers means (which is to say, a second-hand furniture van painted up with the name and address of a non-existent company), Jibsy was delivered handcuffed and blindfolded to the rear of the house in Chiswick via the alleyway, overshadowed by trees and hedges that grew there. Subsequently he was conducted down into the cellars, where he was secured to the same chair that had so recently seen William Grant as its guest. Grant felt an unexpected pang of sympathy for the Australian, a pang that lasted exactly long enough for Jibsy to realise that he could bellow his throat raw and not a soul would hear him. This he took as an invitation to bellow himself raw. Grant, who as a proud Mancunian had been raised not to tolerate "fowk going right mard", gave him a cuff hard enough to send both man and chair onto their sides.

"You bloody coward!" spat Jibsy from the floor. "You'd not be so handy if I were untied!" Then he felt his head squeezed from below by the coldness of the flagstones, and from above by the coldness of a gun barrel, and he grew quiet.

"I'm not playing games, y'Aussie bastard," said Grant, the prospect of violence allowing him the luxury of using his own accent for once. "You'll not find the Marquess of Queensberry in this cellar, I'll tell you that for nowt."

"Steady, mate, steady," said Jibsy, "let's all come to some sort of understanding, eh?"

"Aye, fair enough, and here it is. You tell us anything and everything we want to know, and I don't put a bullet through your brain."

"You wouldn't do it, mate, not you. It's not in you."

"I grew up in Angel Meadow, 'mate', and you don't have the first idea what I've got in me."

Jibsy looked across at Misses Trent and Church. "Are you going to just stand there while he does me violence?"

Miss Church shrugged. "I suppose I could wait upstairs until you've stopped bleeding." She tilted her head to look at him more squarely. "But I shan't. Your employer is a fiend, a creature who is happy to see millions die for nothing, a traitor to his own race. You don't owe him a thing."

"A what d'you say?" Jibsy grunted, unimpressed. "You're spoony. You're all spoony. The boss is just a businessman."

Grant paused, thoughtful. He stepped around the fallen man and crouched to talk more directly to him. "What do you mean, 'a businessman'?"

"Oh, you know." Jibsy smiled at him, the split lip making the sight less chummy than he'd probably hoped. "You're a man of the world, Mr Grant. You know full well."

"A criminal."

"Well, that's a bit blunt, ain't it? He's just a businessman, picking up opportunities as he goes along."

"What about the mine?"

"The mine?" Jibsy laughed derisively. "Luckiest bit o' business he ever picked up, I can tell you. He got those deeds in a poker game. Feller had a terrible hand, at that. The boss was only even in town because we'd been run out of Canberra, had to make ourselves scarce, y'see? Was only looking to set up a house for dressed girls."

"I do not understand any of this usage in context," said Miss Trent.

"He means a brothel," said Grant bluntly.

"Oh," said Miss Church. "But… he's a knight."

"He wasn't then, miss," offered Jibsy from the floor. "Wouldn't be now if he hadn't done such a good job of hiding all that lairy business from the great and good."

"I doubt it's the first time the Queen's knighted a pimp," said Grant "So, he just blundered into running a bauxite mine?"

"It was meant to be a way to cover up the profits from the dollyhouse. The brothel, that is," Jibsy clarified for the elucidation of Miss Trent. "Keep the Excise Men from cottoning on. But, wouldn't you know it? The aluminium business is suddenly going great guns and everyone was crying out for bauxite. What the cats were turning over was small potatoes besides what it turned out the mine was worth."

"Guns? Cats?" said Miss Trent. "Potatoes?"

"The prostitution business was not producing the same volume of profits as the highly successful bauxite mining," Grant translated.

"Why can't humans simply say what they mean?" said Miss Trent.

"Eh?" said Jibsy.

"Never mind that," said Grant, "she was just speaking allegorically."

"Eh?" said Jibsy.

"Never mind. Carry on."

Jibsy wore the expression of somebody who is becoming aware a practical joke has been played upon him, but still isn't quite sure of its nature, only that he doesn't like it. Nevertheless, he continued. "So, the boss sells off the house to some of the local larries, and focuses on the bauxite. His big chance to go clean, innit? All of a sudden, the governor of the territory's his best pal, and the posh folk all want to be invited to his sworries."

"His what?"

"Sworries. It's like a drinking session but everyone stands around and drinks from little glasses."

"*Soirées*," corrected Miss Church.

Miss Trent was unhappy. "This development perplexes me. Becoming wealthy does not remove the fact of his previous criminality."

Grant shook his head. "You have very much to learn

about this enlightened age. Being wealthy allows one to be forgiven well-nigh anything."

"It's true," added Jibsy from the floor. "It ain't what you might call 'moral' exactly, but it's the way of the world."

"But this is not a given," persisted Miss Trent. "It is not a natural law. You have it within your power to improve on this."

Jibsy contorted his face as if detecting a bad smell and looked at Grant for amoral support. "Miss Trent is an idealist," said Grant.

"If you say so, mate. Anyway, so he gets a hankering to return to the old country, ups himself and his house on a steamer and comes home. Buys this place out in Barking, gets hisself knighted for services to British industry or something, and here we are. No treason, no skulduggery, nothing no more underhand than any other feller that's made a few bob in business, and you're cracked if you think different."

"What about the séances?"

"What about them? The feller's wife died, din't she? Can't say I'd've run off to a table-rapper, but not my missus, is it? Grief can do funny things to a feller."

"It's not just the one, though, is it?" said Miss Church. "He's had just about every spiritist in London and the Home Counties at his place, hasn't he?"

"And what if he has? He wants to find the best. He can afford to shop around."

There was a silence for a few moments, and then Grant said, "The session we attended didn't play out like any I've ever attended before. Did anything odd ever happen at any of the others?"

Jibsy scoffed. "Aww, mate, you have to be kidding? We had it all. The white eckyplasm stuff, speaking in tongues, ghosts of druidical fellers going on about phases of the moon and ash trees. Oh, we saw it all. Regular three ring circus, it's been."

"That's not the kind of thing I mean."

"Well, what then?"

"You know full well."

Jibsy had been becoming more ebullient as he had realised that he was unlikely to be murdered out of hand, but now he sobered down again.

"There has been... maybe... a couple of things I can't account for," he said grudgingly. "I mean, I go to the halls, I've seen conjurers. I know there's some tricks I can't really reckon out. But these weren't like that. It wasn't just the 'how' of it. It was the 'why', too. One feller they had to carry out because he was foaming at the mouth. I've seen a crazy man before, and it was exactly alike, but this feller walked in sober as a judge. Something happened during the séance. Something happened in the dark. I'm not a milky tea sort of chap, y'know. I don't balk easy. But that made me feel right off clear down to me belly. Like there was happenings afoot that I didn't understand, but also that I *couldn't.*" He suddenly became energised. "It's that bloody uncle of his! That's it! Everything was properly square between us and the boss, and then that bloody great-uncle of his turns up out of thin air, and nothing's been proper ever since.

That's who you should be looking at. Great-uncle bloody Mathias!"

Every copper knows the asylums and every copper dreads the necessity of visiting them. Bradley was only a uniformed constable for four months when he was called upon to accompany an escaped inmate from the Second Lancashire County Lunatic Asylum back to Prestwich. The man had not wanted to go back, had freed himself of his branks in the back of the Black Maria, and attacked Bradley the instant the doors were opened. Luckily for Bradley, the man had no teeth, which was just as well given how long the bruises from the vigorously applied gums lingered on his arm.

After that memorable first encounter with madness and the mechanisms by which society dealt with it, there was no shortage of sequels, there being no less than four of the Lancashire County Asylums dotted around the periphery of Manchester. London, being a larger city, was possessed of so many more, not least St Bethlehem's, the original "Bedlam". Colney Hatch, otherwise known as the Second Middlesex County Asylum, was a relatively modern building in comparison to St Bethlehem's, being barely over forty years old and thereby having a diminished sense of the Hogarthian about it.

Detective Sergeant Bradley eyed it from the approach, rubbed away the phantom ache of ancient bruises from his bicep, and went to announce his business at the porter's lodge.

After the usual presentation and re-presentation of his

articles of authority to assorted doorkeepers, guards, and orderlies, he was at last ushered into the presence of Doctor Lockley, a man in his late fifties possessed of a downturned mouth and a pince-nez, through which he regarded Bradley after the detective was seated.

"Winston Barnaby," he said slowly and with displeasure, although he gave every impression that this was his usual mode. He examined Barnaby's file. "The *poet* and *medium*," he added. "An interesting case for an alienist, Detective Sergeant, but hardly something to trouble the Metropolitan Police, I would have thought."

"I would like to question Mr Barnaby as a possible witness in a case, sir. He is guilty of no misdemeanours himself that I am aware of."

"Question Barnaby," repeated Lockley as he continued to study the file. He raised his gaze to squint down his nose at Bradley through the lenses of his pince-nez. "You will not learn anything from him. He's quite mad."

Mad seemed a very plebeian term for an alienist to use, and for a moment Bradley was reminded of the American writer Poe and his story "The System of Doctor Tarr and Professor Fether". Might the lunatics have taken over the asylum in reality? He concluded, no, that Doctor Lockley was nothing more than faintly eccentric, and pressed on.

"That's as maybe, sir, but I am nevertheless required to do so. Justice demands it."

"Does it, indeed?"

"Well, my governor does, at any rate, and he's generally right."

"Your governor…" Lockley dropped the file onto the desk and glared at it, perhaps hoping it and Barnaby might burst into flames and allow him to do something less wearing than deal with a policeman. It did not spontaneously combust, however, so he sighed and rose. "I shall introduce you to Mr Sims, the warden of Barnaby's wing."

"Is Barnaby dangerous?"

"Dangerous? No, no. As placid as a duck. Come with me, please."

Bradley followed him, meditating on the serenity of ducks.

Mr Sims, by contrast to his charge, was dour rather than placid, and trundled through the niceties of mannered inferiority towards Doctor Lockley that lasted precisely until his superior was out of sight. "Welcome to the nuthatch," he said to Bradley, "c'mon," and led the way into the wing via double-locked doors and nodded acknowledgements to the individuals that Lockley had called "orderlies", but who looked a great deal like guards to Bradley.

"What kind of patient is Barnaby?" he asked.

"The good kind," replied Sims after a little thought. "The kind what doesn't cause much trouble. Just sits there, mainly. He's allowed pencils, which is more than most are."

"Pencils?"

"Aye. You can do a man a proper mischief with a pencil if you're so minded. High privilege to be allowed them, unsupervised at that."

"And what does he do with them?"

"He don't kill anyone with 'em, which is about the limit

of my interest, sir." He glanced back and saw that Bradley was not entirely satisfied with this response. He sighed and elucidated. "Which is to say, he writes his poems and does some pictures."

"What kind of pictures?"

"Mad pictures. Here we are." They had arrived at a door not dissimilar to the sort of doors sported by police station cells. It was cream, but Bradley got the impression that it had once been white and the colour had curdled over time. Certainly, the difference in shade was distinctive against the fresh white distemper of the hallway walls. "Joe," Sims said to the guard… the *orderly* who had accompanied them from the last locked door, "do the honours, would you?"

As Joe unlocked the door, Sims said to Bradley, "Me and Joe will be right outside. Door stays ajar, all right? First sign of trouble, you shout and we'll be in there quick as Larry."

Bradley was reasonably sure that the phrase was "as happy as Larry", but perhaps Larry was as swift as he was joyful, whoever he was. More pertinently, he asked, "Why would I need help? Both you and Doctor Lockley have assured me that he is perfectly docile."

"Aye, well," Sims gave the open doorway a briny look, "still a loony, ain't he?"

Home to misgivings, Bradley entered the room.

Winston Barnaby was a fine-featured young man, but something – Bradley guessed his incarceration – had taken that fineness and rendered it fragile. He looked up startled from where he had been kneeling to write, using the floor as his desk, and made a clumsy convulsive attempt to cover the papers he was working on with his hands.

"Mr Barnaby," said Bradley, "would you mind if I take a pew? I've been on my feet all day and the dogs are barking." He'd learned the phrase from a cheap American novel about the Pinkertons that somebody had left lying around the office and he had thought rather swish. Looking at Barnaby's blank expression now, he regretted using it. "My feet are tired, that is. Mind if I sit down?"

Barnaby just continued to look confused, so Bradley sat anyway. While it was true that he appreciated the rest, his purpose was to bring his height down closer to Barnaby's and so to appear less intimidating. It appeared to have worked, as Barnaby seemed less like a surprised fawn and more simply confused, which was reasonable under the circumstances.

"My name is Norman Bradley, sir," he said, keen to establish himself as a fellow human being in Barnaby's mind before adding, "I'm a police officer. I was wondering if I might ask you a few questions?"

Barnaby did not seem eager to look him in the face, but instead peeped at him from beneath a lowered brow. "Do…? Do you have any means to show identification?"

Bradley was relieved that the man seemed decently cogent and that he might actually extract some useful answers from the interview. "I do." He produced his warrant card and, with only the slightest hesitation, handed it over.

Barnaby studied it very closely in silence for almost two

minutes, before handing it back with an abrupt carelessness. "It might be a forgery," he said.

"It might," agreed Bradley. "Believe you me, sir, there are some excellent forgers out there. I know people who could make me a card proclaiming me the Great Tippoo and not a soul from the Home Secretary down would be able to find a thing wrong with it. In any case, sir, would I be correct in thinking that you have never actually seen a warrant card at first hand?" This earned him a stare and then a quick nod. "Thought as much. Few have, to state a fact. So, you wouldn't even know what to look for in a forgery. But it hardly matters if it's a forgery or not. The thing is, I have to ask these questions in any case, and I would very much value your patience and your honesty."

The young man thought about this carefully. "I am very honest," he offered, "and I have all the time in the world."

"That's good to know," said Bradley, who didn't have all the time in the world but did not need to share that truth. "Nonetheless, I shall keep my enquiries brief. To wit–"

"To woo," said Barnaby.

"To wit, I am investigating some missing persons."

"Some? That is, several?"

"Just so, Mr Barnaby, and they are all in the same line of business as yourself. Not poetry, mind," he added quickly, gesturing at the sheets of paper. As he did so, he glanced at them and realised that one, partially obscured by the pages bearing poetry above, carried a drawing. It was a busy thing, and he almost dismissed it as a scribble before he realised it was in fact a densely detailed sketch, although of what he could not quite understand. He thought at first it was an anatomical drawing, but he dismissed that idea quickly. There was something very wrong in the proportions and details of it: what seemed to be blood vessels stopped and started abruptly; the musculature – if that's what the waves of flesh represented –did not seem to be uniform in direction and would only be good for contorting the body of whatever it was uselessly. And all the while that he was looking at it, he wished he was not, and so his relief was great when Barnaby finally saw the direction of Bradley's gaze and quickly drew the poetry sheets over it. They looked at one another for the briefest of moments, and in both their faces was a troubled and anxious guilt.

Bradley pulled himself together. "Spiritists, sir. Mediums. Many of your colleagues have gone astray in the past few weeks and months."

"No colleagues of mine." Barnaby took up his pencil and began correcting the copy of the uppermost poem. "There is no more camaraderie there than in the society of hermits. Besides, most of them were frauds." He looked sideways at Bradley. "Did you know many mediums are frauds?"

This was not a revelation to Bradley, but another point had caught his attention. "*Were*, Mr Barnaby? You said 'Most of them *were* frauds' just then. What do you mean by that?"

"Oh," Barnaby crossed out a facile and egregious rhyme and replaced it with something meatier. "They're dead, I think. Something awful has happened to them, anyway."

"How do you know that?"

"I felt their light go out. They weren't *all* frauds, you see."

Bradley checked his notes again just to be sure that Barnaby had been incarcerated early on in the disappearances. He would confirm with Doctor Lockley later that Barnaby had never been at liberty since, but that seemed a reasonable supposition for the moment. "So, some really could commune with the dead? Is that what you're saying?"

"Oh, I don't know about that. It's not an exact science, you see. But there was a certain luminescence about them, so I suppose they might. The ones who were dull and lightless, why, I couldn't suppose what's happened to them. They might have fallen under a train and I would not know of it. Why, have any of them vanished, too?"

Bradley had a peculiar sense that there was something larger lurking behind the disappearance of a few persons of interest to the Metaphysical Investigation Conference. In truth, much of police work was at odds to that of the assorted gentleman detectives, stories of whom had proliferated in recent years. Often, a police detective had a damn good idea who the guilty party was right from the off and it was purely a case of finding the evidence to support that belief within a court of law. Occasionally, however, a case more in the fictional model where the perpetrator was a figure cloaked in the shadows of evidential absence and who would have to be hunted down and dragged into the light came along. Inevitably, he was reminded of his old governor's great triumph of 1889 in the infamous

"Manchester Cab Murder" when Jerome Caminada hunted down and arrested such a criminal based on a good, thorough initial investigation followed up by a strong lead generated by Caminada's voluminous knowledge of the city's underworld, taking him from an apparently insoluble crime to an arrest in a scant three weeks.

It was the kind of performance any police detective dreamed of, but Bradley had been there as a constable and remembered his sense of blank ignorance at the outset. A bustling city, ten thousand suspects at the least, how could anyone focus on the true perpetrator? The possibilities had floated around him like snowflakes in a blizzard and he had felt small and impotent.

He had that same feeling now, except, if anything, worse. The cab murder had been committed for gain, and greed was easy enough to explain. This, though? Why would anyone abduct spiritists? And, if Barnaby was right, murder them? This latter datum, at least, he could take with a good pinch of salt, given that he was interviewing a lunatic. Yet the disappearances were fact, and there was no pat explanation for them he could imagine. Not for the first time, he asked himself inwardly, "What would Mr Caminada do?" and the answer came back, "Use your relevant knowledge to reduce the possibilities to a manageable number". But exactly what relevant knowledge did he have?

"Do you know a Miss Cerulia Trent?" he asked suddenly, the question forming and expressing itself so abruptly within his mind that he was hardly aware of it before he said it.

For the first time, Mr Barnaby seemed suddenly very wary, and Bradley knew he was onto something. "I think so," said Barnaby. "Why do you ask?"

"So, you *do* know her?"

"She's a fraud." As Barnaby said it, Bradley caught in his eyes the furtive look he had seen in the eyes of so many petty criminals when the jig is up and they are not clever enough to realise it. The look of a person seeing if a lie has gained purchase.

"Is she?" said Bradley with mannered slowness, finishing with a significant and magisterial frown.

Barnaby's gaze dropped. "No," he said quietly.

"And has her 'light gone out'?"

"No." Barnaby looked up at him. "But it has changed." He looked down again. "I can't explain how." Bradley watched as he gently skimmed the poems aside with his fingertips until the drawing was once more exposed.

"What is that?" asked Bradley gently. "That drawing… what is it of?"

Barnaby shook his head slowly. "I don't know, but it is the most awful thing in the world, or beyond it. When I saw it, I knew there was no hope."

"You've seen it?"

"In my dreams. In my nightmares. It is coming. They are all coming. I think I am mad now. Doctor Lockley tells me I am mad, and he is a doctor. He tells me that I am prey to fears and delusions that have made me mad." He looked around his cell. "When he told me I was mad, I was happy to hear it. Perhaps my dreams were only the dreams of a madman, and – if they were not – then at least I would be sheltered in a grand place like this with thick walls to protect me from them when they come. But … I see now that there will be no hiding place. I know that now." Barnaby began to weep slow, miserable tears. "I am sorry for Miss Cerulia Trent. They will want her, and when they find her, they will eat her light, too, and all hope will die."

He said nothing more.

"Well, that's that," said Mr Sims from the doorway. He nodded at Barnaby, not without sympathy. "He'll cry himself dry for hours now. Tell you anything useful, sir? For your investigation, like?"

Bradley watched Barnaby sobbing silently, head down in supplication to a threat he could not qualify. "I'm not sure," he said.

Chapter Eleven

GREAT-UNCLE MATHIAS

As councils of war went, it was unusually suburban, consisting of two men and two women gathered around a table in a house in Chiswick, with one prisoner tied up and locked away in the cellar. Upon the table stood a tea pot, but nobody had volunteered to be mother, and it was likely so badly stewed by this point as to be suitable only for the preparation of leather.

"It was always going to come down to this," said Castle. "At some point we knew we'd have to fix bayonets and have at 'em."

"Bayonets...?" said Miss Trent.

"Mr Castle is speaking figuratively," supplied Miss Church.

Castle gave her a look. "I wasn't, as it happens. I'm perfectly serious. Sir Traitor-to-the-Entire-Human-Race there, out in Barking... what, you think he's going to capitulate to some strong words and a wagging finger? No. If we can't dash out his brains with a bullet, 12 inches of good Sheffield steel will do the job just as nicely." He looked around the table and noted the lack of enthusiasm for this eventuality. "Fella on the Whitechapel Road," he continued less assuredly, "I've seen him selling old bayonets off a cart, sixpence apiece or thereabouts." Into the awkward silence that followed his revelation of such a bargain he repeated, a little petulantly, "It was always going to come down to this, and we all knew it."

"Mr Castle is right," said Grant heavily. "There's no point trying to sugarcoat it. There must be violence and blood will be shed if we are to stop him." He looked around the table. "In which case, the situation is hopeless. There are only four of us, and only two of us are men. Two against a small army of hired bullies."

"If, Mr Grant," said Miss Church in a lowering tone, "you are implying that I am somehow too feeble to use a gun, I would point–"

"There are lots more than just the four of us!" interrupted Castle brightly, forestalling the storm. "I mean, we're a secret society. We can field a decent number if needs be, and I would think circumstances like this very much dictate that needs be. I mean, as I've said, when one considers the technicalities of it, we are a sort of cult, really. Although that does sound fearfully outré and a little foreign, doesn't it? I mean, communing with strange eldritch entities from out of the aeons, and all?" He looked at Miss Trent, said "Hello!" and waved at her. She looked back at him perplexedly.

"So, how many men *can* you field?" said Grant.

"If we start sending telegrams now, we could have fifteen to twenty within two days. Although," added Castle, "I feel I must point out that some of those men will be women. But, as Miss Church would surely agree, it doesn't take a man to wield a gun effectively. I mean, look at Annie Oakley. And my Auntie Delilah. She could shoot the knees off a gnat at sixty paces." He nodded, reflecting upon the redoubtable Delilah. "Patently terrifying woman, truth be told."

"Send the telegrams," said Grant. "Sir Donovan plainly knows the game's afoot. He'll try to speed matters up. We can't let him succeed."

Sir Donovan Clay liked his little house in Barking. He found the heart of the metropolis stifling, and was pleased to discover how abruptly the stews of the East End gave way to green countryside. Still, he only had to wander into his garden to see the sky hued so differently, so alien to the west as the great city breathed in coal and workers, and breathed out smoke and profits. When he became as near as dammit a god, he thought, he would like to live somewhere like this. Bigger, of course – what was the point of being a deity of sorts if one did not have a suitably grand home from which to rule? – but not overbearing. Not a palace, but more of a rambling house that bespoke modesty in one so exalted, just a little place that covered two or three square miles. More of a cottage, really.

Of his current house, however, there was one aspect that he did enjoy, and this was the cellar. When he had first inspected the place and declared himself pleased with his agent's choice, the cellar had seemed perfect: a broad chamber supported by columns and thick walls. It was pleasingly cool and dry down there, full of interesting nooks and, in the more open areas, freestanding shelves that bore wooden racks upon which the previous owner had kept wine. And, indeed, the cellar was perfect for the role he had in mind. The racks had been removed, but their shelving retained. Workbenches had been installed, and two powerful electrical generators along with them. He let it be known that he was an inveterate tinkerer in his spare time and that this was to be his workshop where it was his intention to become the British Edison. In reality, the "British Edison" could go hang, along with the American one as well; Sir Donovan's intentions were far grander and, in any case, the workshop was not for him at all.

His men had been told only ever to enter the cellar with his personal permission or in an emergency; otherwise they were to stay well clear of it. This suited his "boys" very well indeed, for there floated about that chamber a psychic miasma as may sometimes be felt on the site of a bloody battle, or in a room where red murder has been wrought. Besides, not a one of them cared to be alone with Great-Uncle Mathias.

"Mathias!" called Sir Donovan as he entered the cellar. And there he tarried on the threshold; he had given Mathias warning that he was there, and now he must sensibly wait. Once, early on, he had hustled regardless to the area of the workbenches without announcing himself, and so caught Mathias unprepared for him. Sir Donovan, not a man known for fragile nerves, had not slept well for a week or more afterwards. At his call he heard movement, sudden as of startlement. Then a more purposeful whisper and huff of heavy cloth being prepared and donned. After a minute, Mathias called to him, "I am ready, Sir Donovan Clay." Without marked enthusiasm, Sir Donovan went to meet him.

The shelves were covered in equipment that Sir Donovan had paid for, but precious little of which he understood in the slightest. Much of it had been rebuilt in any case, and in such a manner that would have baffled the original inventors and manufacturers. Less opaque in all senses were the sealed jars that lined the upper shelves. He made a point never to examine these closely, and even went to some pains to keep them from the periphery of his vision. He was in no sense a squeamish man, but even a butcher has his limits. All these artefacts ranged about the three workbenches that formed the heart of the workshop, organised in a U-shape, with Mathias, standing stoop-backed, in their centre. Sir Donovan noted that the wood of the benches – pristine when purchased only a few weeks ago – now showed scratches, gouges, burns from heat, acid, and (he guessed) electricity, and there were any number of stains the provenance of which he could guess at, given the open roll of surgical instruments that lay nearby, several of their number currently resting blades down in jars of carbolic acid prior to being baked in a fierce little oven of Mathias's design and manufacture for reasons that escaped

Sir Donovan. He could have asked, but then he would have learned, and this he judged to be unwise.

"How goes the plan?" he demanded of Mathias.

His great-uncle – who was not his great-uncle – turned to the large cylindrical device he was building on the rightmost of the benches. "It progresses," he said. His voice was quiet yet penetrating, possessed of no accent Sir Donovan recognised, and any sibilance was replaced with a dull buzzing tone.

"But how quickly does it progress? When shall it be ready?"

"Soon," said Great-Uncle Mathias. "Soon."

Sir Donovan boiled with frustration. "And how long is that? Hours? Days? We do not have infinite leisure, sir! Our enemies are here, in London! They know where we are, and they must know what we're about. They will surely take action. If we can but forestall them by enacting the plan before they come–"

"The device is not the concern." Mathias rested a gloved hand on the device. The shape of the flesh within the heavy leather glove was misshapen. Everything about Mathias was misshapen: swathed in a long, brown shop coat that fell around him like a robe; the shapeless cloth hat that seemed old enough to have belonged to Rembrandt; the cloth wrapping that served as a scarf of sorts, covering the lower part of his face. And that face, what little could mercifully be seen of it, was a yellowish brown, and the eyes bore no obvious pupils, only twin glints of light that were always there even in the shadow of the bulging, shapeless hat. Sir

Donovan could just make out the leftmost edge of the thin-lipped mouth. It did not move at all when Mathias spoke.

Mathias took up a glass rod that contained an irregular and knotted filament embedded in its core, and placed it on a plate atop the device. For a second, nothing happened, but then the filament started to burn with light, growing stronger until it was glowing a dark orange that seemed to dim the air around the rod. Mathias removed the rod from the plate and held it up towards Sir Donovan. "You see. Insufficient. More…" he hesitated, as if seeking the right word. The pause grew out and Sir Donovan wondered if the correct word even existed in English, or any language spoken on Earth. "…energy," said Mathias finally, having given up the hunt for the precise term. "More energy is required." He gestured at Sir Donovan with the rod, within which the unwholesome light slowly dwindled. "You must provide more energy."

Sir Donovan grunted angrily. "Always more! I'm doing the best I can. I have to be cautious. The city's only just calmed down from the Whitechapel murders, damn you. I can't simply pluck people off the street willy-nilly without risking a hue and cry."

"Not my concern," said Mathias. "If you must take fewer, take stronger."

"Damnation, what do you think we've been doing? Why all this rigmarole with séances, eh? How many more?"

"Of the good, one. Two. Of the weak, five. Six."

"Damnation," said Sir Donovan again, but this time without vigour. "Cerulia Trent, would she be useful? She's being watched as we speak. We could take her before dawn if needs be."

Mathias put the rod down slowly and with excess care. "Cerulia Trent is weak. Useless."

"But her eyes…? We all saw it. That light…"

"Illusory effect caused by the Yithian weapon malfunctioning. Cerulia Trent is weak. Useless."

Sir Donovan walked to one of the shelves and took down a curious object that seemed made from twisted roots, some of which had gorgonised into stone, and others into metal. "Can you fix this thing? We might need it."

"Malfunction. Irreparable."

Sir Donovan gave him a disgusted look, and levelled the object at an empty tea chest in the corner. Despite his best efforts to trigger some sort of event, the object remained stubbornly inert.

"If it activates," said Mathias evenly, "it will malfunction again and damage you, as it did the man who brought it here."

Sir Donovan glared at the object yet when he replaced it on the shelf, he did so gingerly. Then he turned his burgeoning anger upon Mathias. "I swear, if you were a man, I would horsewhip you for your insolence and your indolence. We need that…" he pointed at the cylindrical device, "that… thing working as soon as possible. Jump to it, or your masters will want to know why!"

Sir Donovan walked out in a fury, his footsteps heavy upon the wooden steps.

Into the silence of the workshop, Great-Uncle Mathias

said, "I am not a man," and proceeded to remove his hat, his scarf, and, shortly thereafter, his face.

The night and curfew came to Colney Hatch, but sleep did not come to Winston Barnaby. Indeed, he shied away from it as a man might eschew a strange fellow traveller on a lonely byway who walks too close and smiles too much. He knew what awaited him within the soft folds of slumber, and it filled him with a low, sickening fear of the kind that is only forged by the inevitable, because fear is exhausting and unsustainable, and when it finally fades, exhaustion turns to sleep.

He didn't know when he inevitably lost that unwinnable battle, only that he dipped back into the electric waters of dream, silk smooth and oily, and there he sank quickly and deeply. He saw light and he saw darkness, and he could only watch as the latter devoured the former. To the left was the past, and to the right was the future, and between the two he saw a crystal wall spider-webbed with lines of force, and he also saw the things that feasted there. Beyond the wall was only night and extinction, the negative of all. It was a pale that he had no desire to venture past, and yet it stood so close, and his feet bore him onwards though he willed them to drag.

He awoke, finally, his heart beating rapidly and a cold sweat upon him, and he looked about his little hermitage, firm and sober with inherent reality, and it felt like the last night in the condemned cell with no possibility of pardon. Dawn was still hours away, but that did not matter. The execution that awaited him would not be so kindly as if delivered by a workaday Thomas Derrick, he knew that, though he did not know upon which dawn it would arrive. The logical thing to do – the *rational* thing to do – would therefore be to ensure that no dawn of any hue ever arrived, and thus he could protect himself from that awful fate. It was easy enough to do, after all. And so, in the shadows of that small, unfriendly room, he set about doing what needed to be done.

It was the orderly on changing shifts that morning who, during his initial round of his charges, discovered Barnaby silent on the floor of his cell, and – on a short investigation – learned well enough why that was and to send him scurrying for the office of Mr Sims. Sims followed him back at a trot, affirmed the orderly's conclusions, and so sent him running to fetch Doctor Lockley, who came and saw and sighed, because the event would doubtless engender much tedious paperwork. Worse yet, police involvement, for the visit of Detective Sergeant Bradley was still fresh in his mind. Thus, he informed the mortuary and then, with marked reluctance, New Scotland Yard.

A telephone call was made, and an hour later Bradley arrived. He had little time for the niceties, and less still for Doctor Lockley and Mr Sims as they gathered in the asylum mortuary.

"He was always so disinclined towards violence of any hue," said Lockley, gazing at the corpse. "This is very disappointing."

"You told me that he was not at risk of suicide."

"He was not, or so I believed. This is very, *very* disappointing of him."

"And yet ... ?"

"And yet. Oddly methodical, too, for someone taking their own life in a moment of weakness."

"How so?"

"Well," Lockley took a deep breath as he gazed at the cadaver of the very, *very* disappointing Mr Barnaby before huffing it out in an exhalation of mild professional dismay, "it wasn't merely a moment, evidently. He went to the trouble of writing to you, in a manner of speaking." He produced from his pocket a neat square of folded paper.

Bradley took it and, noting his name on the outside began to open it. "You've read it, I gather?"

Lockley shrugged. "It was unsealed–"

"Not much in the way of gum or sealing wax in his cell ..."

"–and was not marked as private or confidential."

Bradley opened it and recognised the drawing Barnaby had been at such pains to conceal the day before. Now he could see that curious organic shape easily, however, he was quite certain that he did not desire to. Instead, he let his eye roam further down to where there were a few uneven lines of writing. It was too dim to fully read them.

"You can see," said Lockley, "that he was distressed from the poor formation of his handwriting. Your visit, detective sergeant, no doubt accounts for that."

"Or that he was writing in an almost pitch dark room," said Bradley, making efforts not to rise to the bait. "I suspect that was the greater factor."

But, based on the appearance of the malformed words, Barnaby may well have been distressed as he wrote and then subsequently took his own life. What Bradley could make out in the dim light was meaningless, and yet, there had to be a rationale behind it, he felt sure. He refolded the paper and put it between the pair of blank postcards he kept in his breast pocket for the express purpose of keeping documents flat. He nodded at Barnaby's corpse on the table. "I would like to have a copy of the postmortem report when it is ready, doctor."

"Fairly evident how he died," said Lockley.

"Be as that may, sir, I am required to be thorough. Please ensure that one is sent to me at New Scotland Yard at your earliest possible convenience."

"As you will. I'll conduct it this afternoon."

"Not you, doctor. Mr Barnaby's death is likely suicide as you say, but it may be contingent to a larger investigation and is therefore a police matter. I shall inform the police surgeon and the local coroner."

Lockley grew red. "That's absurd! I am perfectly capable of conducting a routine postmortem examination!"

"I don't doubt it, but I have my doubts that this is a routine death. Please lock this room when we leave. Nobody is to enter until the coroner arrives. Absolutely nobody else is to touch the body. I hope I make myself plain, doctor."

"Very plain," snorted Lockley. "Very plain indeed, sir!" He turned on Sims. "Out! Out with you!" he cried, as if the man were the source of all Lockley's woes, and he shooed the warden away.

Bradley glanced at the body before he went to the door himself. He was sure that Barnaby's death was as it appeared, and he was just as sure that Craddock would receive a peppery complaint from Doctor Lockley soon. He didn't care about that, not least because he was sure where Craddock's sympathies would lie. What concerned him most was the possibility he was in some way responsible for Barnaby's death. He had brought the outside world into that splendid isolation and reminded the hapless man that he was not divorced from that world and its troubles.

What he had managed to eke out from the blind scrawl on the letter troubled him further still. Barnaby was fragile, true enough, but there had been a definite sensibility there that pertained to something that lay outside Bradley's knowledge or experience. As he edged towards it, he felt that it was like waltzing into a mire, but a mire in which many answers lay.

Surely, he thought, the truth can never be our enemy?

Mr Sims was kept busy all that day, but he still managed to send out a messenger boy to deliver a terse, hastily scribbled letter before noon, and received a rather terser note in reply three hours later. On leaving work that evening, he made his way to a pub just near enough to be convenient while too far from the asylum to be a regular haunt of the staff. Here he waited with a pint of beer and his nerves a-jangle. A quarter hour later he was joined by a large, well-muscled man whose presence betokened violence, but who sat quietly with Mr Sims, and kept his threats tacit.

"Barnaby's dead," said Sims.

"So your note said," answered the large man, signalling to a pot boy to order a whiskey and a small jug of water. "The people I represent are very unhappy about that."

"It wasn't my fault!" said Sims, a man unfond of pain.

"Nobody's saying it was. What happened?"

"Well, he did himself in, didn't he?"

"So your note said," replied the man with characteristic patience. "How did it happen?"

"The doctor let him have pencils. He put a sharp 'un in his ear and fell sideways. Must have been quick."

"Doesn't sound like an accident, I grant you."

"It was suicide!"

"Awkward way to murder someone, too. Yes, I suppose it was suicide. It's a sin, that, you know?" He poured a little water into his glass. "But so many things are. Tell me, Mr Sims, what do you suppose led to it? Anything out of the ordinary?"

"Apart from his being a lunatic?" Sims could see that, no, this would not suffice, so instead he offered, "Well, there'd been a copper sniffing around."

This definitely engaged the attention of his interviewer. "A copper? What copper? What did he want?"

"A detective, from Scotland Yard. I've no idea what he was after. I tried to earwig, but I wasn't alone in the corridor and couldn't get close enough to hear what was said, only a word here and there."

"And what," said the man with dangerous quietness, "did a word here and there lead you to think was going on?"

"I'm... not sure. A missing person, I think."

"A missing person..." The man thought on this for a moment longer, slung back the rest of the whiskey, and slammed down the glass. He reached in his pocket, took Sims's hand, and put a few sovereigns in it.

It was a useful sum, but still well short of what Sims had been expecting. "This isn't what we agreed–"

The man took Sims's hand in a grip so tight that it made him gasp with pain. Finger bones that were not usually near neighbours ground against one another. "I know," he said, "but the deal's null and void, ain't it? The lad's dead, that's no use to us, and that means you ain't much use to us neither, now. So take what you're given, and say 'Thank you.'"

"Thank you," said Sims, on the edge of whimpering.

"You are very welcome, Mr Sims. Don't suppose you caught the copper's name, did you?"

"It wasn't mentioned," said Sims, who couldn't remember if it had been or not, although if it had, he certainly hadn't remembered it. "The guv'nor, Lockley, he dealt with him."

The man rocked his head from side to side as he considered this, never letting up Sims's agony throughout. "Likely doesn't matter," he finally concluded. "But you hear anything else about our Mr Barnaby or anybody else asking after him, you tell me smartish, eh?" He released Sims's hand at last and tapped the coins lying in his aching palm. "Worth a few more of these, eh?"

He got up and left without a farewell or backward glance, leaving Mr Sims deeply regretting ever making his acquaintance.

While Sims made his way home to a warm hearth and a sensibly suspicious wife, the man ultimately made his way eastwards via a peregrinatory course that took in Kensington, finally fetching up at a house on the outskirts of Barking. There he made his way, without preamble, into the study of his employer.

"Well?" said Sir Donovan.

"Barnaby's dead, boss," said Lynch. "Did for himself. Stuck a pencil in his ear and bashed it into his brain."

Sir Donovan said nothing for a long moment, and Lynch knew him well enough not to say a word into the silence. Sir Donovan rose suddenly to his feet and slammed his fist down on the desktop with sufficient violence to dislodge a pen from the inkstand. "Damn him! God curse that effete little worm! Damn his eyes! We needed him! He was our best hope!"

"There's still the Trent woman."

"The Trent woman!" His disgust was patent. "She's a dud. Not worth a bent sixpence."

"What? But she lit up, all aglow! We all saw it! None of 'em have ever done that before!"

"She did, I know. But Mathias says it signifies nothing. She's no more use to us than a rotten log. Forget about her. Call back whoever you've got watching her at the moment."

"Aye," said Lynch in a slow tone that made his employer look at him curiously. "About that, boss. I had McMahon watching the hide."

"And? What about it? Jibsy's a good lad. Reliable. You've said so yourself."

"I have, and he is, but that's not the problem. I went by on the way to talk to my fella from the asylum. Jibsy wasn't there at his post. I thought he might have followed Trent off somewhere or was maybe answering a call of nature down a backstreet or the like."

"But…?"

"But I went by there on the return leg, too, and he was still absent, this being better'n two hours later. Perhaps he was off again for whatever reason, but that struck me as long odds, and he would've got word back to us if he had to abandon his post, I know it. Like you say, he's a good lad."

"An accident, perhaps. Anything could have happened." Sir Donovan rubbed his brow. "It cannot be enemy action. Surely not, not if Cerulia Trent is of no consequence." Lynch saw his employer shoot a glance out of the door ajar towards the door in the hallway that led down to the cellar, and had a good idea what he was thinking. "There was the fellow who followed… whatsisname? Grant? The feller that followed Grant from the library. What was going on there?"

"I couldn't tell you, boss. But I do think that there's a good chance we're not the only ones with an interest in Miss Trent."

Sir Donovan thought in silence for a minute or so. Lynch had been with his boss for a long time and through a good few scrapes together of one sort or another, but had never seen him truly worried before. Then he realised that this was not merely concern but fear, and the realisation shook him.

"If we fail them," said Sir Donovan in a low voice as if to himself, "the consequences will be worse than anything that can be imagined." He looked up at Lynch. "We must assume the enemy know far more of our business than we would like, and that they will act upon it at any time. Warn the boys."

CHAPTER TWELVE

THE ENGLISH CULT

It did not take two days to gather the Cult of the Great Race of Yith. Primed by preliminary telegrams, the members had put their affairs in order, said their goodbyes, and assembled within the house in Chiswick within thirty hours of the word being given. It was true, in a couple of cases, that some members had run for the hills, but most had answered the call faithfully.

Grant had not been entirely sure what to expect of a band of cultists. He had read enough penny dreadfuls to "know" what godless cults in Africa, say, or the West Indies, or the distant Orient might be like: all merciless, armed with curved daggers, and inclined towards enacting human sacrifice at every astronomical oddity to be found in the almanac. With this in mind, and assuming Miss Church and Mr Castle (pseudonyms, he now suspected) were outliers of the clan who were mannered and passable in polite society rather than bloodthirsty fiends, he was therefore relieved – or perhaps disappointed, his feelings on the subject complex – to discover that they were all in reality of a muchness.

Here, he realised, was a cult comprised of artists and accountants, dilettantes and doctors, and their gathering was less a debauched saturnalia than an afternoon tea party that would have gone unremarked in any vicarage in the land. Nor did matters change when the newcomers were introduced to one of their otherworldly sponsors incarnate. There was no debasing themselves or atavistic chants of adoration and submission to the entity currently known as Miss Cerulia Trent. Instead, her hand was shaken, *how do you dos* were exchanged, and polite enquiries were made on how she found the nineteenth century and hopes expressed that she did not find her current body too perplexing. This, then, was the nature of an English cult, and Grant had attended more fevered parish council meetings. Shocking as it seemed, it appeared that the yellow papers had lied to him.

As the meeting wore on, he began to wonder if a pack of foreign degenerates might actually have turned out to be more useful in the coming battle. They were brave to be there, he knew, but they were not, by and large, warriors. They had brought weapons, which was a relief, but as he watched them load revolvers and shotguns, it was plain that such activity was neither familiar nor natural to them. There was a former captain of the army who went around, helping the others prepare and dispensing advice, but he was the only one there with the slightest experience of war. Grant himself knew enough to load a revolver without embarrassing himself, but he had never had cause to fire a weapon in anger, his criminality being of a less violent bent, and he had no idea how he would fare against Sir Donovan's band of hardened bully boys. He could only hide his concern behind a veneer of paper thin confidence and hope he did not make too dreadful a hash of things when the moment came. He wondered if that was the sort of thing that went through the minds of cultists in the stories he had read; they were all nervous, but no one wanted to let the side down, so they behaved in a beastly fashion out of a misplaced sense of *esprit de corps*. Across the room, he watched a seemingly calm estate agent thumb rounds into the cylinder of his Webley revolver, but Grant could see the sweat on his brow and the small tremor in his hand. It is a poor turn to be terrified, and a worse one to have to hide it.

Castle came to sit by him. "I say, look at this awful act I have visited upon some poor gunsmith's finest." He showed Grant how he had sawn much of the barrels and most of the butt from a double-barrelled 12-bore shotgun, sanding down the wood to make a handle and transforming the weapon into a great ugly pistol of sorts. "Once met an interesting little man in Birmingham who showed me how to do this. This ungainly loop of cord running through the wood lets me carry the thing slung over my shoulder and dangling down within an overcoat. Apparently cowboys do this sort of thing in America." He looked morosely at the contrivance. "Small miracle any of them are still alive, really, if they insist on visiting this sort of brutality upon one another." He looked sideways at Grant, and Grant saw, just for once, the light hearted affectation running thin for Castle.

"You'll be all right," he assured Castle, surprising himself a little with the confidence in his voice.

Castle smiled a tight, hopeless little smile. "Oh, I doubt that. I doubt very many of us are coming home after this. But truly, that doesn't matter. We have to succeed even if it costs the life of every blessed one of us. There is so very much at stake. You know, chaps like Pendleton over there," he nodded at the captain doing his rounds of the pocket army, "I've never understood 'em. Joining the army or the navy. Whatever for? If the land itself is in danger, then yes, by all means, let the old queen slap a shilling in my hand and I'll be in the front rank to see off the invader, you just watch me. But that's not been the case since they packed off old Bonaparte to St Helena, and no, Napoleon III doesn't count. I simply don't see the allure of signing up just to go tramping all over somebody else's back garden, bashing in flags all over the show, calling it patriotic, and then getting upset when the locals get in a bate about it and fight back. To my mind, that's just frightfully poor manners on our part."

"You're a radical?"

"I don't see much radical in simple good neighbourliness. 'Do unto others', eh? What's happening here, though, well, it's unique. Humanity as a whole has never been at the receiving end of an invasion. At least, not to my knowledge. If we mess this up, the enemies of Miss Trent's crowd will murder her people into extinction and, in the process, perform a hecatomb of mankind for the ages. For the survivors, a planet of horrors." Castle's smile had quite gone as he focussed on the floorboards between his feet. "I don't want to die, but if anything in the history of humanity was ever worth fighting for, it's this."

The soldier, Captain Pendleton, clapped his hands for attention. "Everyone! Well, we all seem to be armed and have a decent understanding of how to use our weapons." He coughed. "By and large. I shall now go through the plan I have developed from the reconnaissance material we have, courtesy of Messrs Castle and Grant, the last of whom has actually been inside the house. Once I've laid that out, we can discuss any questions that may arise. Then, when we are settled and in agreement, I suggest we eat together before those who are staying in hotels disperse for the remainder of night. Tomorrow, we rendezvous in Barking Town, and we attack an hour before dawn."

The plan was simple, and that was sensible given that hardly a man or woman in the little band of twenty had ever fought before. It would hinge on the two advantages of surprise and of numbers. There was no reason to suspect Sir Donovan had brought more men into his circle, not least because it was unlikely he would trust anyone enough to draw more in at such short notice. That still left a force of perhaps ten, or nine now that they no longer had the services of Jibsy, who was still a prisoner in the cellar. But even a force of two to one may not be sufficient if the one is determined and experienced enough. Having seen those men at first hand, Grant could easily imagine a single one of Sir Donovan's fellows ploughing through their entire force with abandon. Surprise, then, was their talisman and was to be maintained to the last possible moment. As many of the enemy would be dealt with as rapidly as possible (where "dealt with" was the tacitly agreed euphemism for "killed"), and the rest mopped up while they were still in a state of confusion. "Don't expect that to be more than a minute at the very most," counselled Captain Pendleton to those who had stayed at the Chiswick house overnight. "These men are hard-bitten survivors, and they have not reached that state by being subject to panic. If they get even an instant to rally, they will do so and be entirely ruthless in the counterattack. We must not give them even the slimmest chance. It is a harsh thing that we must do, but it is a thing that is forced upon us."

And so, with this exhortation to slaughter ringing in their ears, the Cult of the Great Race of Yith went out into the streets of London and bought railway and bus tickets to usher them to the distant battlefield of Barking.

The pocket army, labouring to seem just a gaggle of assorted middle class and trades folk out for a jolly in the country, gathered at Barking Town Station and, when they were reasonably sure that all were present, they broke into groups that would form the two pincers that would take the house and a small reserve. The primary aims of the operation (eliminating every Australian to be found there being secondary, although important, to their survival) were simply to find and kill Sir Donovan, and burn Elmwood House to the ground. This, it was hoped, would be sufficient to nip the enemy's plan in the bud. One factor that might prove vital was the mysterious Great-Uncle Mathias. After some thought, Miss Trent had arrived at the conclusion that the temporal barrier was simply too far beyond the wit of Sir Donovan, and that he must have sought help. "Mathias", then, was this help. Miss Trent referred to him without irony as a "wizard", a term that had caused both Grant and Castle some consternation. Grant had carefully explained that there was no such thing as magic. Miss Trent concurred and asked him how he would then describe psychic time travel and lightning guns. This, he was at a loss to do, and Miss Church clarified that, in her opinion, science remained magic until its underlying principles were well understood and the knowledge disseminated. Mr Castle agreed and said that he had no idea how the telephone worked, so that might as well be magic as far as he was concerned.

Semantics aside, they all agreed that Mathias was likely a scientist whose immense knowledge outpaced the current scientific establishment. This "wizard" was considered extremely dangerous and to be eliminated on sight. "When push comes to shove," muttered Castle to Grant as they walked along the quiet lane towards the house, "I hope I'll be able to do the deed. Pendleton's a good sort, but he's no Shakespearian King Hal. My courage doesn't feel even adjacent to the sticking place. How about you?"

Grant thought of the strange figure of Great-Uncle

Mathias and how he had felt unnerved in such a way that the sensation had felt imposed upon him rather than coming from within his own body. "If we see Mathias," he said, "leave him to me. I would be happy to put that man down like he was a frothing dog."

Castle gave him a curious look. "He really rattled you, didn't he?"

"I don't deny it. There is something very peculiar about that man. Something I can't explain, but something that shouldn't be. This *wizard* business… I've always thought a wizard would be like Merlin, performing miracles with a smile and a wave of a wand, just like a stage conjuror. But that's not what magic is like at all, is it? It corrodes those who practice it. Mathias has made himself into a monster. I take no pleasure in it, but he must be removed just as a surgeon might cut out a tumour."

"Wish we still had the lightning gun. That would settle this in a twinkling."

"You only had one?"

"Alas, yes. They're the absolute devil to make, you see. Modern day science is barely able to provide the materials required, and even then not to the ideal purity. It was an absolute labour gathering it all and then building the wretched contraption. When it worked, it was a marvel, but it often didn't. Not the ideal state of affairs in a battle, is it? When the Great Race fought the enemy, their guns were entirely reliable. I envy them."

"You realise Sir Donovan's probably got the wretched thing now?"

"Yes, much good may it do him. I hope he tries to use it and blows himself to kingdom come in the process."

"And what if his 'Great-Uncle' has repaired it for him?"

Castle paled a little at that thought, then bestirred himself with a wan smile. "Then we all die, old man, but we do it in a blaze of glory."

Previously, the journey to the house had seemed longer than it needed to be, but to Grant's perception it seemed that they had hardly left the station than they were close enough to see the house, louring behind its hedges in the thin light of the dying night. The sun was still a good way below the horizon, but the promise of day was already there as the dawn light gathered. Grant and Castle's contingent had set off a few minutes before Pendleton's, the intention being to come around the far side of the property, gain entrance to its land and approach the house through the cover of the copse of trees on the eastern side. By the time they were in position, Pendleton's contingent would have arrived, and they would try the garden door and, if that were locked, use the drive gate. The garden gate was preferable as it would allow them to use the flora to hide their approach, but the drive would do if needs be.

This, then, was the plan, based as it was on limited knowledge of the battlefield and of the enemy. Far too limited, it transpired.

The first problem Grant's half of the pincer encountered was that the only access they could find to the eastern part of the property was actually a door set into a wall of privet that might have last opened freely around the time of the

Siege of Paris. It was partially overgrown with immense foliage and resisted fierce pushing and shoving. "I think it's giving," said Castle as he wrenched the door back and forth in its frame. Grant could see that, but could also see that it was only by a small degree. He dearly wished they had a pair of secateurs with them.

"We have to be in position in…" he checked his watch, "three minutes! Is there another way in?"

"How would I know?" Castle continued to lean back and forth on the door.

"There's a four bar gate over here!" said one of the others, appearing around the curve of the hedge at a dogtrot.

"Come on," said Grant, and led the way, fuming as he did so that they'd wasted a precious couple of minutes doing the equivalent of pushing on a door labelled "pull" when there was an easier way available the whole time – something that would have been apparent if they'd had the opportunity to carry out a proper reconnoitre. His father had been in the army, and he had been very happy not to follow in those footsteps. Playing soldiers in this extreme was more exasperating than he could easily encompass. He was only glad that Miss Church – by her own admission a nurse and not inclined to violence – had agreed to stay with Miss Trent in the reserve group to the south.

"If we lose her, we lose everything," he had told Miss Church privately. He was not clear in his own mind, either then or later, whether he had meant Miss Cerulia Trent or Lizzie Whittle. In either eventuality, Miss Church had agreed to stay close to her and get her away should things go awry.

As he clambered over the four bar gate at the eastern end of the property and advanced through the small copse of trees beyond which lay the house, Grant already had a sense that things were going awry. The scent of imminent catastrophe was strong in his nostrils and if he could have sent up a flare and called off the attack, he would have done so in the instant. No such useful piece of equipment was to be had, however, only the Enfield revolver in his hand and the clasp knife in his pocket. There would be blood spilt that morning, he was sure, but whose exactly was a concern to him. His little group of seven came to a halt at the edge of the trees and looked to the house. No lights burned there, which was good news, but the silence of the place was foreboding.

"Seems a bit unsporting to murder 'em in their sleep," whispered Castle.

"They'd cut your throat while you slept without hesitation and laugh at you while you drowned in your own blood."

"Would they?" Castle glared at the house. "The rotters."

"What's taking Pendleton so long? I thought they'd start the attack while we were still coming up, but we've been here a couple of minutes and nothing is happening."

Castle took out his pocket watch and squinted at the dial in the poor light. "You're right. We got here a minute late. The curtain should have gone up three minutes ago." A shot rang out. "Oh, speak of the devil."

"Wait," whispered Grant. "Listen."

Only Castle heard him. The rest of the group was spread out along the line of trees and out of earshot. At the sound of the shot and obedient to Pendleton's plan, they broke cover and rambled across the open lawn. Halfway across, the crossfire began.

From the bushes and shrubs that marked the northern and southern boundaries of the lawn, guns spoke, muzzle flashes blinked, and Grant heard the uncompromising sound of lead furrowing the air. The man closest to Grant out on the lawn, a haberdasher from Bermondsey, stopped suddenly as if he'd forgotten something, and then quietly folded down as a corpse on the dark grass.

"Ambush!" cried Grant, forgetting his own safety in the shock and fury of the moment. "It's an ambush! Fall back, you fools!" He fired at the bushes, two, three times, and then pulled Castle with him back into the trees.

"How could they know? How could they know?" Castle was babbling as Grant pushed him furiously through the copse.

To Grant, the answer was plain. Of course, Sir Donovan and his men had to suspect that action would be taken against them shortly, and that they would attempt to expedite their plans. So, he had taken out a map of the area, set it upon his desk, and considered how he might execute such an attack given that it was to be launched by an amateur group with little military experience.

A staging at Barking Town was therefore a likelihood, and how difficult would it be to place a watch there with a bicycle and instructions to hie themselves back to the house at the first sight of a strange gathering of disparate and probably nervous types? Now Grant thought on it, he remembered seeing such a diminishing figure upon the road when he had first emerged from the station building to find the others milling around in the most obtrusively unobtrusive style conceivable. It had taken another ten minutes to rally the troops, and then they had walked to the house. Sir Donovan must have had the best part of twenty minutes to send his men to their predesignated places, there to await this army of lambs. Whether this was the actual sequence of events was academic; all that mattered was that they had been handily outmanoeuvred.

And what had happened to Pendleton? There was shooting from over that way, the timbre rendered more hollow by the extra distance, but it was not as intense as that immediately in their wake as they ran through the trees. Pendleton's group had probably been flanked, too; the western approach was so obvious that even Grant could imagine how easily they might hide in the field across the way, wait for the invaders to go by, and then fall upon them. He did not fault Pendleton for that. It was not overconfidence or incompetence nearly so much as a lack of time forcing them into a precipitate action, an action that had doomed them and would therefore ultimately doom so many more. The hopeless Battle of East Barking would never make it to the history books, should history books ever be a feature of the uncertain and unfriendly future. Sir Donovan did not strike him as a great reader.

"I say, old man," said Castle who had slipped back into his wake, "I think perhaps you should just trot along without me. Feeling awfully short of breath all of a sudden."

"Don't be a bloody fool! They're right on our trail!"

"Yes, well, you see, felt a bit of a slap on the back a minute ago, didn't think anything of it, but… you know, I think I've been shot…"

"What?" Grant stopped, grasped Castle and turned him around. High on his back and just below his shoulder blade, a ragged wound stained the cloth of his coat red. "It's nothing," lied Grant, "just a scratch. We must keep moving!"

"Oh, bless you. Bless you for that. 'Just a scratch'. I like that. Yes, well, I'm going to sit down now and… what do you call it? Sell my life dearly. Yes, that's the thing. That's the ticket. You just cut along and find some other way to save the world, there's a good fellow. Right. Yes." Castle slumped to the floor. "Prop me up against a tree, would you?" he gasped out, his voice weakening by the second. "Can't do my 'Horatius on the bridge' business if I'm all of a puddle on the sod, can I?" Grant dragged him to the base of an elm and set him there. As he made sure the man's little automatic pistol was ready in his lap and the mutilated shotgun in his hands, Castle said, "Go now, Grant. Run along. Do whatever it takes. Nothing's more important in the world now."

Grant could hear cautious footsteps approaching through the trees and knew that all the men on the lawn were dead. "One thing. Is your name really 'Castle'?"

"What? Yes, of course. Why do you ask such an extraordinary thing? Oh, tell me later. Shoo."

Grant fled, feeling wretched yet relieved, which only

made him feel more wretched. He ran in a low sprint and vaulted the gate the moment he reached it. As his boots landed in the lane beyond, there was the boom of a shotgun roaring from both throats and then a crackle of responding fire behind him. He spat a curse then and swore he would bring down Sir Donovan, the fate of the world having no part of it.

He retraced his steps around the southern part of the periphery, back past the jammed door in the hedge, and back down to rendezvous with the tiny reserve force. He had left four there. Now there was only a frantic Miss Church. "Where are the others?" he demanded. "Where's Lizzie... Miss Trent?"

"The captain's dead!"

"They're all dead. Where is Miss Trent?"

"When we realised it was a trap, she ran in. I think she wanted to warn you!"

Grant grabbed her by the elbow and dragged her around the hedgerow and into the southern side of the field, putting a finger up to his lips for silence. A moment later, they heard footsteps in the road.

"No one here," they heard a rough male voice say.

"We have to make sure. Follow the lane right round and back to the drive. We've to make sure we got every one of 'em."

"Some fight, eh?" The first voice laughed.

"Fish in a barrel, mate. Fish in a barrel."

The men moved onwards, their voices diminishing.

Grant turned to Miss Church and found her weeping

silently. He felt he might join her if he let himself, so instead forced himself into gruffness. "Stop that. What's done is done. We have to get away from here."

"We've lost," she whispered. "It's hopeless. They're all gone, even Miss Trent. What can we do?"

Grant thought of Castle; ridiculous, blasé Castle, sitting there in the light of a new day, the end of which he would never see, calmly awaiting his death with composure and a sadly debauched shotgun. He thought of what he had said. "We do whatever it takes," said Grant. "There is nothing more important in the world now."

CHAPTER THIRTEEN

A CLATTERING OF JACKDAWS

Detective Sergeant Bradley received a letter that morning. The outer envelope was good quality vellum and he recognised that somebody was trying to impress him with it. Opening it, he realised why; it contained a letter from Doctor Lockley, director of the asylum at Colney Hatch.

Lockley's letter was brief and to the point, explaining that he had insisted he be present at the postmortem carried out upon the body of Winston Barnaby and that the police surgeon, Doctor Andrews, agreed that the death was likely a suicide, there being no signs that Barnaby had been restrained at the time of his death.

Bradley was impressed that, in so few words, Lockley implied his own lack of culpability for the death. Clearly, according to Lockley's written implications, Barnaby's death was probably Bradley's fault – how dare the detective have the temerity to trouble the asylum's daily routine – and finally that nothing of further relevance had been discovered in Barnaby's cell. That, Lockley strongly hinted, was the end of any possible police interest, and clearly Lockley wouldn't give a tinker's cuss if he never saw Bradley again. Bradley was inclined to gratify him in that.

Barnaby's note was lying unread in his desk, not through forgetfulness on Bradley's part, but simple lack of time. He now took the note from a drawer and held it for a moment before taking a deep breath and unfolding it.

He was not looking forward to studying the strange drawing of something like a diseased organ or a carcinoma of some description on the sheet again, but, happily, he had the reasonable excuse not to peer at the image in more than passing by dint of the lines Barnaby had added to the bottom of the sheet. In the sullen dimness of the mortuary, they had been all but indecipherable, but in the good light of the CID office, the light pencil strokes gave up their meaning easily.

Sir,

I have aways been a good judge of character, and I see that you are a good man. I am not insane, but I am a coward, and I cannot bear what I know is our future. The weight of it is too much. You will see.

There is a terrible king, the king of the world. His time draws close. The world's king shall rise from a house of clay and death shall be his handmaiden. It is too horrible. It is too horrible. A kingdom of blood and bones. I can already smell its stench. I thought that perhaps I might hide from it, but there will be no hiding places, such shall be its totality and ubiquity.

They will come for me, just as they came for the others.
I have no power left, except to deny them my light.
Perhaps I am not such a coward after all. Perhaps this
is the most courage I shall ever have. Good luck, sir,
and may a good God bless you.
   Faithfully,
   Winston Barnaby

It was not the sort of note he might have expected from the inmate of an asylum given his previous experiences of inmates, but he knew it was folly to take any of it at face value. Then again, the passage about how "they came for the others" troubled him. His desk still contained a large packet of missing persons reports, after all. He hadn't had time to study them as closely as he might have liked, but he was beginning to think perhaps he should find that time.

As he thought about the case, his gaze slowly crept up the sheet until he was looking at the abominable thing Barnaby had drawn there. He was, unfortunately for Bradley, a decent artist, and the sketch bore a vivacity Bradley found troubling, as if such an awful thing had been drawn from life. Then, as he unwillingly studied it, Bradley made a discovery. The thing, the cancerous organ or whatever it was supposed to be, did not stand alone, but against a shaded background. At first Bradley had taken this to simply be a way of highlighting the thing itself, but now he noticed small specks of paper that were very deliberately not shaded and, with a small shock, he realised that they represented stars. The background was not simply there to set off the drawing, it was a drawing itself, of a night sky. But that, he thought, was absurd. That would mean that the thing was floating in space.

The shading was not uniform, but turned paler at the base, and here the stars were drawn in, not absences. Almost against his will, Bradley pulled out the stationery drawer in his desk, removed the hand magnifier he kept there, and studied these tiny markings more carefully. They were not stars at all, he realised. They were human figures. Which meant that the cancerous organ must be some sixty feet high or more, and some twenty-five feet at its widest point. There also seemed to be some suggestion that it reached down to the ground, but the pencil strokes grew fainter there, as if Barnaby had been unsure of his vision.

Bradley realised that he had forgotten to breathe.

The fanciful vision of a diseased mind it must be, he informed himself firmly, drawing in a deep breath as he did so. No such thing could possibly exist. Not even a blue whale could encompass such a horrible cancer. He was smartly folding up the sheet to add it to the file when he overheard Detective Inspector Craddock say the words "clay house".

"I beg your pardon," he said, rising and going to where Craddock was talking to DC Hamer, "but what did you just say about a clay house?"

"Sir Donovan Clay's house, sir," supplied Hamer. "Out in Barking."

"The local constabulary had a complaint about Sir Donovan holding a shooting party this morning before dawn," explained Craddock, "apparently to deal with a parliament of rooks that were wrecking the garden. The local constable went around, spoke to Sir Donovan, tug of the forelock, word to the wise about being a good neighbour, and away again. That should have been the end of it, but the complainant is Sir Eberhard Jackson." Here Craddock paused significantly, as if that explained everything, but Bradley could only look at him blankly.

"*His Honour* Sir Eberhard Jackson," supplied Hamer. "Recently retired. Terror of the High Courts. There's not a lag for fifty miles didn't sigh with relief when he gave up the wig."

"Ah," said Bradley, beginning to see.

"From what the local station has told me," said Craddock, "Jackson regards Clay as an arriviste. Apparently, he has Australian connections and has heard stories about Clay's activities out in the Antipodes. Not a fit man for a knighthood and certainly not someone he wants for a neighbour, even though they don't live *that* closely together. In any event, he wants CID to take an interest and he has the heft to insist upon it."

"He wants a detective to investigate the shooting of a few birds?"

"He does, although the way he describes it, it sounded more like a restaging of the Battle of Rourke's Drift."

"Does it have to be today, sir?" Hamer appealed to Craddock. "I've got this business in Norwood to attend to…"

"Ideally. Could you go on after Norwood, perhaps?"

"Actually," interrupted Bradley, "I could go, sir. My afternoon's all paperwork, and nothing pressing at that. I wouldn't mind, and besides, if Sir Donovan Clay is potentially going to be a nuisance, it would be as well if we got the measure of him now." As he spoke, he glanced at the file on his desk. Craddock followed the glance, and nodded slowly.

"That's very true, Bradley. It may well prove useful in the long run. Very well. Hamer, off to Norwood with you. The wilds of East Barking for you, Bradley, and make a point of talking with Judge Jackson before you speak to Clay. I want verbal reports from both of you promptly on your return, understood?"

Bradley took his lunch at his desk and ate a cold pie with pickles washed down with strong tea as he went carefully through the missing persons reports and regretted not having time to have done so sooner. Coincidence certainly exists, and a policeman must take care not to see wilfulness in the hand of happenstance. "Reasonable doubt" is the measure of trial by jury, after all, and if the diligent detective cannot discern mere coincidence from true cause in the case he presents, he may be very sure that the defence barrister will. Closer examination of the reports had shown that coincidence was being drawn too thin even for the tastes of the most optimistic defence brief, however. No less than three of the reports – the only three that had gone into the activities of the missing in the weeks before their disappearances in any detail – mentioned visits to a client in Barking, two explicitly mentioning Sir Donovan Clay, and the third – while not naming the client – supplying enough indications that were in common with the other two to make it highly likely that it was again Sir Donovan.

So, Sir Donovan Clay was in the habit of inviting sundry psychics to his house, who would then go missing shortly afterwards, and who had that very morning apparently fielded enough guns to besiege Sevastopol in an effort to drive off a few birds. Perhaps this lattermost incident was simply eccentricity on the part of a man wealthy enough to indulge such impulses without ending up in a place like Colney Hatch, but Bradley had been asking around, and the consensus was that Sir Donovan Clay was a hard man, a ruthless industrialist, and not the sort of fellow to indulge in fancies. If his explanation of the morning's activities was true, therefore, the rooks must have numbered in their thousands and been the size of albatrosses. Bradley felt sure somebody might certainly have mentioned such a phenomenon. Sight unseen, he was evolving a distrust of Sir Donovan Clay.

Before he left for the station, he had a quick word with Hamer about Judge Jackson, an unknown quantity for Bradley as Jackson had retired around the time Bradley had first come to London. "An even-handed sort of cove," was Hamer's opinion. "Scrupulous about fairness in the trial – he threw plenty out for lack of evidence or poor preparation – but the old lags were afeared of his sentencing. If you robbed for a career, you could expect him to chuck the whole book right at your head."

"A 'firm but fair' kind of feller?" asked Bradley.

"'Fierce but fair', more like," said Hamer, and it was with this description in mind that Bradley went first to call on the retired judge.

The judge's house was about ten minutes' walk from Sir Donovan's, he noted; close enough to hear gunfire in quiet before dawn, but a little too far to easily investigate. It was a pleasant little redbrick villa with roses around the door, and one would not have guessed it was the home of a feared former judge and scourge of London's underworld. On calling and submitting his credentials, Bradley was also favourably impressed by Jackson's old world civility. He was brought into the sitting room and had tea pressed upon him. He sensed a certain gleeful energy in the judge when the reason for his visit was made plain, the joy of a retired gun dog unexpectedly called upon to hunt once more.

Having taken down a statement on the specifics – and Sir Eberhard Jackson was *very* specific, having noted to the minute when he heard the gunfire and a second burst two minutes later – Bradley asked him about what happened subsequently. "Well, I sent my man Noakes over at nine to tell Clay what a damn impertinence it is to rattle off gunfire at such an hour in what is, after all, a London suburb, near as dammit. I knew Noakes would couch it more diplomatically than that for me. It's one of the great virtues of the man. He comes back with some cock and bull story about rooks or jackdaws or some damnable nonsense. I may be retired, sergeant, but I am by no means senile nor, I flatter myself, have I ever been a fool. Those were full-throated firearms. Now perhaps that's what they use for birding in the Antipodes, but it's a blasted rum show for the metropolis. Besides, his plot is a small garden and a patch of woodland; what exactly were these remarkably resilient birds feasting upon? The place doesn't have a kitchen garden and those trees are no orchard."

"Did your man notice anything else?" asked Bradley. "Anything that struck him as out of the ordinary?"

Sir Eberhard smiled. It was plainly a question he had been hoping for. "Noakes is a remarkable feller, detective sergeant. A born diplomat, as I've said, but he has a good pair of eyes in his head, and he knows how to employ 'em."

"He should have been in the force."

Sir Eberhard barked a laugh of delight. "He *was*. I sent him down a dog's age ago for a petty larceny. Six months of hard labour. I didn't have a choice; you cannot have police officers break the law and not be seen to be severely punished for it. What sort of message would that send, eh? But I know a moment of weakness when I see one, and a ruined character for life seemed a disproportionate punishment to me. Therefore, I employed him when he came out of the Scrubs. That was… oh, twenty years ago now, and I have never had a moment of regret about it. But we digress. What Noakes observed certainly interested me. Firstly, this blessed garden of Sir Donovan's that requires an artillery fusillade to protect it from a vast flock of greedy birds that no one else in the neighbourhood has seen. Noakes reported it as being in a poor state. By his evaluation, it hasn't seen a gardener since Sir Donovan moved in. What little work has been done looked grudging and amateur. It seems strange to me that this ragged plot was worth him marshalling his men out in the early morning to protect."

"It does seem peculiar. Was there anything else, sir?"

"There was. As he approached, he noted a scattering of sawdust in the lane. He took a moment to investigate it and saw it was bloodied. He then went to the house to register my disapproval of their nighttime activities. He didn't see Sir Donovan himself, but met Sir Donovan's… well, major domo, I suppose you might call him. A man called Lynch. Noakes's measure of the man was that he was talking to an inveterate criminal, and I am inclined to trust his judgement in such matters. It seemed Noakes had been observed studying the sawdust and this man Lynch was at pains to explain that there had been a delivery of meat that morning and the butcher's van had leaked a quantity of blood in the road."

"What was Noakes's opinion of that?"

Sir Eberhard snorted in amusement. "Utter eyewash. As if a butcher's van would carry meat still thick in gore! No, the butcher would have had to slaughter an ox right there in the road to require that much sawdust. Besides which, it wasn't in a single location. Patches had been scattered across the road. How do you explain that, eh?" He watched Bradley's face as he arrived at a particular solution. "Yes. That's what I thought. One doesn't like to think the worst of a knight of the realm, especially when one is such a thing oneself, but, nevertheless…"

"It's a very serious thought to bear, sir."

"Oh, don't I know it? And yet… all his peculiar comings and goings, the collection of thugs with which he's surrounded himself. Why, even the weather has behaved oddly hereabouts since he took residence." He leaned forward and lowered his tone. "I know a villain when I see one, detective sergeant. Trust me when I say that I've donned the black cap for better men than Donovan Clay. When you go to interview him, keep your wits about you. You may be sure that this is about far more than an inconsiderate neighbour and a flock of birds."

When Bradley took his leave, Sir Eberhard saw him to the door. "Sir," began Bradley, but the judge forestalled him.

"If you're not back in an hour, I shall telephone New Scotland Yard and report your absence and my suspicions to… you're under Craddock, aren't you? A good man. I shall give Detective Inspector Craddock chapter and verse upon what we have spoken about this morning. I think the danger is small at present, but real. Clay gives me the sense of a man possessed by a growing desperation, but I do not think he is quite at the point of doing something so stupid as to antagonise the police. Not yet, in any case. That said…"

"I shall be cautious, Sir Eberhard, and thank you."

There were still traces of sawdust in the lane, but Bradley went to pains not to be observed studying them. His camouflage would be that of a put-upon copper sent out by overbearing superiors to satisfy the whim of a former judge. He would embrace generalities, eschew specifics, and observe tacitly. He would, in brief, project the air of a man with better things to do.

He was met at the door by a man braced with muscles, and coated in superciliousness and a suit worth more than his soul. Bradley took him to be the infamous Lynch and, if so, he agreed with the assessment of Noakes. Blandly, he stated his business, and was brought into the hall while Lynch confirmed his identity with a handshake and went to inform his master that the police had arrived.

As Bradley waited, he took in the hall and what he could discern about the inhabitants. There was dust denoting a level of recent slovenliness in the running of the household that was echoed in the garden. There were magazines lying on window nook, and even an abandoned teacup. Beyond this evident slackness, however, there was little else to observe until he happened to note what seemed to be the door to the cellar. It was a fancy arched door of a quaint old design, all painted in black, even the door irons. It was also slightly ajar, and Bradley got the impression that he was being observed through the slim crack between the door edge and the broad, arched frame. As he watched, the door swung slowly to, and the latch clicked shut.

He was still wondering at this when the man who might be Lynch returned to shepherd him into the presence of Sir Donovan Clay.

"It's very good of you to speak to me, Sir Donovan," said Bradley, projecting the air of a bored timeserver who can't wait to get back to the station for a cup of tea.

"Not at all, not at all," said Sir Donovan, coming around

his desk to shake his hand. "Anything to help the forces of law and order." Apparently realising that this was perhaps suspiciously ebullient, Sir Donovan adopted a slightly pained expression, withdrew back behind his desk, and sat down. "I understand this has something to do with our little shooting party this morning?"

"It does, sir," said Bradley, drawing out his notebook, and writing out the date, time, place, and situation as he spoke. "We've had complaints about the noise, I'm sorry to say."

"Complaints? Plural?"

Bradley ignored the question and ploughed on. "I know it looks rustic out here, but practically, it's in the suburbs, sir. Letting off guns willy-nilly, well, it's a little frowned upon."

"So it would seem," said Sir Donovan, all conciliatory and keen to get rid of him. "You have my apologies, detective sergeant. It shall not happen again."

"I'm glad to hear it, sir." Bradley was writing with glacial slowness in his notebook all the while. "What was the trouble exactly?" Sir Donovan looked at him blankly. "The shooting, sir. Why was it necessary?"

"Birds. There was a flock of birds that had taken to roosting in the trees. They made an awful din in the morning, and were quite laying waste to the garden. We really needed to shoo them off."

"Magpies, was it, sir?" asked Bradley, writing *Magpies* at a speed commensurate to chiselling it in stone.

"Jackdaws, sir," said Lynch, who was standing by the door moved into Bradley's eyesight. "It was jackdaws."

"Ah," said Bradley as if receiving great wisdom.

"Jackdaws." He slowly crossed out *Magpies,* slowly wrote in *Jackdaws,* and then slowly underlined it to mark its significance. The only sounds in the study were the slow drag of his pencil lead on paper and the quiet fuming of two very impatient observers.

Into the pool of silence, he dropped a pebble. "I'm sure I read somewhere that you have an interest in the formulation of explosives, sir. Is that so?"

"Explosives? Why... yes. Yes, for mining operations, you understand."

"Do you have a laboratory, sir?" Bradley saw Lynch tense, but made no sign that he had noticed the reaction.

Sir Donovan scoffed. "A laboratory? What? Here?"

"Well, a lot of these houses have good-sized cellars beneath 'em, sir, and I noticed a door out in the hallway that looked like it might lead to one such. I just thought that, since you have an interest in chemistry, that you might have established a laboratory down there."

"What a novel thought. No, there's no laboratory down there. Just bric-a-brac."

Bradley sniffed as he continued to write with all the gusto of a sedated sloth. "Just as well, really, especially with explosives. You'd likely blow yourself to kingdom come." Bradley sighed when he placed a full stop to conclude the last sentence, exhausted at the finish of his magnum opus. He looked up. "Might I see the guns, sir?"

"The guns?"

"The guns that you used this morning to drive off the..." he consulted his notebook, "...jackdaws."

"Oh." Sir Donovan shot a cautious glance at Lynch that Bradley pretended not to notice. "Yes, of course. By all means." He rose and went to a cupboard that Bradley had taken to be a locked bookcase. On opening, however, it was revealed to be a gun cupboard containing four shotguns. "These are they."

Bradley sauntered over and regarded them without enthusiasm. "I see, sir." He started writing again. "Two double barrelled twelve bores, a double sixteen, and a single twenty. Is that right, sir?"

"Yes, that's right. You know your firearms."

"Experience, sir." He pocketed his notebook and pencil, and – without seeking permission – took down one of the twelve bores, a Purdey, broke it and sniffed at the chambers. He closed it, replaced it, and repeated the performance with the twenty bore. All he could smell in either case was gun oil. "Freshly cleaned, sir," he said, as he put back the twenty.

"I take good care of my guns, detective sergeant."

"Are these all of them, sir?"

"Yes. Well, I have a revolver in my desk, but that wasn't used this morning. Why do you ask?"

And why do you *ask?* thought Bradley, but he said, "Only that the complaints suggested a long and busy period of firing, sir. I'm surprised only four guns with seven shots between them could keep up that sort of din."

"Oh, well, you know how people are, exaggerating for effect."

Bradely closed the gun cupboard. "Very true, sir, very

true." He turned to Sir Donovan, smiled pleasantly, and asked, "May I see the bodies?"

In his peripheral vision, he saw Lynch straighten up, a sudden tension apparent. Even Sir Donovan noticeably paled beneath what remained of his tan. "Bodies?" he said, less of a question, and more a ghastly echo.

Bradley raised his eyebrows, the very epitome of innocence. "Of the jackdaws, sir. With all that shot flying, you must have a fine pile of the noisy little devils."

"The jackdaws!" said Sir Donovan with very poorly concealed relief. "Oh, we didn't shoot straight at them, you know. That would have damaged the trees. We just fired into the air beneath them. We only wanted to startle them, you see."

"Very humane of you, sir." Bradley glanced sideways at Lynch to nod convivially at him, but really to enjoy watching the man come down from tenterhooks. "Why strike down God's creatures when it's not even for sport, hmmm? Very humane indeed. Well," he made a last few tortuously slow notes and finally flipped his notebook shut to the visible relief of Sir Donovan and Lynch, "that all seems very much in order. I shall take my leave now, and do so with the advice that, should you ever be troubled like that again, you should just bash together a few pots and pans. You'll get much the same effect, and you're that much less likely to rouse the neighbourhood."

"Thank you. Thank you, detective sergeant. I shall certainly bear that in mind. I can quite understand the desire for quietude in retirement. Good day."

Lynch waited for Bradley to reach the lane before he finally closed the door, and Bradley could all but hear the whole house exhale with relief at his departure. He went by Sir Eberhard's house to assure the judge of his return and briefly agree with his analysis of Sir Donovan, stopped at a tearoom in Barking Town to write up his notes properly, and then caught the train back into the city. As requested, he went straight to the office of Detective Inspector Craddock to give him a verbal report.

"Well?" said Craddock. Bradley took out his notebook, but before he could open it, Craddock added, "He's a wrong 'un, isn't he?"

Bradley lowered the notebook and nodded. "A very wrong 'un, sir." He stood awkwardly, a man plainly wanting to say more, yet held back by professional reticence.

Craddock nodded sympathetically. "Be at your ease, man. You haven't reached where you are today without seeing things most citizens would dismiss as inconceivable in a civilised society. They don't appreciate just what a thin coat of varnish civilisation is. At least part of what we do as diligent coppers is to maintain the illusion that God is in his heaven and that, but for the depredations of a few criminal types, all is well in the world. But, it's not true." He looked ruminatively into the fireplace and watched the flames purr around the coal in silence for a few seconds before continuing. "A few years ago, I was involved in a murder inquiry. Retired soldiers being done to death. I was a very no-nonsense sort of feller at the beginning of that with a very clear belief that I knew the way of the world."

He looked sideways at Bradley, and it was very evident in his expression that old memories continued to torment him to that day. "I knew nothing. Nothing at all. None of us do, not really. Forget every word they taught you of history at school. Half-truths are no better than lies, but it was never intended to enlighten, only to be an ingredient of that civilised varnish. Because if people ever see past the shellac…" He shook his head. "We preserve the illusion of normality, Bradley. If you don't see that now, you will soon enough, because I have a very unpleasant intuition about Sir Donovan Clay. I can only advise you to keep a broad mind and to be wary of dismissing the remarkable as the impossible simply because it is outside your experience. Not one of us on God's Earth knows everything and we should be very grateful for that, because some knowledge is too dreadful for the mind and conscience of mortal man to bear." He smiled, but he seemed to have grown older and more weary for the recitation. "Well, I've said my piece in the hope that you might understand me. What do you say, Bradley?"

Bradley thought on Craddock's words for a long moment, then said, "May I alert the Thames River Police to be on the lookout for bodies bearing gunshot wounds, likely dropped into the estuary at Barking shore this morning, sir?"

Craddock nodded, quietly pleased. "You may, Bradley. You may."

CHAPTER FOURTEEN

THE ENEMY

"You must be careful," said Mathias to its guest. "You must not be observed."

Miss Trent was sitting on a box by the shelves, placed such that she might rise quickly and hide in the shadows should Sir Donovan appear at the head of the cellar stairs. "I had to see who it was. I think it was a policeman."

"I do not know the term *policeman*," said Mathias.

"A security agent for the state."

"A security agent." Mathias digested this for future reference. Its learning of English was still very much a work in progress, and there were still many unexpected gaps in its vocabulary. "An enemy of the Donovan-man?"

"Sir Donovan has a lot of temporal power here. The security apparatus may be corrupt in his favour. But I do not think they were pleased to see the policeman. Perhaps Sir Donovan's plans are compromised."

"That would be supposition," said Mathias. Here, outside the view of weak-minded humans, it was at liberty to shed its face and the pretence of being descended from apes, or a mammal, or even being a member of the animal kingdom. Miss Trent was only human in form; her race had known of Mathias's for unimaginable eons. Its great fly-like corpus formed from fungal protein sheets and bundled hyphae, the creature known for convenience's sake as "Mathias" stood a shade over five feet high, possessed six limbs – the middlemost discreetly tucked away under its shapeless coat when in polite company – and elements of physiology that brought the *crustacea* to mind, although the ellipsoid head furrowed with brain-like convolutions was not known on any terrestrial species. Beneath the head, a cluster of damp, worm-like cilia dangled and flexed. Its brethren could lay claim to large, functional wings, but Mathias only bore stumps roughly where a man's scapulae would be. Presently the cilia moved in slow, long sine waves, an indication of thought.

The attack had gone terribly wrong almost immediately. Miss Trent's little reserve group heard the sounds of struggle in the direction of Pendleton's group. "They were waiting for us!" Miss Church had said in dread realisation, as two members of the reserve ran up to relieve the captain's group. That was when the shooting broke out.

"Mr Grant's group must be warned," said Miss Trent. "Stay here!" And, so saying, she had run through the gate and up the drive. Almost immediately firing began close at hand, and she had spied Sir Donovan's men shooting from cover at the rear lawn. At the same time, she heard the rest of Sir Donovan's crew coming up behind her and, across the front garden, she saw the hedge door opening. Caught in three directions, she had fled into the fourth – the house itself. Seeking a quiet place to hide in the hope that she could steal out again later, she tried the cellar, and there found that she was not the only non-human entity in the building. Mathias had shown as much dismay as its species were capable of showing upon seeing her, but it led her quickly into the dark places at the rear of the cellar, and then innocently resumed work at its usual place. Presently, Sir Donovan's men had dragged down some wounded souls with the instruction that "Sir Donovan says make use of them", and then they had been left alone.

Since then, she and Mathias had spoken quietly and at length. Miss Trent's current psychic tenant came as no surprise to Mathias. It had known since the night of the séance. The chair contained an apparatus to detect and, if need be, tap into the psychic energies of its occupant. Mathias had seen immediately that her reading was far beyond the common human capacity, so high that it strongly doubted she was entirely human at all. That she was possessed by one of the Great Race of Yith had seemed most likely, and so it had lied to Sir Donovan about her capability. Why, hadn't it even grabbed Grant as he carried Miss Trent during the darkness and forced him out of the French windows and into the night?

Mathias had come to Earth in the time of the pharaohs, seeking the source of a curious etheric disturbance it had detected from space. Borne on its great membranous wings, it had discovered the abandoned Yithian city in the place now called "Australia", and descended into the catacombs to search. There it had encountered the ones the Yith called "the enemy", and they had taken it prisoner, tearing away its wings to prevent escape. The logic of Mathias's race was not that of humans, or even the Great Race, but it had nevertheless dispassionately reached a state of what humans would characterise as an undying hatred towards the enemy and to their human agent, Sir Donovan Clay. Even by its curious ratiocinations the maxim "My enemy's enemy is my friend" held a certain truth, and so Miss Trent was preserved against discovery.

"I have done what I may," said Mathias, "but I cannot delay indefinitely. Though they bring me such poor materials," it gestured at the human remains arrayed in the jars upon the shelves, "the device must inevitably reach a state of sufficient operational energy. The Donovan-man is human and therefore of limited intelligence, but it has the cunning of a lower species. I may not prevaricate very much further. The device must be activated soon."

"If you do, the enemy shall commit genocide upon the Great Race of Yith," said Miss Trent. She said it in a colourless tone, because it was no more than the truth and the truth needs no colour. "Furthermore, you will still be the prisoner of the enemy or their agent."

"What course do you suggest?"

"The one you have already considered and discarded because you have been given insufficient time to attempt it."

"The time remains short."

"But now you have aid."

Mathias did not hesitate. It was not in the nature of its race to quibble in the face of the rational. "There is a small table in the corner. The Donovan-man never ventures that deeply into the cellar. You may work there."

Miss Trent did not thank Mathias, because this innately understood plan was the best of both their hopes and fit the needs of the Great Race of Yith. Gratitude was a human sensibility. Instead, she said, "I shall require sustenance, or this body will fail."

In answer, Mathias took down one of the jars and handed it to her. She nodded, and took it to the small table in the corner to dine.

Grant reconnoitred the area around the house in Kensington carefully, both from the perspective of thoroughness and the desire to avoid being seen. He went around, left for a while, came back, repeated his search, went away again and then, after the third circumnavigation of the house, decided that it was no longer a place of interest for Sir Donovan Clay.

He did not go directly up to his rooms, however; it was by then mid-afternoon and he had realised he could not remember eating at all that day, or the previous. There was a little back street cafe he knew that would give him a quiet respite in which to restore his humours before... what? He had no idea. A doomsday was coming, and he had not the foggiest notion how to interfere with it. It was entirely possible that, when the barrier was thrown up, he might be one of the humans whose body was occupied by an unwilling member of the Great Race, and he would find himself swapping places and end up permanently encased in a body that was not his in a time so long ago he could not imagine it. He would be trapped there forever when "the enemy" destroyed his former body in their frenzy of revenge. As he was shown to his favourite table in the cafe, he thought that might happen to any of them there: the other diners; the chefs in the kitchen; the dour waiter.

Grant ordered and, as he waited for his meal to arrive, he sank into a bleak contemplation of his limited options. He had left Miss Church at the house in Chiswick. She would draw together what was left of the cult in Britain, and there were other agents coming from abroad. They would take too long, though, Grant was sure. By the time they arrived, what was to happen would have happened. It would all be far too late. In any case, Miss Trent was lost, and that meant so was Lizzie Whittle. What did any of it matter anymore?

He was so submerged in his black mood that he did not hear the waiter engage in a short conversation with a new diner, nor the man wave the waiter aside, and it was not until the phrase, "Ah! There you are, Grant, old man! I thought I might find you here!" was uttered close at hand that he troubled to look up and was duly horrified by the sight of Detective Sergeant Bradley drawing up a chair and making himself comfortable at his table. His smile for Grant was broad and honest and the model of friendliness, but only Grant heard him say in an undertone, "Don't make a scene. It will go badly for you."

He was too surprised to make a scene, though, and – in

any case – any last traces of vigour had been drained from him by recent reversals. All he could do was regard Bradley lividly from his inner swamp of resentful ennui. "Bradley," he said listlessly. "What a delight."

Bradley accepted the menu from the waiter and, as soon as the man as gone, muttered, "We must talk, you and I."

"How did you find me?"

"Came over to see if you were in at home, but, as I approached, I was treated to the sight of you skulking around, so I followed you."

"For how long?"

Bradley shrugged. "An hour," he said, and ordered the liver and onions.

"An hour?" Grant, duly appalled, said as soon as the waiter was away again.

"You were hunting for watchers, not pursuit. Don't take it so ill. All's well that ends well. I was looking for you and I found you. Just imagine if it had been Sir Donovan's men, instead." He smiled warmly, a friend chatting with a friend. "They'd have murdered you, you know."

Grant blanched. "I don't know what you're talking about."

Bradley's smile faded a notch. "Here's the thing, Grant, I truly don't have time for your nonsense. That man Clay's up to something and, whatever it is, it's on a grand scale. For the moment, he's as greasy as a fairground pig; we can't lay hands on him because, well, he's a knight and the Exchequer is fond of him. My governor tried to get a search warrant to have a look at his place in Barking, but walked into a brick wall. 'Sir Donovan Clay? *The* Sir Donovan Clay? Involved in skulduggery, detective inspector? And where is your evidence?' And that's the rub. All we have are the gravest suspicions and a few bodies dredged out of the Thames, with nothing but the most circumstantial link to Sir Donovan Clay. It's not enough. The thing is, he must know it's only a matter of time before we get that search warrant, but he isn't shifting. It's as if he knows it won't matter soon. I can't imagine anything short of a successful rebellion that might give him that degree of immunity, but I also can't imagine how he might manage that with just a handful of Aussie convicts."

"And what makes you think I might?"

"Coincidences. Many, many coincidences. Far too many to ignore, and they keep touching on mediums and séances and the like. Your name and that of Miss Cerulia Trent have come up more than once. Speaking of whom, where is the remarkable Miss Trent?"

Grant blinked, caught off guard by the question. "She's gone to the countryside. To recuperate," he said, and the desperation of his tone and the glibness of the lie were all too apparent to him as he said it.

And, it seemed, just as apparent to Bradley. The last wisp of a smile dried from his face. "Bollocks," he said. "This would all go much more quickly if you'd just accept that I'm cleverer than you and, it seems, much better at my chosen employment. Drop the act, man. You're no more a Londoner than I am. When you're flustered, as you are this instant, your accent comes right out. The mud of the

Meadow is there on your boots for anyone to see. It's also as plain as a pikestaff that you're frightened, and not of me. Or, not *just* of me." He looked at Grant narrowly. "My God. You were there, weren't you? You were there when Clay's men committed murder."

Their food arrived. Grant looked at his plate as if it bore broken glass and ashes. "I can't eat."

Bradley meanwhile was energetically jamming his napkin in his collar to protect his tie. "Gravy gets everywhere," he explained. He gestured at Grant's plate. "Eat, man. You're clemmed, I can tell it; your stomach's been growling all the while. You're neither use nor ornament to me if you're starving yourself to death. Eat. We can talk afterwards."

The flat seemed alien to Grant now, a long way from the pleasant nest he had made of it. The knowledge that Lizzie's rooms were directly above his own and just as cold as she probably was by this juncture depressed his spirits to the edge of despair. He sat down heavily in what had been his favourite armchair before all the world and beyond had decided to burden him with its woes, and buried his face in his hands.

Bradley, like all his contemporaries in CID, had been a beat copper before he dropped the serge and beetle-crusher boots and became a plainclothes man. He had seen his share of domestic tragedies and been called upon to act as honest broker, intermediary, or a shoulder to cry upon any number of times. He looked at the figure of misery before him, nodded, and said, "I'll make some tea."

There was no milk to be had, but in Bradley's estimation, that seemed low on Grant's list of things to complain about. Certainly, he accepted the cup and drank quietly. This acquiescence to the reality of his situation Bradley took to be the first dribbles of water that warn of a collapsing dyke and, sure enough, a few moments later the levee broke entirely.

"Lizzie's dead," said Grant, quietly and with little intonation, despite which Bradley caught a waver of bone-deep misery in his voice. "Dead or worse."

"Lizzie?" asked Bradley gently.

"*Miss Cerulia Trent.*" Grant spat the name from his mouth like a dead fly. "That were all flash and palaver. She were Lizzie Whittle."

Bradley noted that he wasn't even attempting to hide his Mancunian accent now. Grant was a broken man, and it gave Bradley no pleasure to see him reduced thus. "Tell me what happened, mate. Every detail. Leave nothing out." He produced a notebook. "Anything that goes in my police notebook is a matter of record. This *isn't* my police notebook. This is my own. I have a feeling whatever you tell me would cause ructions if it were part of the official record. In which case, we'll play this by ear, eh? So, tell me everything."

"There's a lot to tell."

"You've a lot of tea in your caddy. We'll make it through somehow. Now," he licked the tip of his pencil and readied it above the blank page, "in your own words."

Grant obliged to tell his story, by chapter and by verse,

and Bradley never interrupted him except for points of clarification. He didn't ask for more incriminating details with respect to their adventures in mediumship, not least because he was unconvinced there was any real crime there worth pursuing, given that "Miss Cerulia Trent" had certainly possessed abilities of some sort. Mindful of D.I. Craddock's advice to maintain a broad mind and accept that what he knew fell well short of everything that there was to know, he accepted the description of the fateful séance, curious lights and all, without demur. Perhaps there was a simple scientific explanation, perhaps there was not, but he reminded himself that he was there to record, not debate, and his pencil skittered onwards.

He was quietly amused and found himself warming to Grant on hearing that his opinion of the great Sir Donovan Clay was commensurate with his own, and saw that Clay was truly the nub of the case, as he had recently come to anticipate. Grant was a small man who'd been dragged into the gears of a big machine, and it was this machine that represented the threat, whatever that might be.

When the threat was defined in Grant's narrative, however, it took every sinew of Bradley's self-control not to slap his notebook shut, take Grant by the ear and dispatch him to Colney Hatch to make the acquaintance of Doctor Lockley and a nice, warm cell. Instead, he steadfastly ploughed on through a sea of tripe about unlikely concepts that included ancient inhuman races, time travel, and Australia.

The existence of some sort of secret society, however,

did have evidence to support it; specifically, three bodies, all peppered with ball and shot, fished out of the estuary. The River Police had only been set to search for such things specifically on Bradley's own suspicions about Sir Donovan. Even if all the twaddle about monsters were only that, it didn't preclude the possibility of some grand "madness of crowds". He himself had been involved in dispersing a mob in Manchester who'd managed to convince themselves there was a "boggart int' ginnel" in Ancoats once, which is to say, a goblin in a back alley. He'd seen sensible men in that crowd, wide-eyed with uncritical fear and anger that the supernatural had set up camp in their backyards. The irrational, he reminded himself, can take a grip of anyone. History is not short of examples, after all. Even in the region of Manchester, the fate of the Pendle witches was a matter of shame to that day. He took a moment to sharpen the pencil, and carried on.

He thought he had done well to weather that part of Grant's tale without interruption, but he had to gird his loins all the more when Grant described the preparations to attack Sir Donovan's home in Barking. He knew how that had worked out, but even so, listening to how this secret society had decided to murder a knight and his entire retinue and to do so without comment caused him much internal stress. He may not have been entirely successful in hiding this from Grant, who paused in the telling, and glared at him. "What would you have had us do?" he spat. "Go to the *police*?"

Bradley's immediate response was to say, "Yes! Of

course, you bloody fool!" But he did not, and in that moment understood what Grant had really meant and how inarguable it was. Given Sir Donovan's wealth, influence, and reach, there was not a single reason to believe that he would have been informed immediately if even a guarded report on his activities had been made. Sir Donovan might be *nouveau riche* with all the associated social opprobrium that came with such status, but the *riche* part of the equation was colossal and went a long way towards minimising the former. People might sniff at the mention of his name, but they still invited him to their parties and were eager for acceptances. In Grant's view of events, the establishment would conspire in the destruction of the world out of politesse. If Grant was right about all the grander details Bradley did not like to think too heavily upon, then Bradley conceded that he had a point; the Earth would die curtsying.

Finally, sometime after six o'clock, the story was told. "Miss Church and myself are all that are left. She tells me that others are coming from other parts of the world, but it will be too late." He shrugged. "Run me in, copper. Do what you like. None of it matters. In a month this won't be a world you'd recognise anyway."

"Well, let's see about that," said Bradley, finishing his last notation and stowing away the book. "I need to talk to your Miss Church and to this man you kidnapped."

"He's scum."

"And that from a son of Angel Meadow. You are off the Meadow, aren't you?" Grant nodded. "Thought so. You've done well to get so far from it. Anyway, to get back to the point, if he's one of Sir Donovan's chaps then, oh yes, he is scum, I don't doubt it for a moment. I still need to talk to him."

Grant looked at him for a long second and shook his head. "You don't believe a word of what I've just told you, do you? It's mad talk, I know. Why would you? Still," he took a deep breath and Bradley saw him visibly relax on the exhalation, "I'm glad I said it to someone. It's been an awful burden, and all the while thinking, 'Have I gone mad?' Listening to myself talking to you, yes, I think I have. It is a relief to me to know that."

Bradley laughed as he took the tea things into the small kitchen. "Let me tell you a couple of things, William Grant," he said on his return. "First thing is that mad folk don't tend to know it. They're positive their delusions are real and everybody else is wrong. That's what marks them out as insane. Mad folk don't tend to sit there, stroking their chins and saying, 'I sound mad'. That is, as I understand it, very much the mark of someone who isn't. Mad, that is. You may be mistaken. You may be deceived. But, mad? I'm not convinced of that. Not that I'm a mad doctor or anything of that sort, but in the job, you meet all sorts. Which reminds me of something." He started searching in his inside breast pocket. "Second thing is that, since I joined the CID, I've been lucky with my governors. Both of 'em great believers in keeping an open mind. We see some odd stuff on the job. I've never seen nowt I couldn't explain, even if maybe I couldn't explain it right there and then. My current guv, though, he tells me he's seen some stuff that was beyond any explanation. So, I've long been prepared for that day to arrive. Perhaps you really are mad, Mr Grant. Or perhaps today's that day. Oh, here it is." He fished out a couple pieces of card held together with India-rubber bands to sandwich a piece of paper and keep it flat. He extracted the paper. "Brought this along with me as it was possibly germane to what's been going on with you. Here…" He unfolded it and held it out to Grant. "That mean anything to you?"

Grant looked uncomprehendingly at the image of some sort of cancer-riddled organ dripping from a night sky. Then he saw the figures where the lower "limb" of the abomination touched earth and so understood its scale. Bradley watched the colour drain from his face and was assured the reaction was in no way affected. Grant believed the reality of what he was seeing.

"Oh, dear God," said Grant in a small, terrified voice. "The Enemy."

CHAPTER FIFTEEN

ON THE RIVER

Miss Church's poise at a detective turning up on the doorstep of the house in Chiswick was careful displeasure. "Who is he?" she whispered *sotto voce* to Grant as they assembled in the murky hallway, lit by a single candle on a side-table.

"He's the police, madam," said Bradley with dry affability. "Don't you worry – Mr Grant here and I have had a frank discussion about recent events, up to and including your little society's playful attempt at lynching a knight of the realm and the subsequent sad massacre of your colleagues."

She glared at Grant. "What possessed you?"

"Not one of the Great Race of Yith," said Bradley, answering for him, "I can tell you that much. No, more like desperation, I would say."

Miss Church's face fell. "You told him of the Great Race?" Grant looked wretched. She turned to Bradley. "Most people have… difficulties accepting such things."

"Perhaps so, miss, but I'm a Mancunian." He said it as

if it explained everything, and perhaps it did. "You have to understand, it doesn't matter a farthing if I believe him or not. The point is that Sir Donovan Clay clearly does, and that belief is informing his actions, which go up to and include what would seem to be an ambush and mass murder in Barking, of all places. Now, I understand that you have one of Clay's fellows locked up in the cellar. I should like a word with him. And, yes, kidnapping is a very serious offence, I don't dispute it, but I have a sense that the relative severities of assorted crimes in train here will be something to be sorted out afterwards. Right this instant, I am on the hunt for clarity, and the more voices I hear, the more I know. So… the cellar, madam?"

Miss Church glared at him for a moment, but then the fight quite left her. "I don't suppose it matters very much now, in any case," she conceded, to which sentiment Grant slowly nodded his head in agreement with her. Her shoulders drooping, she followed as Grant led the way down into the house's vaults and the small room therein that served as their prisoner's cell.

When he heard approaching footsteps, "Jibsy" McMahon was tensed and ready for the door to open. As it did so, he burst through it with a war cry and his fists balled, all set to fight for his freedom. What he was less ready for was the man outside the door to step lightly aside as he bulled past and then apply a truncheon to the back of his skull with a tap of scientific precision both in terms of placement and pressure. The world flickered for Jibsy, and his next coherent memory was of lying face down on the cellar floor with someone kneeling on his back and handcuffing him.

"Now then, sir," said an unamused male voice he had not heard before, "let's have no more of that silliness, eh?"

"Who are you? What are you? A copper?"

"Decently sure you're not in any position to be asking the questions, sir. Whether I am a police officer or not is moot, given that you're not under arrest. Amusingly, I have more legal restraints placed upon me when you *are* arrested than not, so the fact that you are currently not under arrest… well, sir, let's just say I wouldn't take that as a good sign if I were you."

"Hey, hey!" Jibsy had not enjoyed his incarceration and wasn't going to let go of his outrage quite that quickly. "I'm the victim. I was kidnapped!" He squirmed his head sideways to where he could see Grant and Miss Church watching the proceedings with plain misgivings. "Them! They're the ones you should be arresting! They kidnapped me!"

"So they did. Will you be pressing charges, sir?"

"You're bloody right I will!"

"Well, that's capital, sir. I'll take you all in and you can give me a highly detailed statement, explaining all your activities since you set foot in England. Oh, actually, I've got some questions about your time in Australia, too."

Jibsy belatedly realised the situation was not playing out quite as he'd hoped and expected. "Eh? What's that got to do with anything?"

"Context, sir. Context is everything. For example, you

will be able to provide the context by which there is a perfectly simple explanation for why you had a house in Kensington under surveillance."

"Surv...? Look, I was just standing there when–"

"You were just standing there in Kensington when you are resident in Barking, sir? Pull the other one, sir; it is bedecked with bells."

"Eh?"

"Tell me about Sir Donovan Clay."

Jibsy grew still. "So that's what this is about, is it? Well, you can bugger off, copper. I ain't going to bleat on me boss."

"Your boss, who cut you loose as soon as you got yourself taken? Yes, he feels a strong duty of loyalty to his men, I can tell. He's under surveillance himself at the moment, you know. Suspicion of crimes against the state."

"What are you talking about?"

Bradley brought the truncheon down smartly on the bricks of the cellar floor right in front of Jibsy's face, making him flinch. "Treason. We have reason to believe that your boss plans treason."

"Spoony," muttered Jibsy to himself. "Everyone's gone spoony."

"He's a knight, though, so I expect he'll just get a nice quiet beheading in the Tower. No fuss, no palaver. His men, though, fellers like you, they'll make an example of you."

"I don't know what you're talking about," snapped Jibsy, but there was a sparking emphasis in his speech that was new. Bradley knew the sound of a slow or gullible man finally starting to add things up and not enjoying what the sum came to.

"I don't know if it's still on the statute books, but have you ever heard of something called hanging, drawing, and quartering, sir?"

"Oh!" said Miss Church, who had. She covered her mouth in unsimulated horror. "They wouldn't, surely?"

"I honestly don't know, miss. But even beheading's not as terrifically swift as you might expect. I'm told it took Jack Ketch four or five goes to get Monmouth's head off, and he was a duke. Monmouth, that is. Not Ketch. Ketch was an incompetent. You know, I would say the French were onto something with that guillotine thing of theirs, but, well, that's the rub…" he shrugged expressively and grimaced, "it's French, isn't it?"

"You're trying to frighten me," said Jibsy. "It won't work."

"Frighten you?" Bradley looked suitably philosophical as he sat on Jibsy's back. "Oh, chum, we don't have to frighten you. Look at the situation you're in. You're in a lovely deep cellar that could host a German band concert and the neighbours wouldn't hear a note, the only people who know that you're here are here with you, and none of them like you much. We don't have to try and frighten you; you'd be a bloody fool if you weren't frightened anyway. So… I know about this feller Mathias. How about you tell me all about what led up to his appearance. What exactly went on in Australia?"

"I told those two, I don't know! I wasn't there!"

"But your mates were. What happened?"

Jibsy hesitated. "It's crazy talk."

"Well luckily, I'm very much in the market for crazy talk. Been hearing a lot recently and I think I've developed a taste for it. So, tell me."

As Jibsy began spilling his guts, far away on the Thames, the pleasure steamer *Kingfisher* was on her last leg of the day, back out of town and so hugging the northern side of the estuary until she made her way past the river mouths at Holehaven and then Hadleigh Ray. She'd drop off the last of her passengers at the end of Southend Pier, see them away on the pier railway, and then return to her overnight mooring at Leigh-on-Sea. Her master, Kerwin Gibbs, was a careful skipper, made more careful still by being on the river, man and boy, and having seen too much of the grief inattention can bring upon the water. He was especially mindful that the *Kingfisher* performed very much the same route as the tragic *Princess Alice*, lost thirteen years ago. The *Alice*'s eastward destination had been Sheerness on the southern shore rather than the *'Fisher*'s upon the northern, but they both terminated west close by one another, the *Alice* at the Swan Pier and the *'Fisher* a little further upriver at Blackfriars. That had been an awful day for all on the river, the day the *Alice* was cut in two by the collier *Bywell Castle*; hundreds died, and all due to a moment's confusion.

The years after had been difficult, too. People were chary about travelling by steamer, be it for pleasure or necessity, and things had been hard. But, with patience and diligence, the trade was repaired, and if the public's confidence was ever dented again, it wouldn't be by the actions of Captain Gibbs.

He knew some of the younger crew thought it comical that he treated a jaunt up and down the river as seriously as if he were circumnavigating the globe, but they hadn't helped with recovering the bodies thirteen years before, so what did they know? A gnat's eyelash above nothing, that's what. He stood on the bridge watching the progress of every vessel in eyeshot, and inwardly reckoned what to do if one was piloted by a fool. The *'Fisher* was rated to carry 600 passengers, and that was a lot of lives for which to be responsible.

There were barely sixty aboard that evening, but every one of them was some mother's son or daughter, and he would get them to the pier safe and sound, as was his duty. The sun was down, and he was scanning ahead with his binoculars, looking for navigation and bridge lights, but the broadening horizon of water as the river grew steadily wider was blissfully clear of them for the moment except those clustered along the banks. Gibbs envied them; soon enough, soon enough, he reassured himself. He did not like the look of the weather. The barometer had assured him of clear skies, and yet there was an ugly, ill-tempered squall rolling in from the sea. It was peculiar, a freakish local sort of upset, like a storm that soaks one end of a street and leaves the other bone dry. Indeed, there were areas ahead over the Thames that looked as if the clouds had touched the very surface of the river.

"What do you make of that?" he asked Jones, his first officer.

Jones squinted into the darkness. Then he borrowed the captain's binoculars and squinted again. "Well," he said finally, "bless me." Jones came from a Welsh family and had been raised strictly chapel. "Bless me" was a bloodcurdling oath coming from him. "If we were out and properly into the North Sea, I might say waterspouts, but whoever saw such a thing on the Thames?"

Gibbs took back the binoculars and looked again. Then he called to the helmsman to reduce speed to *Slow*. As the telegraph clanged, he said to Jones, "Can't see a blessed thing through them, whether they be spouts or cloud."

"We're in the southern channel, sir. The path ahead should be clear."

Gibbs grunted. "Should be" assumed the absence of fools. It was, however, the only assurance he would be likely to get, and – combined with the prudence of reducing speed – he might have to hope that this would suffice. "Eyes peeled until we're by, Jones."

"Aye, captain. Coldharbour turn ahead."

The air grew colder as they closed on the strange weather, and worse, it became fetid. The Thames was never a flux of rosewater at the best of times, but such delicate scents as the waters gave up, rivermen such as they had long since grown inured to. This, however, was something very new, and the novelty was not enjoyable.

"Do you smell that, sir?" asked the helmsman, gagging slightly as he did so.

"Hard to miss it. What on Earth is that? Horrible factory smell, is it?" It was a reasonable assumption; the smell was not especially organic, but a chemical scent that started sharp and then coiled itself around the parts of the brain dedicated to smell that were rarely visited. It smelled unearthly, it smelled ineluctably amiss, and in some ancient cloister of cerebral architecture inherited through countless generations, it sounded a warning bell. "Whatever it is, it bodes ill." From somewhere close at hand, he could hear what he took to be factory whistles, but they blew incessantly, and their tones warped and mingled and changed such that he didn't know what he was listening to, nor wherefrom it came. Only that, as they closed on the curiosity in the river, the whistling grew louder, and the strange scent strengthened with it.

He scanned the river ahead. The view was still unaccountably shrouded by shadows, but he reckoned he could see far enough ahead to risk passing this peculiarity at a faster pace. "Take her back to half ahead. The sooner we're by this, the happier a man I shall be."

The helmsman did not quibble with the order by even half a moment; none of them on the bridge felt comfortable in that place. Gibbs went out and looked down the side of the boat. The passengers were gathering at the rail, pointing ahead at the pocket squall. He looked too, and saw that Jones's "waterspouts" were becoming more defined. The more he looked, however, the more his heart quailed in his breast. There was no sense that they were spinning, as was the usual way with whirlwinds and waterspouts, but only standing there atop the water, and where the river was cut by their points of contact with the surface, there was no spray. Instead, the water broke around them – three in number, he now saw – as if these were great structures standing in the river and not whirling above it.

He looked up into the bodies of these whirlwinds in all their terrible stillness, and he saw no air and water whirligig-ing around, but what he did see made his eyes widen with a terrible realisation. Not only was he looking at the whirlwinds, but they were also looking at him. He burst back into the wheelhouse, almost incoherent with dread. "Full speed ahead! Give it every ounce, man! Full speed! We're in danger! Such danger!"

Neither Jones nor the helmsman were used to seeing Gibbs in such a state, and it was understandable that the latter looked to Jones for confirmation. Jones looked up into the confusing mass, and as his mind unwillingly resolved it, he saw teeth set in wet gaping mouths wide enough to eat a carthorse for a morsel, and he saw the eyes, filled with a weird light that told of inestimable depths of hatred and an unfathomable capacity for cruelty.

Jones swore the first real oath of his life. That was enough for the helmsman, who rang for full speed on the telegraph, set his eyes firmly on the river ahead and not up at the sky that had so utterly disordered two of the soberest men he knew. "Aye, sir!" he called, and steeled his grip on the wheel.

"Well," said Detective Sergeant Bradley over tea, "wasn't he the charmer?"

Jibsy had, in Bradley's estimation, "cracked like a nut" when the correct pressures were brought to bear. Only a particular variety of interrogation is given the sort of acceptable leeway Bradley had just employed, but he had stopped short of any form of torture. Threats of torture, however, were of fair use and Jibsy, like many if not most of his ilk, was ill-prepared to weather that possibility. Thus, he had told them what he knew, divulging things he had not previously to Grant, and, by Bradley's estimation, laying out many truths he had not himself realised that he knew. Sir Donovan's deep criminality was no surprise by this juncture, but now it was possible to guess at his actions that had led to the present day.

Jibsy had never been out to the mine – what interest could he have in a pit? – but kept himself in town as much as possible. Thus, his intelligence pertaining to events was secondary. There had been a disaster, he said, or so they thought, and then it turned it out, yes, it was a disaster, but not quite of the nature expected. "Y'see, y'say 'mining', and people get a picture of a coal pit in their heads, but that's all wrong," Jibsy had explained, rendered unexpectedly loquacious by the prospect of explaining industrial extraction techniques. "It's what they call 'opencast mining', y'see, which is more or less like quarrying. There's no big pits or tunnels."

Or, at least, there weren't supposed to be, but a tunnel is exactly what was exposed during the expansion of the bauxite pit.

"They didn't like it, the locals didn't. Got very upset with us."

"In the town?" asked Bradley.

"The town? That's two miles away if it's an inch. The Aborigines." Jibsy curled his lip. "Not like proper people, that lot. Not like you or me."

"Ah, you," said Miss Church sourly, "a shining paragon of civilisation."

"Eh? Anyway, the locals had been a bit batey about all the digging and blasting out there, and when they found out about the tunnel, well, they carried on and on. Said the land was… eh, what did they call it?"

"Sacred?" offered Bradley.

"Cursed. Yeah, that's the one," said Jibsy brightly. "And now they said there were sleeping devils down under the land and they'd come out and eat the world if they weren't kept asleep. All that sort of bilge. Made a big noise about how only they could stop the devils until finally Sir Donovan… well, he were just plain 'Mr Clay' then, still… he agreed to go into the tunnel with the local leader. Terrifically old feller he was. Huge beard, old as Methuselah. Just to show there weren't nothing to be afraid of. They went in… hours they were down there… and then Mr Clay comes out all on his lonesome." For the first time, something like a reasonable suspicion crossed Jibsy's face. "Funny look he had when he came out. Sort of scared, but excited. Said there'd been an accident and the old feller had copped it in the tunnel. Said it was dangerous in there and he wouldn't allow anyone to go and fetch the feller's body. Well, you can imagine the fuss that caused. So…" Jibsy looked off into the distance, "Mr

Clay said they had to go. He said he didn't want a single local within twenty miles of the mine."

Now, talking through the testimony of Jibsy McMahon, Detective Sergeant Bradley carefully replaced his empty teacup upon his saucer and said, "He meant Sir Donovan ordered every Aborigine within twenty miles to be murdered. I have no doubt his men fulfilled the order efficiently and even with enthusiasm. Impossible to prove at this time and distance from the event, but I think you might have trouble finding a judge and jury in the territory who would convict in any case."

"I don't understand, though," said Grant. "Why do something so horrible? What threat were they to Clay?"

"Not to him," said Miss Church. "To his new masters. The local people had been there for heaven only knows how long. They *must* have found those tunnels a long time ago and discovered what lay down them. They found some way to keep the Enemy dormant or imprisoned or both. It made no sense to them that any man would ever want to free such monsters, but they had never met the likes of Donovan Clay before." She looked at Bradley. "You must mount a police raid on his house, detective sergeant! You must! Once your superiors see what's in that house, his plan will be nipped in the bud."

"Oh, miss," said Bradley as he refreshed his cup from the pot. "I admire your faith in British justice, and, in all honesty, there is much worse in the world. But at the very least I need a warrant to mount a raid, and who is going to sign a warrant for a search on the basis of conspiracy with unearthly monsters to usurp the rightfully elected government of the United Kingdom? In all honesty, I've no reason to be convinced, even in myself. That you and Mr Grant obviously believe all this and have answers to almost everything is seductive in itself, I admit, but when I stop to think on it, there is very little solid evidence for all this. Sir Donovan is as crooked as an old man's stick, I am convinced of that. But there would be a lot of resistance to raiding the home of a knight, for heaven's sake. It would take damning evidences and time. We have neither."

"What if I could show proof of the existence of the Great Race of Yith?" said Miss Church suddenly.

Both men looked at her. "How?" said Grant. "They became extinct millions upon millions of years ago. What? A fossil?"

"No! Come with me!" Suddenly excited, she led on and was followed by the two mystified men. Back down into the cellars they descended, but she went right before they had gone left to Jibsy's confinement. In a dank vault apparently used as a workshop, she indicated a set of ancient shelves up against one wall. "Push it! To the right!" They did so, and found it ran on casters set onto grooves set in the mortar floor. Behind the shelves was a door, which Miss Church unlocked and led them through.

Beyond was a square room perhaps twenty feet long by fifteen wide. It was dry in there, illuminated by electrical light when Miss Church twisted the switch, and all cluttered with equipment of unguessable purpose. The centre of the floor was clear, however, but for a heavily-built mechanical pedestal upon which was mounted a bulky device that looked like a sculpture wrought from ten thousand brass pipes each little more than a tenth of an inch in diameter. Against the wall at an angle was a second, freestanding wall, not very expertly built and just as inexpertly painted in white distemper.

"You see?" said Miss Church, excitedly pointing at the device as if it were as vindicatory to their cause as a confession of all his sins signed by Sir Donovan Clay. "You see?"

"What is it?" said Grant, who did not see at all.

"It's… oh, look!" She stood by it, said "Watch that wall!" and touched something nestling inside the device's Gordian innards.

Without fanfare, the device spat lightning and blew a hole clean through the freestanding wall. Both men jumped back in astonishment. "A lightning gun!" cried Grant. "I thought the only one had been lost when Lizzie and I escaped that night?"

"No, it's not the final version. This was just to see if the principle of it worked. It weighs half a hundredweight and its range isn't much further than those few yards to the wall. But did you ever see the like? Either of you? You would agree that this is not the work of man?"

Bradley, his curiosity overcoming his amazement, had advanced to look at the weapon closely, albeit careful to avoid the twist of pipes that represented the gun's equivalent of a muzzle. "Ah, but that's the pity of it, miss. It *is* the work of man. I can see manufacturers' marks on several of its component parts."

"Yes, but ..." Miss Church foundered, realising her error.

Grant shook his head, sympathetic to her plight. "You and I both know it is of the Great Race's design, but we live in an age of wonders. Who is to say some brilliant, human inventor did not happen to discover its principles? It is amazing, but it proves nothing. The only real proof of Sir Donovan's evil lies in his house in Barking, and by the time we have enough hands to try another assault, it will be too late."

Bradley was quietly and thoughtfully gazing at the prototypical lightning gun. "It may not necessarily convince a judge, but – for whatever it's worth – it's convinced me. Up until now, this could all have been the result of a great, shared delusion. Now, however..." he looked at the hole in the target wall, smoke still curling up from molten brickwork, "well, that's quite forceful. Yes, Sir Donovan requires a forceful visit, and very soon. Your international friendly society won't arrive for days. There will not be a warrant for a police raid forthcoming in a timely fashion. We are thrown back on our own resources, and these seem thin for the task in hand. We may be able to scrape together weapons, but with only we three to bear them, it will be a short engagement."

"You don't know any coppers who might ... ?" said Grant.

"Who might what? Risk their lives, careers, and liberty on a venture like this? I don't think so. I'm still fairly new at Scotland Yard, in any case, still the bumpkin northerner to half my colleagues. I've had more respect from the criminals, to be perfectly frank."

Grant nodded. "When I first came down, those were the circles I moved in, too. For a while, at least."

"Oh?" said Bradley, taking a professional interest. "Where were you? I was placed with H Division for my probation. I think the logic was that if a bloke can handle Spitalfields and Whitechapel, he can handle anything."

Grant laughed. "You were in the station on Commercial Street? With all the chimneys?"

"A great many chimneys," agreed Bradley. "I don't remember seeing your face around there. I think you must have moved on before I arrived."

"This is all very heartwarming," said Miss Church in a brittle tone, "but might we perhaps–"

But suddenly the smiles fell from both the men's faces. "Nine-Fingers!" they chorused.

"I *beg* your pardon?" said Miss Church.

Chapter Sixteen

COLDHARBOUR MUD

Coldharbour is little more than a meander in the Thames before the river finally blunders into the southern reaches of the North Sea, and that is nearly all that there is to be said about it. A few fishermen's shacks here and there, mostly abandoned and falling down, and little else to speak of. Certainly, Detective Inspector Craddock knew little enough about the place when he went out there in response to an unusual report that had crossed his desk.

"Not been out here before," he said to the uniformed sergeant who'd accompanied him. The sergeant, the most senior officer available, had no idea why a full-blooded Scotland Yard detective like Craddock was out there now, but he kept his curiosity to himself, largely.

"Not many do come out here," said the sergeant, looking mournfully at the river, running oily and serpentine below them. "Even most Londoners'd be hard pushed to find Coldharbour on a map if you asked 'em, sir. Not for a mug of ale and a cigar, they couldn't."

"Usually quiet here, then?"

"Like a grave, sir. Must admit, if you don't mind me saying so, sir, I'm a mite surprised they'd send a detective out here. I mean, I can't account for it, but it's a nine days' wonder when all is said, ain't it, really, sir?"

Craddock smiled at him and nodded down at the river. "London's lifeblood, that is, sergeant, and anything that interferes with navigation up and down the river needs to be investigated. I think that you're right and there's nothing out here that will matter in a week, but I have to be sure. Those upstairs would have my guts for garters if I didn't look into everything properly."

As was well known and understood, "Those upstairs" were the bane of every honest working soul in the land and the invocation of the name put the sergeant firmly on Craddock's side.

"Oh, well, there it is, then, isn't it?" he said, nodding sagely. "Those upstairs." He joined Craddock to look at the grey moiling waters. "Don't know much about what happened on the river last night, sir. Only what I was told at a remove by the River Police."

Craddock didn't need to hear any of that again. He'd studied the report carefully and knew all about the uncharacteristically hurried arrival of the pleasure steamer *Kingfisher* at the end of Southend Pier, where she disgorged several dozen distressed passengers and her no-less distressed crew. Statements were varied in the extreme, the only thing they had in common being that there had been "something awful" over the river – clouds, or clouds of teeth, or swarms of eyes or stars. Already the deadeningly soothing gruel of officialdom was being fed to the public, that a combination of noxious gases rising from the riverbed and an unusual weather condition plus the poor visibility that evening had combined to wreak havoc upon the perceptions of the poor passengers and crew.

On being told this explanation for what he had seen the previous night, Captain Kerwin Gibbs had some choice words indeed, until it was explained to him that, if that was not the case, then he had certainly been drunk and his licence would regretfully have to be withdrawn with immediate effect. Captain Gibbs had some choice observations to make about that, too, but he changed his statement, nonetheless.

It was just as well, therefore, that Captain Gibbs had no idea about what had been discovered and reported at Coldharbour.

"What do you make of that, eh, sir?" said the sergeant. They were close by the crest of the headland that extended into the Thames there, and in the small hollow of the land, rain had gathered and made mud, A little off centre in the mud patch was what looked for all the world like a footprint, although what sort of creature might leave a symmetrical footprint bearing five great toe marks spaced evenly around it, the whole being some two yards across, was certainly a puzzler.

"It's a hoax," said Craddock without hesitation. It was the only option in such situations. If the sergeant had shown him the second coming of Christ Almighty, attended by cherubim and seraphim all upon clouds of glory, he would have said the self-same thing. What alternative was there for a busy police officer? "Some silly beggars have been down here and made those marks."

"But… why, sir?" said the sergeant, somewhat crestfallen.

"Why do hoaxers do anything?" said Craddock, and then masterfully deployed his trump card. "Probably to make the local constabulary look foolish. London is hip-deep in such petty anarchy these days. Anything that may bring the forces of authority down in the respect of the citizenry is to be embraced by these people." He shook his head at such naughtiness.

The sergeant's moustache bristled angrily that some collarless anarchist gang had tried to make him and his colleagues look like bumpkins. "The dogs! We should ignore it, then?"

"To an extent. This needs to be recorded if only for our own reference. Do you have a man who's handy with a camera?"

"Walters, sir. He's a good man, and a fair devil with a camera."

"Perfect. Get him out here immediately with a dozen plates. Photograph this thoroughly from all angles and keep a yardstick by it so we can reckon the scale from the prints. When he's done, destroy this. We don't want it leading people astray. Then send the plates on to New Scotland Yard. Every one of 'em, mind, and undeveloped! I don't want any images of this going anywhere else, you understand me? People see a thing they don't understand, it's like a poison in the mind. Every one of those plates will be developed at the Yard and go directly into the records."

"Of course, sir! I'll put matters in motion right away."

As the sergeant stumped off to shout at his constable, Craddock turned back to the river, withdrawing his notebook as he did so. He opened it and took out a square of paper on which he had copied a sketch from the report of Captain Kerwin Gibbs. It was a good representation of the river's meander at Coldharbour, as might be expected of a man who'd sailed up and down that stretch more times than might be served by memory. It was easy enough to find the spot in the river where Gibbs had marked an "X" to represent where he, his crew, and all sixty or so passengers had sighted the effects of river gas, darkness, and tiredness congealed into three otherwise indescribable monstrosities. He sighted the spot carefully on the river, then turned as exactly as he might a full one hundred and eighty degrees. Now, lying dead before him, was the mark in the mud. He raised his gaze and looked off into the distance, imagining a line drawn neatly through those two points. He would have to sit down with a map and a straight edge to be sure, of course, but in his mind's eye the line ran straight through the east of Barking.

Charlie "Nine-Fingers" Briggs had a police file thick enough to stun a reasonably resilient ox, should one allow you close enough to whack it over the back of the skull with such a hefty document. Spitalfields born and bred, or perhaps spawned and grown, Charlie had never set out to become any sort of criminal mastermind, and this was as well because he would never be any sort of mastermind. He was, however, of more than passable cunning, and this, combined with his gregarious and generous personality, his extensive web of criminal associates, and his easy recourse to terrifying violence had conspired to make him a personality of a type deeply fascinating to the mechanisms of law enforcement. Yet, he had managed to stay out of Her Majesty's Pleasure in venues such as Wormwood Scrubs or Dartmoor Prison. Although he wouldn't have recognised the term, he was a "gangster", and one of sufficient superiority in the complex underworld of East End London to be kept clear of most of the actual criminality from which he ultimately profited. Indeed, he was seen as a benevolent presence amongst the poor of Spitalfields and neighbouring Whitechapel; a crook, yes, of course, but a decent one who listened to grievances, put flowers on his mother's grave every week, and was not party to the many injustices that the poor already suffer.

"Charlie'll see you right," was heard often enough in the pubs along Commercial Road. Why, hadn't he put a stop to the Whitechapel murders? Well, the rumour was he'd killed a chap and had his body dropped in the Thames, and nothing more had been heard of the Ripper subsequently, so that had to mean something, surely? That he'd killed the feller for something else entirely was neither here nor there – Charlie Nine-Fingers had stuck a chiv in this feller's ribs and then stamped his head flat with his big boots, and then the Ripper murders had stopped, so QED, patently. The man was a hero. "How Charlie Nine-Fingers did for Jack" was taken as gospel in the locality, and Charlie was loved for it by nearly all.

But not quite all. Commercial Street also carried in its upper reaches a large and impressive police station, home to H Division and, as previously mentioned, a great number of chimneys. The coppers of H Division had their own opinions of Charles Briggs Esquire, and they were of the less flattering variety. While they were aware of the gossip pertaining to Charlie's inadvertent feat, no body bearing a stab wound and a head as flat as a pie crust had been discovered in the river or its estuary, and they presumed on this basis that the story was wholly apocryphal, not least because it was so injurious to the pride of the Police Force should it be true. Besides, Charlie was at least as much a legitimate businessman as he was a criminal and, as his career matured, that ratio only improved as is often the way among career criminals. There comes a point where it's just a great deal simpler, safer, and very nearly as lucrative to stay within the law, and Charlie could see that fulcrum drawing closer by the day.

For the moment, however, he was distinctly not an entirely legitimate businessman, and that evening was to be found in a farrier's barn off Brick Lane where, unobserved, he and his lieutenants were engaged in divvying up a misappropriated cargo from a ship just that morning arrived from distant Ceylon, via Wapping.

"Feller to see you, Charlie," said one of the lookouts,

sticking his head around the door. "Manchester Grant. Says it's urgent."

"Bill Grant?" Charlie was a big, heavily muscled man who did not project an air of intelligence, but this would be a misapprehension on the part of the observer. While not of overarching intelligence, he was possessed of a fair portion and combined it with a sharp wit and enough cunning to have stayed out of chokey for most of his adult life. Part of his arsenal of mental weapons was a good memory for names and faces, and a moment's furrowed brow was all it took to bring William Grant and such details as Charlie knew of him to mind. "Come out east again, has he? All right, Sedge, let him in."

Sedge did so, and Grant, dressed down for the locale, entered. "Evening, Charlie," he said. "Thanks for talking to me."

"Haven't talked to you yet," pointed out Charlie. "You told my boy it was urgent. What's it about?"

"I need your help. It's very important. If I told you how important, you'd say I was mad. But I'm not. I've never needed help from somebody as much as I do from you right now."

Charlie frowned, put down the bolt of gorgeously patterned cloth he'd been examining, and came around the table to meet Grant in the middle of the brick-floored shed. "That's a bit of a speech, ain't it, cully? When all's said and done, I'm just… well," he looked over his shoulder at where his men were sorting the mass of stolen goods, "a businessman, ain't I? What kind of help are you talking about, eh?"

Grant had been hoping to lead up to this a little more gently, but he could see Charlie Briggs was not in a patient mood that night, so he said, "I need a house to be raided. I need the owner done in. He's got some likely bullies with him, so they'll need sorting out, too."

Briggs looked at him with unabashed astonishment. "You 'maze me, Bill, you fair do. I don't see you for a dog's life and then, next I do, you're asking me to war on some poor bastard? Who is this you want doing?"

Grant looked at his boots, took a deep breath, looked Briggs in the eye, and said, "Sir Donovan Clay."

Briggs looked at him speechless. One of his lieutenants at the table snorted in derision on his behalf and said, "You what? Sir Big Aluminium Nob himself? Are you cracked?"

"James there has the gist of me own thinking neatly summed up, Bill," said Charlie. "Are you bloody cracked? We'd have every bluebottle from here to John O'Groats down on our neck. What did he do? Cut in ahead of you at the opera or something?"

"He killed Lizzie."

The mocking smile that had been forming on Charlie's face faded quickly. "He did what?"

"It's… oh, God, Charlie, it's so complicated. We found out what Clay was up to and a bunch of us went out to his place in Barking to have it out with him. He had his bullies ambush us. There was shooting."

"Shooting? Why haven't I heard anything about this?" Briggs turned to his men. "Any of you lot heard anything about a shooting match out in Barking?" Heads shook. He turned back to Grant. "Mate, you can't have carryings on in Barking like it's the Wild West and nobody hear about it."

"Somebody did. Remember Eberhard Jackson? The judge?" Now heads nodded. Criminals don't forget feared judges easily. "He's retired near there. He complained. Clay said they were scaring off birds. Jackson thought that was donkey stones, but how can you prove it?"

"Beak Jackson weren't never no fool," said one of Charlie's men. "He sent me down for a hard stretch once, I know him."

Another said, "Charlie. A little bird told me the River Police had been told to look for bodies downriver from Barking a couple of days ago. Bodies with shot in 'em. They were told if a word got breathed to the papers, they'd all be looking for new jobs in the morning, too."

"What kind of little bird?"

"A sandpiper."

Charlie nodded thoughtfully at this, and Grant took it to mean that "sandpiper" was his gang's cant for an officer of the River Police.

"And…?"

"And they found three."

"Jesus Christ." Briggs looked back to Grant. "Lizzie's dead?"

"I don't know, not for a certainty. We got separated. But Clay's men killed better'n a dozen. That I know for sure."

"But why, mate? What's this bastard up to?"

Grant thought about how little he really understood of the details, and how blessed a state that was. Even in the broader strokes, however, there was plenty that he didn't think Charlie would accept willingly if at all. "It's complicated. Truly complicated. What it is in essence, though, is that Sir Donovan Clay reckons he sees a way to become king. And… he might even be right about that."

"King of where?"

"*Here*, mate! England! Great Britain! The Empire! The whole bloody lot!"

Briggs grimaced at him. "Don't be stupid. What about the Queen?" Grant spread his hands. Briggs's eyes bulged. "Are you bloody kidding, Bill?" he snarled. "Kill the *Queen*? How? He'd need a bloody army!"

"He's got one. He met some people in Australia. Foreigners. They're going to set him up." He thought about what Bradley had told him a couple of hours earlier about Craddock's expedition out to the wilds of Coldharbour that morning. "They're already in the country. They're just waiting the word, and that's going to be soon, Charlie. Really soon."

"This is crazy," said the man who'd been sent down by Judge Jackson. "What are you doing here when you should be telling this to the police?" Some of his fellows shot him glances. "I'm not saying they don't have their uses," he added in a placatory tone.

"You think I haven't tried, chum? The police know, and they think the threat's real enough, but what can they do? The man's a knight! They can't raid him as easily as they raid anyone else. What if they get it wrong? The commissioner would have to hand in his resignation the morning after.

The Grand Poo-Bahs want evidence in triplicate, signed, sealed, and delivered on tablets of stone from Mount Ararat before they'd sign a warrant. And *there is no time left*."

Charlie rested one massive four-fingered hand on Grant's shoulder. "Are *you* sure, Bill? About all this? Would you swear your life on it?"

"Every word, Charlie. If you don't come, I'll go by myself and die there. If you come with me and everything isn't kosher and just how I told you, you can put a shot through my head with my blessing. I swear it's all true. If Clay isn't stopped and soon, you won't recognise the world this time next week."

"I don't give a monkey's balls about the world, Bill. I care about my country and Her Majesty." He looked at his men. "Fellers?"

They looked uncertainly at one another. "We're not an army," said one. "We're just…" he shrugged, "we're just a gang, Charlie. We can't go to war."

Charlie nodded. "He's not wrong, Bill. Even if everything you say is true, you're asking us to risk our lives. Even if we get away with those, we'll get our arses slung in gaol. There's no winning for us in this bloody mess."

Grant saw that it was time to play his only ace. "What if I could guarantee to keep you out of the jug?"

"That's a miracle to suddenly come out with, mate."

"I said the police know. I've spoken with them. Their hands are tied, but there's some things they can do in the lavender, if you take my drift."

"I ain't sure as that I do, mate."

Grant sighed. "What if, the morning after, somebody goes into the police records to find your file, Charlie... and it's gone missing?"

"Missing?"

"Just vanished, like morning mist."

"You know coppers who are willing to steal my file," said Charlie, wagging his finger for emphasis as he spelled out the offer in detail, "just so I'll help you with this?"

"There's no 'just' about this, Charlie. It's the end of everything if Clay gets his way. It's the best offer I could get out of them and – if you want my opinion – it's a pretty bloody good one. Your record ends up in the furnace in Scotland Yard's cellar."

"What about ours?" said one of Charlie's men.

Grant's heart sank. "Oh, for crying out loud."

Charlie nodded in their direction. "What about theirs? Five files go up the flue, and you get your army."

Grant thought about it for an awkward moment. He knew how Bradley would take this given how difficult it had been to talk him into destroying even a single file as a bargaining chip. "I can but ask."

Charlie slapped him cheerfully on the shoulder. "Ask tonight, pal, 'cos this time tomorrow we'll be burning down the crib of Sir Donovan Clay, and it'd be nice to know before then, eh?"

Chapter Seventeen

MAD AMBITION

That which lived within the former residence of Miss Elizabeth Whittle was no tyro when it came to piloting humans around. It had been chosen for this mission precisely because it had experience both of the species and of this time and culture. If it were to steer Miss Elizabeth Whittle out to Kings Cross Station and travel to Edinburgh, it might seek out an academic at the university who, some twenty years earlier, had suffered a peculiar fugue that changed his personality to the extent that he unexpectedly dropped physics in favour of a particularly abstruse arm of archaeology and spent the next year haunting the banks of Loch Feinn, turning up menhirs that had at some time in antiquity been toppled and buried. How he discovered five with disconcerting alacrity and accuracy troubled the more pedestrian halls of the discipline, and there was general relief when, after that year, he suddenly dropped all interest in archaeology and returned to his laboratory, claiming a profound amnesia now obscured those strange months. Lizzie Whittle had never been to Scotland and never met the scientist, but if she did so now, she would recognise him from the mirror. More to the point, he might instinctively recognise her, and that was a happenstance to be avoided.

In any case, Miss Elizabeth Whittle or, in her professional moments, Miss Cerulia Trent would not be tripping lightly off to Kings Cross Station or, indeed, anywhere else for the time being. The house of Sir Donovan Clay was constantly busy, and the tread of Clay and his men could be heard at most hours. Miss Trent (for let us call her that, a name as alien to her true self as the intellect that occupied her) was trapped in the cellar with only Great-Uncle Mathias – who was not human either – for company.

Miss Trent was thoroughly absorbed in the task he had set her and was making leeway towards an effective conclusion. The alliance was of a purely practical nature, of course. The Great Race of Yith had little time or tolerance for the fungal forms that littered the outer edge of that solar system, and had studiously kept its distance from their interest on primeval Earth. Besides, the fungi maintained a very limited interest in the planet; its atmosphere was difficult for them, both to breathe and in which to manoeuvre, and the Earth contained the Enemy, and their relationship with the colossal polypous creatures was almost as fraught as that experienced by the Great Race itself. They had little in common, then, but for an animosity towards the interloping Enemy, but alliances have been forged from far less.

Mathias's plan was simple enough in principle, but simplicity had not lent it certainty and its execution offered many pitfalls. Indeed, Miss Trent was currently working on the second iteration. Miss Trent had asked to see and examine Mathias's first, failed attempt, but Mathias had not been able to locate it in his workshop, a failure that concerned them both; the race of Mathias was not prone to absentmindedness, and he had been certain as to where he had placed it, but now it was gone. There was nothing to be done about it and, as Mathias said, the monkeys often stole things to play with them. There was no possibility that any of them might divine the device's function, but it was a nuisance nonetheless. Miss Trent, with her better understanding of the mentality and unexpected ingenuity of said "monkeys", was less tranquil about the loss, but there was nothing to be done about it, so she persevered with the work in hand and hoped against hope that the missing artefact was simply gathering dust somewhere, being used as a paperweight or a geegaw.

She heard the latch of the door to the cellar lift and instantly doused the oil lamp she was using to illuminate her worktable. It was irritating that humans had such poor vision in low light, but then again, they had opposable thumbs, which was a nice innovation. She sat in total silence as heavy footsteps descended the wooden staircase into the cellar. There was a smell of expensive but poorly chosen cologne, and between the weight of the steps and that scent, she knew it was Sir Donovan Clay come to demand what was taking so long, as if such demands might speed up the process.

"Mathias," said Clay, and Miss Trent knew he was standing with his balled fists upon his hips, his splendid waistcoat on display, and the diamond in his tie pin twinkling in the subdued light; she had watched him often enough from the shadows as he made such visits two or three times a day. "Mathias, how goes the device?"

Miss Trent looked at her own work, carefully lifted a cap she had turned that morning and slid it on, securing the inner mechanism. It only needed testing, now. Such a small thing, no bigger than a matchbox, but it might change everything if it could be placed correctly and in time. Her skirt had pockets, which was apparently an extraordinary thing according to Miss Church, but Miss Trent had insisted they be installed. It seemed absurd that such useful accessories be largely the domain of the human males. Into one such useful accessory, she carefully placed the mechanism.

"It is almost complete," said Mathias, adjusting his face.

"It's been almost complete for a while now, hasn't it?"

"The final adjustments are critical."

"Yes," said Clay, looking at the machine on the workbench. "That is very much what you said last time I asked. And the time before."

"They are critical," repeated Mathias with slow emphasis.

"The thing is," said Sir Donovan, "they're here. On schedule, right to the dot. And we are not ready. The device isn't ready, and we still do not have quite enough energy to make it work even if it were. They were not best pleased with me when I told them that, but then we had ... well, *talk* is the wrong word, so we shall say we communed for a little while and I explained that you have been rather laggardly at finishing it, so now they are not best pleased with *you.*"

Mathias regarded him silently, and Miss Trent held her breath. "The device must not be rushed, or it may not work," Mathias said finally.

"Very true, very true." Clay walked to the workbench and ran his hand along the surface of the machine. It was misshapen and looked oddly organic under his hand, although it was purely steel and crystal on the outside, arranged around a core of more organic components culled from the cream of Home Counties mediumship, albeit unwillingly. "Curious thing, to my eye. My untutored human eye. All of a piece, but for this." He leaned over it and tapped an odd protrusion in its side, about the size of a matchbox. "Tell me, Mathias, why is that? Why is there just one place that a component may be added? That confuses me."

"The element is prone to failure. In rendering it modular, I have rendered it replaceable," said Mathias curtly. Miss Trent thought she detected an undertone of tension in his usually dispassionate voice.

"Failure. Hmmm. I see. Well, that seems eminently sensible." In a sudden motion, Clay withdrew the element from the device's side and studied it under the gaslight.

"Be careful," said Mathias. "It is fragile."

"Oh, I am very careful, great-uncle. It's how I've stayed alive as long as I have. The things I've done to stay alive, the so-called 'friends' I left in shallow graves in the Outback.

You have no idea." He looked Mathias in the face. "You have *no* idea. But, as you know, I am no scientist, and as you also know, there is no man alive who could make head nor tail of your device. Your knowledge is not our knowledge, not yet. That probably makes you feel very superior over me, doesn't it?"

Mathias didn't reply at once. Then in an undertone, "I have work to do."

"I'm a very ignorant fella, Great-Uncle Mathias," said Clay, ignoring his words. "Perhaps you can educate me, and explain to me in nice, simple words, why this ..." he placed the freshly extracted element on the workbench by the device, "should look so very remarkably different from *this*." He reached into his pocket, extracted something, and placed it by the element. Even from where she hid, Miss Trent could see that it was the missing prototype to the apparatus currently residing in her skirt pocket.

Mathias did not hesitate. "The device is a new and untried concept. I approached the resonance generation differently to begin with. The results were unsatisfactory. I employed a second approach, and this garnered superior results."

"Well, then!" Sir Donovan was apparently delighted with this. "That explains everything! Thank you for bringing clarity to my thinking and dispelling my confusion, Mathias. That all makes the most perfect sense to me." His smile faded. He picked up the prototype module. "Except it's hogwash, isn't it? I showed this to, ah ... my *patrons* last night. They don't pretend to your levels of genius, of course, but they knew enough to tell me that they had no idea what this thing is for, but that it certainly has nothing to do with creating a barrier in time." He tossed the prototype onto the workbench. "As I said, I'm always careful. Just what are you up to, you damnable mushroom?"

Once again, Mathias did not hesitate. He rushed at Sir Donovan. His hands fell away and pincers snapped for the man's throat. Clay gave a cry of furious astonishment and fell back against the edge of the workbench, evading the attack. He ducked under the assault and punched Mathias hard in the upper stomach, a blow that would have doubled up any man. Mathias was no man, but while the blow did not wind him as it would a human, it did push him back and so afford Sir Donovan a moment to reach into his pocket and produce a double-barrelled Lancaster pistol. Its barrel was sawn down to little more than the length of the cartridges within, lending it an ugly and brutally functional appearance. He raised the weapon and fired at Mathias's head. The pistol was not loaded with bullets, but .410 shotgun cartridges, and the small cloud of lead it projected caught the side of Mathias's human face, tearing it away and about a fifth of the fibrous mass of the head beyond it. A green ichor sprayed across the shelving behind Mathias, and some of the sample bottles smashed, sending a rivulet of fingers and eyes to the brick floor.

Mathias's race, however, maintained that the head is primarily a place to keep a few sensory organs and the mouth; the brain was dispersed across a larger area, primarily in the torso, and the loss of a section of head was not as devastating an event as it would be for a human. This,

Sir Donovan did not know. He had had occasion in the past to shoot violently argumentative folk through the head and had always found it a sovereign resolution to disputation. He wrongly assumed this would be the case now, and was therefore unprepared when Mathias rallied and rushed back at him. They struggled, Mathias's pincer-like claws shredding the tweed of Clay's jacket, tearing through cloth and skin to draw blood. Clay roared with pain and anger, found space to position the Lancaster against the spongy mass where a godlier creature would keep its ribs, and fired the pistol's second barrel. The lead tore at what served as a nerve ganglion, and Mathias shrieked a high, ululating scream and fell back onto the floor where he thrashed in agony.

Dropping the empty gun, Sir Donovan looked around and, seeing a crowbar used to open a packing crate still lying carelessly across the angle of the crate sides, snatched it up and charged at the helpless creature with a roar that betokened an ugly death. He got halfway towards Mathias when a darkly clad form burst out of the shadows between the shelves and ran headlong into him, knocking him sideways against one of Mathias's workbenches. Caught by surprise, he lost his grip on the crowbar, and it clattered off across the bricks.

Clay was baffled by this intervention for a moment, doubly so when he recognised Cerulia Trent fiercely clawing at his face, but while Clay may have been a knight, he was certainly no gentleman. The realisation that he was fighting a woman did nothing to mediate his strength when he pushed her away from himself and then struck her hard enough across the face to send her to the floor in an insensible daze.

He barely had time to take in the changing situation; Mathias was climbing clumsily back to its – it was no longer possible to consider the figure in terms humanistic enough to permit the use of "he" as a pronoun – feet, clicking and grating out sounds that might be meaningful words on the edge of the Solar System but were purely barbaric atavistic noises filled with hateful menace when uttered in the cellar of a house in Barking.

Sir Donovan cast around for another weapon and saw on a shelf the strange thing they had taken from the false cab-man less than a fortnight ago. Glinting under the lights, it was a combination of an ancient future and modern materials, a thing that looked like a plumber's nightmare but that might be his only hope. He ran for the shelves, shouldering Mathias aside as it swept a claw at his head, took the lightning gun down, and aimed it even as his fingers followed its curves and dips and found a small metallic stud nestling in a hollow formed by fine silver and glass pipes, alternating in a wave. Hoping that his luck was with him, Sir Donovan braced himself and pushed down the stud.

It was hard to know which was more terrible – the blinding or the deafening. Both were sudden and violent as lightning erupted from the weapon's tip, bisecting and burning Mathias, and thunder cracked loud enough to shake dust from the cellar's supporting beams. Glassware exploded around them, but Sir Donovan hardly cared as he fell, stunned by the Brobdingnagian concussion, the weapon slipping from his nerveless fingers.

Lynch was the first down into the cellar, closely followed by two more of Sir Donovan's men with whom he'd been smoking and playing cards upstairs. He took the scene in and, while he did not pretend to understand every element of it, he could draw enough sense from the tableau to act upon it. "You two! Hold that woman! She's going nowhere!" He rushed to Sir Donovan's side. His employer was groaning and there was blood running from his nostrils and more wetting the bricks under his upper back, but the vital spark seemed fairly secure in him for all that. "Boss! What happened? Are you all right?"

Sir Donovan's eyes flickered open, rolled in their sockets for a moment, then found Lynch and focussed upon him even as Sir Donovan started violently as if waking suddenly. "Lynch! Oh, dear God! Tell me true, man, am I wounded?"

Lynch carried out a swift inventory of injuries. "Nothing serious I can see, but you'd better get those tears on your shoulders cleaned and bandaged up right smart or they're fit to get nasty. What was that bang? It threw me and the fellers out of our chairs, as if a giant had tossed the house like a prospector's pan! Never felt such a thing before!"

"Man, you'll have to speak up. My ears are still ringing. The bang, you say? That gun! The lightning gun. The one Mathias told us was too dangerous to use, that lying garbage!" He nodded to the charred and disunited body of Great-Uncle Mathias. "That thing was dragging its feet all along, swinging the lead because it wanted us to fail. It had its own plans. Its own secrets."

Lynch tried to keep him lying down while he recovered himself, but Sir Donovan was too angry to be coddled. He staggered unsteadily to his feet, pushing away Lynch's restraining hand, and advanced on where Cerulia Trent was held by two more of his men.

"Ugh!" He angled his head. "This blasted ringing in my ears. It's clearing, but too slowly for my liking." He stuck a fingertip in one ear and waggled it fiercely, saying as he did so, "Well. Miss Cerulia Trent. An unexpected pleasure. Great-Uncle Mathias swore blind that you were nothing but a mountebank and a dodger, yet here you are. Lynch, be a good fellow and find out who or what else might be lurking back there. Take a pistol."

Lynch, demonstrating a degree of forethought, had a small five shot revolver in his pocket. He drew it, nodded to Sir Donovan, and vanished into the darkness between the standing shelves. "I can't imagine when you got in here, Miss Trent," said Sir Donovan. He thought for a moment and then corrected himself. "But, yes, of course I can. You were with those fools we killed the other day, weren't you? Nobody in the house but Great-Uncle Mathias while that was going on. You must have come up the drive, all alone. Looking for your Mr Grant, were you? Well, I wasn't expecting him, so we weren't looking for him at the time, but if he'd been among the dead from the ambush or one of the survivors we drained of their potentiality later for Mathias's machine, I would have recognised him. That's bitter, isn't it? You came here to save him even while he was abandoning you." He frowned. "What confuses me is why you came here at all? What would that little band of useless incompetents want with you?" The frown cleared as an idea dawned upon him. "Oh, but wait. What if…?"

He was interrupted by the return of Lynch. "Nobody back there, boss, but I found where'd she'd been hiding." He looked uncomfortable. "Boss, I can't be properly sure, but there were a couple of those specimen jars Mathias used for his… whatever he kept them for. They were empty, just a few bones. I mean to say, I can't be *properly* sure, but…"

"You don't expect a lady to starve, do you?" Sir Donovan was smiling, his gaze never moving from Miss Trent's face as he understood the boon that a perverse yet kindly fate had bestowed upon him.

"Oh, but boss, that's not proper!"

"It's not cannibalism if it's not your own species, I suppose. Very smart, very sensible."

Lynch looked at Miss Trent with an expression that spoke of a sense of horror that was evolving within him, first this way and then that. "You can't mean…?"

"Did you find anything else back there?"

Lynch dragged himself with difficulty away from the trail down which his thoughts were taking him. "A work table. I didn't understand what was being made on it at all. All bits of metal and crystal and such."

Sir Donovan nodded and stepped closer to Miss Trent. "You were helping him, weren't you?" She said nothing, but only looked him steadily in the face. He laughed. "I don't need you to say a word to know it. Here's what I think, Miss Trent, or whatever your real name is. Even if I heard it, I doubt I could say it. I think that gadget is done and ready. I think it's been ready a good while, and Mathias kept lying to us. I think the only thing he told us the truth about – and even then only because he didn't need to lie about it – was that it didn't have enough energy to do its job. He needed it to work in case our patrons wanted a look at it. To us poor stupid humans, it's just a box of tricks. But our patrons, *they'd* know if it was anything other than what they'd demanded. But then he needed some extra time to come up with some little alteration that would make it do what *he* wanted." He picked up the prototype external module from where it lay on the ground and showed it to Miss Trent. "This thing. I think you helped him finish it. Then – and, oh, the bloody arrogance of it – he left it out in the open because he was so sure we poor stupid humans would never guess he was up to something."

He looked at the ruins of Mathias. "Well, we poor stupid humans have a saying about pride and what goes before, but I don't suppose they've heard it out amongst the stars, more shame for you." He returned his attention to Miss Trent. "And here we are. We have a working machine that will help snuff out your lot like the tricksy vermin you are, Mathias's betrayal…" he held up the prototype module before her face, dropped it, and then ground it into metal fragments and powdered crystals beneath his heel, "…has come to naught, and best of all…" he tapped her on the forehead with the tip of his index finger, "…we have more than enough mental energy to operate the device. The fall of the Great Race of Yith will be initiated by one of their own. I hope you enjoy the irony, madam."

He addressed the two men holding her. "Take her up and tie her into the big chair. And tie her in tight and keep a close bloody eye on her! If she gets loose, what I will do to the brace of you will make what we did to the Aboriginals back home look like a kindness, you understand me?"

Chapter Eighteen

LIKE PIRATES

The thudding at the door was unexpected and, given the timing, unfortunate. Lynch went to answer it as Miss Trent was dragged into the dining room, struggling all the way. He returned to the cellar a few minutes later looking worried.

"It's that judge," he reported, "wanting to know what all the commotion was about."

"Tell his man we had a small accident with…" Sir Donovan glanced around, looking for inspiration. His eye settled upon the gas mantel. "…with the gas. All attended to now, and nothing to concern his nibs with."

"It's not his man," replied Lynch. "He's come here himself!"

Sir Donovan closed his eyes, took a deep breath, and reminded himself that all he had to do was keep affairs on an even keel for an hour or so longer and then he could do what he liked. "Give me a minute to get a fresh jacket," he said as he shrugged off the ruined one and dropped it carelessly on Mathias's corpse. "I'll speak with him. But first, make sure that woman's gagged. I don't want her screaming while we've got a bloody judge on the doorstep."

A few minutes later, a smiling Sir Donovan Clay went out to the porch to talk to retired judge Sir Eberhard Jackson. "Sir! My apologies for keeping you waiting. You'll understand that the house is in a bit of an uproar at present."

"The entire neighbourhood is in an uproar, sir!" snapped Sir Eberhard. "Gas, your man said. Is that so? You should evacuate immediately and call for the corporation engineers to make good! Stuff's poisonous, after all, and you haven't opened a single window! Thought you had a smattering of chemistry about you, sir."

Sir Donovan realised that his impromptu tale of a gas leak was not going to impress Sir Eberhard, a man possessed of a mind too analytical to be fobbed off that easily. "Gas? Is that what Lynch told you?" He paused to look up the darkening evening sky as if in thought. "No, I understood why he said that. Good man." He looked Sir Eberhard in the face and leaned forward a little. "May I be candid with you, sir?"

"About what, pray?" said Sir Eberhard with evident suspicion.

Sir Donovan stepped out into the porch and said in the low tone of one extending a confidence, "This is all very *sub rosa*, you understand? Out in Australia, I dabbled in the formulation of explosives for the purposes of mining. Well, I made a discovery, a formula for an explosive that is far more powerful than, say, dynamite, but as stable."

Sir Eberhard's eyes widened. "You cannot mean to say

that you are continuing to conduct these experiments in this house? Are you quite mad?"

Sir Donovan chuckled, although he wanted to throttle the judge in that moment. "Not at all, but I have had a eureka moment of sorts. The explosion you heard was caused by a scrap – barely more than a nail's paring, sir – of what I took to be a failed experiment. In Australia, where I mixed the stuff, it was all but inert. But somehow, in the intervening months, it has undergone a metamorphosis and... well, you heard what an accidental detonation can be wrought by such a minute sample. This is a tremendous breakthrough! If I can reproduce the effect, think what it will mean to Britain! Why, a single shell of the stuff could finish an enemy ironclad or one of the new first-class battleships! Entire enemy strongholds, brushed away in a twinkling with a single artillery salvo! Think of it!"

Sir Eberhard breathed heavily through his moustache. "All very wonderful, I am sure, but I am more concerned with Barking being *brushed away in a twinkling,* sir! You will conduct no more experiments until the War Office has been informed of your invention and the proper facilities made available, ideally in the wastes of the North or Scotland or Wales or somewhere else that no one would miss. I shall speak to the necessary authorities in the morning. You should prepare yourself for an official visit from the War Office, sir!"

Sir Donovan beamed even as he fantasised about hands around the judge's throat, and the pleasure to be had in watching the old man's eyes bulge, his tongue protrude, and his skin turn puce as he died. "Thank you! That would expedite things enormously. Thank you, sir."

A few minutes later, Sir Donovan re-entered the hallway, his expression foul. "I hope that sanctimonious old bastard survives this night," he said to Lynch. "I want to kill him myself."

"Is it going to work?" said Lynch.

"It has to, but I think the odds are better than even. The best thing would have been to scoop that little girl's brains out and use 'em direct, the way Mathias did, but how to do that died with him. But I know enough of how the apparatus works to know the big chair we used for testing the mediums can tap that energy, too. Might not do so good a job of it, but if she's one of the Great Race – and I am damn'd sure that she is – she'll be awash with the stuff, and we don't need so very much more for the device to work. It's not a sure bet, mate, but it's not a bad shot either. If it goes wrong, I reckon I can talk the things into giving us more time –they're brutes but they're not stupid, and this is their best chance to destroy their enemy. If I can't… well, we'll all die and it won't be pretty. But," he grasped Lynch's shoulders and looked closely at his face, "if it comes off, mate… if it comes off…" He let Lynch go, and grinned. "We'll be kings of the world." He rapped Lynch gently in the chest with his knuckles. "You're my right hand, my pal. Where d'you fancy for your kingdom?"

Lynch hadn't really thought about it. "Dunno. China?"

"It's yours, mate. It's yours."

•••

Unlike the previous incursion, Charlie Briggs's men knew better than to simply decant themselves from Barking Town Station and mill around like workers awaiting a charabanc tour. Rather, they arrived by divers means and made a point of avoiding even exchanging meaningful conspiratorial glances. They were, after all, professionals at avoiding interest, and they performed such avoidance easily and with a certain criminal panache.

Sir Donovan Clay was not the sort of man to lack for prudence and, despite having seen off one assault, he was not so complacent as to dismiss the possibility of more. Thus, he still maintained a watch upon the town. This had served him well the previous time, less so this time, when his sentry, lolling bored at the corner of a side street across from the station entrance was accosted from behind, quietly strangled and chloroformed into unresisting stupidity. Charlie Nine-Fingers wanted to slit his throat after a brief interrogation, but Detective Sergeant Bradley (who had thought it prudent to shadow the corps of bullies to the house and was now doubting the wisdom of that decision) intervened with the admonishment that the real enemy was at the residence, and killing the sentry would be an unnecessary stain upon their (and his) souls. Charlie Nine-Fingers responded that it was a bloody war and it was traditional in wars to bloody well kill people, but grudgingly admitted that it was also traditional to take prisoners. The hapless if ultimately lucky sentry was tied and dumped in a field, and the little army swept eastwards by highway and byway.

En route, they saw an approaching figure and dispersed en masse as shadows into the nearest field. Bradley, however, recognised the figure and stepped out to address them.

"Sir Eberhard? Might I ask, are you coming back from the Clay house?"

Sir Eberhard Jackson was understandably taken aback to have a Scotland Yard detective leap out of a hedgerow at him, but marshalled himself and replied, "Detective Sergeant Bradley? What on Earth …? But, yes. Yes, I've just come from that blackguard's house. He's letting off bombs in his cellar as far as I can make out. What sort of fellow does something as half-witted as that?" He squinted into the darkness of the field and fancied he saw crouching figures there. "What's this about, sir? Do you mean to raid him?"

Bradley hesitated a moment, and then decided that, under the circumstances, sacrificing his career was a reasonable price to pay. "I do, Sir Eberhard, but you have to understand, it is of an extra-judicial sort. There is no time left, and therefore we have no choice but to step outside the law. We have reason to believe that Sir Donovan intends to commit an act of grand treason tonight."

"Good God!" The judge regarded him as if looking upon a man quite bereft of reason. "Treason? Are you quite sure?"

"Very sure, sir. We know for a fact that Sir Donovan has been directly involved in three murders in recent days, and we suspect perhaps a dozen more. His ambition is grand, and he has the means to realise it. He has no reason to wait beyond tonight and every reason to act immediately. The situation is desperate."

"And why are you telling me this?"

"Because everyone in the area is in danger. I beg of you, go to your home, gather together your household, and send them away at least as far as Barking Town. Ideally further. Once they're on their way, you, and whatever men you trust to act quickly and sensibly, must go to every house within a mile of here and send every soul you find a safe distance, too. Sir Donovan knows his life is forfeit if he doesn't succeed, and his men are entirely loyal to him. They have nothing to lose. There will be a terrible butcher's bill to be paid tonight."

Sir Eberhard did not trouble to hide his consternation. "It's an incredible tale, lad, and you are asking me to accept a great deal on trust. Sir Donovan Clay a *traitor*? Is it true? Are you *sure*?"

"I wouldn't throw away my career like this unless I was entirely sure, sir."

"Good Lord." Sir Eberhard looked upon him in the thin light of a gibbous moon as a father might look upon a son going to fight in a hopeless war. "Win or lose, the mandarins of Whitehall will surely throw you to the lions." He nodded at the dark forms in the field. "You can't go running around the suburbs with a private army and expect to get away with it scot-free, lad."

"I know, sir. I'll be lucky if I stay out of gaol."

Sir Eberhard nodded. "Well, time is wasting, and then only to the advantage of Sir Donovan." He thrust out his hand. Bradley took it and, as they shook, Sir Eberhard said, "I'd hoped I was wrong, but that man Clay, he's a wrong 'un, ain't he?"

"The wrongest I've ever met, sir."

He watched as the judge hurried away into the darkening lane and waited while the larcenous shapes rose from their hiding places. Grant and Charlie joined him. He heaved a sigh. "Well, that's that. What you can smell here, lads, is the scent of my last bridge burning down."

"Go with him," said Grant.

Bradley looked at him curiously. "What's that you say?"

"The judge. Go with him. Do your job. Help get folk away from here."

"But you'll need me at the house."

"Nah, son," said Charlie, cracking seven knuckles. "It'll be dirty business there for a certainty."

"I can fight dirty if needs be," said Bradley, wondering even as he said it why he felt it an insult not to be considered sufficiently barbaric.

"I don't doubt it, but I was thinking having a copper along might put me boys off their stride. Believe me, mate, you're not required on this voyage, so go on," he said kindly, "bugger off out of it."

There was sense in what they said, and he would have been lying to himself if he didn't admit to qualms about what was likely to be a slaughter without conscience. He shook Grant's hand. "Good luck," and then extended his hand to Charlie. "You, too, Charlie." Then he ran into the night in pursuit of Jackson.

They watched him go for a moment. "You're no fighter neither, Bill Grant," said Charlie from the corner of his mouth.

Grant looked up at him sharply. "You're not sending me away."

"Wasn't going to. You got a dog in this fight, my lad. That Clay did for Lizzie Whittle and as like as not never would've swung for it. So, you got a public duty to perform. Me and my lads won't get in y'way."

Grant drew breath to reply, but realised anything he had to say was redundant, so he only nodded. Charlie nodded too, then to his men said in a *sotto voce* tone that would have scared a drill sergeant, "Form up, me buckos. Just as we planned. Do as you've been charged, watch out for your mates on left and right, and don't give 'em dogs a second's rest nor mercy, savvy?"

The little army of two dozen reprobates sallied forth to save the world.

The atmosphere in the house of Sir Donovan Clay was curious and febrile; Clay himself was in ebullient good spirits, his path to a power unimaginable to every human who had gone before was clearly apparent and gloriously simple.

All he had to do was to connect Mathias's device to the big chair at the head of the table in the dining room via the hidden cables that had once similarly connected Mathias's instruments when it had been used to assay the psychic energies of assorted mediums, true and false. It was delightfully straightforward, for it is in the nature of devices as they become more capable to become simpler in their operation. The cable fixings were of specific types, and it was child's play to connect them correctly. Then he would use the bayonet switch to connect the unfortunate Miss Trent to the device, it would drain her energies for its operations, and the temporal barrier would be raised. It need only operate for the smallest fraction of a second to be entirely successful; whether the barrier was a tenth of a second thick or an hour, the "Great" Race of Yith would batter helplessly against it and be forced to occupy a good fraction of the human race, with only those in the immediate vicinity of the device being protected from that outcome. Sir Donovan's vilely polypous patrons would seek out the possessed and destroy them, and then they would be content to let Sir Donovan run the planet for them, since they had not the slightest interest in such minutiae. Earth, it seemed, was important strategically, or so he understood; a crucial piece in some unimaginable chess game of the gods.

Sir Donovan's imagination did not extend nearly far enough to encompass it, nor did he care. No, he just wanted the world and its surviving people. The death toll was unimportant – there were far too many people in the world in any case – what mattered was that only he would end atop the globe, emperor of all the world with his men as his tyrant kings beneath him. Lynch would do well with China, he was confident.

His men were blissfully unburdened by the details, only

aware that there was some grand plan, that it was godless in any sense that they understood, and that they would do very well out of it. That was enough for them. They would have followed their boss into Hell for half as much. It made them a little skittish to be quite so unsure of the exact shape of their future, but that it was golden was an article of faith. Crusades have been fought for less.

The first of those men to discover that the path to such a future was strewn with dangers unseen was a former sheep thief by the name of Harry Belker. He was out in the garden smoking a pipe when it struck him that the weather was changing with remarkable rapidity. It had been a day of patchy cloud punctuated by blue skies, but now the sky had curdled into clouds as glutinous as porridge and a strong breeze had come up out of nowhere. There was a chill to accompany the wind, and Belker clamped his pipe stem between his teeth and turned up his jacket collar as he looked up to examine the slow whirl of cloud that seemed to be placed exactly over the house. Around him, the night wind got in amongst the trees and shrubs, making the leaves susurrate harshly like foam on a pebble beach. His chin was up, the pose of a man exposing his throat to the kindly barber's blade, but it was a less kindly hand that clamped over his mouth then, knocking his pipe to the grass, and a less kindly razor that drew over his throat and so murdered him. He was held down while he kicked and pissed himself in his last throes, and his carcass left obscured and abandoned between the rose bushes.

Charlie "Nine-Fingers" Briggs noticed William Grant

breathing heavily, pale as a fish under the fitful light. "He'd have done same to you soon as look at you," he whispered to Grant. "You going to be up to this, boy? There'll be more claret before night's out, y'know. Lots more."

"I know. That was coldly done, though. Never seen the like. But when we get to Clay," colours flushed back into his cheeks, "that'll be different."

"That's it, my lad. Get some fire in y'belly. We're going to take this house like pirates taking a merchantman, a proper roaring fight. Brace y'self for that."

As Sir Donovan attended to the last of the cables (how the metal glistered in a way he had never seen before, silvery and liquid as if the light was mercury darting around the wire braiding), there was a pull upon the doorbell.

He swore. "Good God, why are our neighbours taking such an interest in us this evening? Lynch! Send them away, whoever they are."

"Aye, boss," said Lynch, and he went to the front door. He half expected to find Judge Jackson once more upon the doorstep to deliver a homily beginning "And another thing!" He was, however, surprised to find a large man wearing a billycock hat that was perched upon his head at a jaunty angle, and a pipe sticking out of the side of his mouth. His cheery smile wrapped around the stem.

"Whatever it is, we don't want none," said Lynch, looking around for Harry Belker who he'd seen go out earlier to enjoy a pipe of tobacco in the evening air. Why hadn't he intercepted the big man? Then he glanced back at the visitor and recognised the pipe he was sucking on as Harry's.

"Evening, squire," said the man, whereupon he raised a pistol and shot Lynch clean through the forehead.

The shot signalled the beginning of the hostilities proper. Bottles filled with lamp oil and with burning rags tied around their necks sailed through the kitchen and study windows. In the latter case, the bottles failed to break and lay there, dripping burning fuel onto the floor and ruining the parquet. The one in the kitchen, however, hit the edge of the hearthstone and shattered most satisfactorily, a pool of flames spreading out from it across the brown rustic tiling.

In the dining room, Sir Donovan heard the shot and the shattering of glass a moment later and realised he had been optimistic in believing the Cult of the Yith had been stamped out for the short term. He strode to his study, saw the guttering fire bomb, tossed it back out of the broken window, took his revolver from the desk drawer, pocketed it, and took down one of the shotguns from the gun cupboard.

A big man in an appallingly uncouth hat appeared at the study door. Sir Donovan loaded and slammed shut the shotgun, thumbed back the hammers as he brought it to his shoulder and gave his target both barrels. The big man, for his part, fired a shot from his own revolver more in hope than expectation as he saw the shotgun rising, then slammed the door and dived aside as two 12-bore cartridges worth of shot tore through the wood at chest height. Charlie Nine-Fingers decided discretion was the better part of valour, and certainly preferable to being eviscerated by an angry knight and trotted back into the porch, skipping lightly over Lynch's corpse as he did so, and thence vanished into the dark, to move around the house and strike elsewhere. Charlie had been a boxer in his youth and knew that one should try to avoid being where somebody with a heavy punch expects you to be.

In the shadows, he encountered William Grant. He laughed, delighted to be afforded such a grand opportunity for violence and for it to be, as he understood it, on the side of the angels for once. The novelty was pleasing, and he felt he owed it all to Grant. "Met your Sir Lah-di-dah Bastard," he said. "Feisty sod, ain't he?"

Grant's eyes grew dead. "Where?"

"Front door, step over the dead feller, into the hall, room on the left. Can't miss it –hole the size of a pig's head clean through the door."

Grant nodded, hefted the pistol he'd been given, and headed for the entrance.

"Watch yourself and good hunting, mate!" Charlie called after him. "Tally-bastard-ho!"

Chapter Nineteen

TRIUMPH AND DEFEAT

The taste of triumph had been so clear to him, so present and vivid, Sir Donovan had been able to savour it like a copper coin upon his tongue, redolent of cold blood and hard enough to bite upon. Now, at the very moment of victory, this reversal, so unlike the previous sally against his redoubt and so utterly unexpected, conducted by people who knew what they were doing. He'd chased the man in the billycock hat out into the hallway, but he had halted, disbelieving and horrified to find Lynch wide-eyed and quite dead upon the porch tiles, lying in a blood and brains omelette. By the time he gathered himself, the big man was gone, and he became aware of shouts and cries from all around the walls.

He burst into the kitchen to find two of his men fighting a small fire there. "There's nothing for it to burn, you damn idiots!" he snapped. "The house is under siege! Take guns and defend it! Don't leave the building, just stop them getting in!"

Somebody tried the back door and Sir Donovan fired

three bullets through the wood, though he doubted he'd hit anyone beyond. Leaving his men to defend that quarter, he went to rally the rest of his troops.

He ran back into the dining room to find Miss Cerulia Trent still restrained but wearing an indisputable expression of triumph. He tore the gag from her mouth, its usefulness now moot. "Your people?" he snapped at her.

"I do not know, but they seem very intent upon killing you. I cannot help but approve."

"Well, I'm not done yet." Behind a section of panelling was a small, concealed cupboard, presumably once intended as a store for the table silver or the decanters. Whatever its original purpose, Mathias had reworked it as a relay and control box connecting the great chair and the laboratory below. Sir Donovan had been looking forward to making a ceremony of this, but instead it would do well at this juncture as a small act of retaliation that smacked of spitefulness. There was a rotating spidery contact disc, its contacts like silver legs, mounted upon an oaken board. He twisted it from its customary position, connecting the chair to the sensory equipment where it could assess the supernatural potentials of media and spiritists, to a position that connected the chair to the psychic capacitors powering the barrier device in the cellar. Mounted on the cupboard wall by it was a bayonet switch above from which a light began to glow dimly. This, Mathias had explained with painful slowness the week before, indicated the apparatus was working; the light would abruptly glow at full intensity when the capacitors were fully charged. Not that he needed any such assurance that the chair was doing its work; the low groan of pain from Miss Trent was enough to satisfy him of that.

"Mathias told me that the extraction process would be agony. Good. He also told me that when the machine has extracted every drachm of psychic energy from its subject – from *you* – you will crumble into dust and bones. I shall admit, I am very much looking forward to seeing that. Congratulations, Miss Trent – you shall be the first of your race to die in the coming holocaust. But very, *very* far from the last."

One of his men rushed in at that moment of triumph to sour it somewhat. "We can't hold them, boss! They're coming at us from every direction, and I think they outnumber us! They're sure to get in!"

"We're not done yet, lad! I've a trick or two up my sleeve. Back to the fight, but on no account leave the house, understand? Tell the others that, too!"

As the man ran out, Sir Donovan took something from the cupboard, walked to the great chair and crouched by it to look Miss Trent, her head lowered in pain, in the eye. "Recognise this?" He held up a cube of a greenish stone, perhaps three inches along a side, the sides crisscrossed with shallow grooves incised in a complex weaving pattern. Miss Trent glanced at it and her eyes widened enough for him to know that he had managed to disconcert the usually serene mind that dwelt within the frame of Miss Cerulia Trent. "I see you do. Then you know what's coming. There is no hope for you here, Yithian."

•••

Cerulia Trent watched Sir Donovan stride from the room, leaving her abandoned in the partial darkness of the dining room. She could feel the chair leeching her energies and, despite her most concentrated efforts, she could not slow the process at all. It is a vile thing to be offered hope at the eleventh hour only to have it snatched away; a false pardon on the morning of execution. Things might still go wrong for Sir Donovan. His plan had been thrown into disarray by the attack and that increased its chance of failure, but she knew that the odds still stood at better than even. The attack had come as a small miracle, but perhaps too small to change anything.

Then a head appeared furtively at the door and in a moment William Grant was at her side. "Lizzie! Oh, dear God! Lizzie! I thought you were dead, girl!" He saw her bonds and started trying to release them. "Let's get you out of here. Oh, by all that's good, I thought I'd lost you, Lizzie Whittle!"

"Donovan Clay…" she managed to gasp past her agony.

"I came looking for him. Got into a bit of a scrap in his study. Laid some feller out. Then thought to look–"

"No!" she snapped, silencing him. "Clay will kill us all… one chance left… you must do as I say…"

"Whatever you want, Lizzie, just as soon as I get you out of this chair." He fumbled with the straps, but they were strong, and, he was belatedly realising, locked. He would have to get a good knife to carve through the leather.

"No!" she said, and he stopped and blinked at her. "I do not matter. Save my people, William Grant. I beg you, save my people."

"But Lizzie…"

Since Lizzie Whittle had ceased to be Lizzie Whittle in any true sense, it had been painfully apparent to him that "Miss Cerulia Trent" was not only not the same person, but barely a person at all. She thought and acted on the basis of pure logic and curiosity, and there was barely a flicker of anything called "emotion" in her now. But perhaps, in the same way that one's behaviour may change to more closely match the mode of new clothes or a new home, a little of Lizzie Whittle had somehow rubbed off onto the mind that possessed her body now.

"Please," said Miss Cerulia Trent, and there were tears in her eyes.

William Grant looked into those eyes for a moment, then nodded curtly. "What would you have me do, Cerulia?"

Sir Donovan Clay, a traitor to all but himself, gained the house's attic room and went swiftly to the circular gable window there. Beyond it, swathed in night, were the fields and commons eastwards of Barking. And out there in one such field…

Sir Donovan held up the strange cube of stone, and he contemplated it. It was not quite a cube in reality, the angles being slightly off. The asymmetric weave of lines inscribed across its surface seemed random at first, but on closer inspection, a pattern became apparent in his mind. And as the pattern grew clearer to him, so the pattern on the cube shifted slightly to accommodate his perception of it. He disliked the cube, disliked how studying it generated ideas in his mind that were smooth and soapy and slipped away when he tried to examine them, first one or two, and then multiplied until his mind felt as active as a goldfish pond at feeding time, and with as little discernible pattern. He loathed the sensation, but he understood its necessity because it meant the cube was drawing from him in its own small way in much the same fashion as the machine was currently draining Miss Trent. He would get a mild neuralgia at the end and his sanity would be slightly abraded by the experience, although he never noticed this because how could he? It would be worth it, though. It *had* to be worth it.

The alien thoughts multiplied and swarmed and, finally, they slipped from his brain and his mind and his skull, and darted off unseen into the dark night.

If they stayed still and thought particular thoughts, the stupid apes could not see them.

So, the one, and the other, and the other other stood in the day and then in the night and thought particular thoughts and the few stupid apes who had come by had barely glanced in their direction. The ones who had wiped their eyes and rubbed their skulls as if something was awry there and not noted the presence of the one nor the other nor the other other, had not noted how the light distorted there, or how no birds would fly nearby or how there were three great solitary footprints in the field, as broad as a tall man is tall with five toe marks set around, regularly spaced.

Their history since the Great Race of Yith had

abandoned a long past present was not heavily marked with event. There had been the fungus who had come to the abandoned city beneath the desert sands from distant Yuggoth, and that they had captured and mutilated that it might never leave again. There had been the apes who found the city a millennium or two ago, and these the ones had handily slaughtered. The apes, showing an unexpected and unwarranted sophistication had set psychic wards and defences against the ones and they had found it difficult to wander from the city. Then, fortuitously, another clan of apes had arrived – pale, and loud, and smelling of smoke and solvents – and they had ventured down. The ones had largely slaughtered these apes, too, eager to be left in a morbid peace, but one had contrived to communicate and shown fitting subservience in slaughtering several of the other apes, thereby lifting the bounds that had been placed upon the city.

Further negotiations were conducted, and the stupid ape agreed to help them in a plan that had been maturing since they captured the Yuggothian. The ones were not capable of lying – the creative act of mendacity was both beneath and beyond them – and they had explained what the appalling cost to the ape's fellows would be, how many millions of them must die. This, the ape concluded, was acceptable as long as it got to rule the survivors. The ones did not care about which stupid apes ruled which other stupid apes, and so agreed. The true prize was the planet's strategic significance, after all, not which tribe of idiot primates was in ascendance over the other idiot primate tribes.

They had given the leader ape an artefact that made it think in a way that was useful to the ones. It had required several attempts, but now the creature could gaze at the artefact and have its thoughts reordered into a practical pattern that allowed the feeble matter of its simian brain to resonate at a frequency perceivable to the ones. It was akin to the yapping of a servile dog, and it had brought them from halfway around the world to the edge of the smoking mess the apes flattered themselves was a city. Now they heard the yapping again and sensed a note of desperation within it. The ape was failing in its task.

The one, and the other, and the other other ceased troubling to think themselves invisible, raised their cyclopean five-toed feet, and advanced towards the source of the signal.

The weather was becoming angrier by the second, a great circling wind around the house of Sir Donovan Clay making the trees sway and sweep across open grass, making it appear like a wave. While the weather was curiously oppressive, however, it still gave the sensation of being natural, but summoned up by unnatural means.

There was nothing at all natural about the wind that struck Alfie Moyes and two more of Charlie Briggs's men as they ducked around the outside of the property and advanced on the house, looking for an unattended room to break into. They had disturbed some of Sir Donovan's men, who had fired blindly into the night, forcing Alfie and the others to seek shelter back at the edge of the copse of trees. Seeing that they were not being pursued, they then advanced cautiously across the croquet lawn when Alfie had the strangest feeling that they were being watched and not with benign interest. He looked up and saw what he at first took to be a cloud of smoke, but before his gaze, it solidified and he became aware of eyes in the cloud looking back at him, of slowly whipping flagella, of teeth and a strange disassociated hatred that tasted like vinegar in his mind. Then the awful teeth grew further apart, the whistling that he had taken to be the high wind in the house's eaves grew suddenly so much more intense, and he realised that the smoke had a mouth. The smoke breathed out upon him and his comrades, a cone of whirling destruction that stank of the seabed and grave damps and possessed of a violence that made a hurricane seem the slightest zephyr in comparison.

Alfie did not die immediately, but he was so concussed by the fury of the blow that he was barely aware of his eyes exploding, his eardrums collapsing, of the very clothes being stripped from his flesh and then the flesh from his bones. He scattered, no more than debris from a butcher's floor, while one of his comrades was thrown over the hedge a quarter of a mile down the road, and the other ended up tangled and impaled in a tree. This was the least action of the first of the ones, and the actions of the other and the other other echoed it in dispassionate ferocity.

"What in blue-blazing buggery is *that*?" demanded Charlie Nine-Fingers of no one as he rounded the corner of the house and saw a cloud of half-seen meat extend a tentacle and impale one of his men, and then casually fling his corpse so high into the air that it was immediately lost in the darkness. Charlie made his decision immediately – it was one thing to go up against a comparably sized gang of treasonous Australians, but nobody had mentioned the Aussies might have forms of distilled nightmare at their beck and call, nor yet that these entities might be so remarkably good at killing.

"Fall back, lads! Save yourselves! The battle's lost!" Obeying his own orders, he ran back the way he had come, and looked for safe passage from the grounds of the house. This, he realised, might be more trouble than he'd anticipated; two more of the awful things had taken station beyond the garden hedges, cutting off their retreat. His surviving men rapidly gathered around him and, in desperation as much as trust, awaited his command.

Charlie was famously cunning rather than clever and right then he felt how a fox might when cornered by no less than the hounds of three hunts. There was only one thing for it. "We go to ground, lads. Those things are big and we're small. Salt yourself away in any corner you can find. It's hide and go seek for your lives, boys. Don't make it easy for 'em!"

Sir Donovan Clay watched the forces of his oppressors scatter like chaff before the attentions of his patrons, and he saw it was good. He mused on that phrase as he descended through the house; it might be useful to create a religion around himself. People are far less likely to question the utterances of a holy figure, especially when he has supernatural forces at his beck and call to smite the unbelievers. He would have to make some notes; he had been so very focussed on ensuring his victory, he had not fully considered how he was to run the world afterwards. Divvying up the planet amongst his men (his surviving men, he reminded himself. Poor Lynch. Now somebody else would get China) was very nearly the limit of his planning and he could see now that it was inadequate.

Yes, he would say that what had gone before had been evil and decadent and he had torn down these houses of the wicked to take the world into a brighter future. That would do it. If people were told on a regular enough basis that it was the truth, they'd start to believe it as their memories of the old world faded. Perhaps he could even manage to herd the world into some sort of golden age. "Donovan the Good", the history books would call him, even if he had to write them himself to make sure of it.

Such happy musings carried him down the stairs and back to the dining room. A couple of his men accosted him in the hallway, wide-eyed and fearful that "There's something proper crook going on outside", but he told them that it was all part of the plan, and that they were safe as long as they stayed inside the house until told otherwise. In the meantime, they were to watch from the windows for any further enemy activity.

In the dining room he found Miss Trent still secure and still in pain, which cheered him further. "Not long now, my dear," he said, addressing the vessel rather than the content.

He went to stand by the switch, taking the revolver from his pocket as he did so. He reloaded the spent cartridges as he spoke. "I regret to tell you that your friends have suffered a small reverse. They're currently dying horrible, horrible deaths." A scream sounded close by in the garden, making Sir Donovan jerk his head that way, his expression aghast. The scream ended suddenly with a wet ripping sound. Something heavy and inert fell in two pieces on the grass. Sir Donovan forced a smile upon his face and insouciance into his voice. "There goes another one." He closed the revolver.

Sweat ran down Miss Trent's brow. "They... will kill you... too."

"Oh, no. We have a deal, but I know that doesn't count for much. More importantly, we have a common purpose. They wish to eliminate your people, and in doing so, they will eliminate many of mine. After that, they want the planet, but they have no great interest in running it. But they do want it run. It may still be a useful asset to them. At the very least they will require cities to be built. Great windowless basalt affairs, I understand. Not very aesthetic, you may think, but really have you *seen* them? Putting them somewhere without windows seems an excellent idea. Humanity shall raise these cities for them, as they once built the pyramids for more human masters, although," he dropped his voice to a confidential, conversational tone, "from what I gather, I'm beginning to wonder about even that." He examined the light above the bayonet switch, but its glow was still subdued. "This is taking forever, and I am not a patient man. You cannot fight the device, madam.

Give up your vital energies and let us be done. Resistance at this time seems only inconsiderate to me."

"Clay!" Sir Donovan looked back to see William Grant in the doorway, a revolver pointed shakily at him. "Let her be, you bastard! I swear, I'll kill you if I have to!"

"Mr Grant," said Sir Donovan, turning to face him. Too late Grant saw the pistol in his hand. Sir Donovan shot him without hesitation.

Grant's revolver tumbled from his fingers to clatter uselessly to the floorboards. He fell to his knees, then pitched forward onto his face.

"An idiot to the very last, Grant," said Sir Donovan, coming over to kick Grant's pistol away. Grant groaned miserably, breathing in small, ragged gasps. "You should've just fired, you know. Now you're going to bleed to death while your lady love here turns to ashes, and I win. I want that to be your last thought, you ridiculous little charlatan. *I win.*" He glanced back at the bayonet switch just as the light flickered and suddenly blazed strong. He grunted with satisfaction, went to the cupboard and laid his hand upon the switch handle. "Perhaps I should give a little speech at this time; it seems the done thing. But, since my entire audience will be dead very soon and my words will be lost, I don't think I shall bother beyond repeating what I now realise is my favourite phrase in all the world." He grinned fiercely at Mr William Grant and Miss Cerulia Trent. "I *win!*"

He threw the switch.

CHAPTER TWENTY

ANCIENT RIVALS

Instantly the switch was closed, the wind died away and the house was suddenly quiet, the only sound being the nauseating fluting of the three great sentinels that patrolled the surrounding lanes, searching for the attackers. But, as the silence of the elements quietened, so did they, and they drew to a stop.

"There," said Sir Donovan Clay. "All it took was for the device to work for the briefest part of a second, and the barrier in time is now impassable. Your filthy race is even now finding itself in human bodies, Miss Trent. You tend to be helpless for a little while, I understand? For days or weeks, even, in some cases. My patrons will find you and destroy you before your kindred have that period of grace. Even now, they are seeking them out."

He went to the window and looked out. Across the way, the great form of one of the alien monstrosities was outlined against the night sky, elements of its flesh fading in and out of vision like Pepper's Ghost viewed through a kaleidoscope. It seemed in no great hurry to go seeking out anything at all, but only turned this way and that, apparently scanning the skies, although it was possessed of such an embarrassment of eyes it was hard to be sure. "At least," said Sir Donovan, his bluster faltering, "I was given to understand that this was their plan."

He looked into the sky then himself, and saw that every cloud had vanished away as softly and as suddenly as a Boojum snark straight from a Carroll tale. The sky was naked of clouds, and he had the strange sense it was even naked of air. He had never seen the sky so black, the light of the stars so sharp, not even while out deep in the Outback. A misgiving stirred in him then, a misgiving that quickly escalated into a grave suspicion awful enough to hollow his heart and lace it with fear. "What have you done?" he said quietly. Then, more loudly, "What have you *done*?"

Something skittered across the boards of the floor and fetched up against the side of his foot.

"There," croaked Grant. "You're going to die, Clay. We all are, but I cherish your miserable, painful death so much more than my own survival." He grimaced and it may have been the pain, or a smile, or simply the bared teeth of a cornered animal.

"I, too," said Miss Trent through the pain as the chair continued its dreadful work. "You... are the greatest monster here... your death is... is a blessing..."

Sir Donovan reached down and picked up the item Grant had thrown across the floor. He had seen something like it before. Indeed, hadn't he killed the traitorous Mathias for intending to replace this very item with something else, the function of which he had never divined? So, if this was here, what was in the device in the cellar? He guessed whatever it was, it was a close cousin of the trinket for which Mathias had died. He thought of Miss Trent, salted away there in the corner, working diligently on something.

Of course.

Of course, she had sent Grant to carry out a substitution. Of course. It was all so clear to him now that it was impossible to do anything about it. He considered the irony. If the Yithian had occupied a male body, Clay would have ordered a search, but some last faint glimmering thread of social courtesy had driven such a thought of having Miss Trent thus discommoded from his mind. He laughed a little humourless laugh. What was about to happen had been allowed to happen because of a stupid instinctive act of unthinking chivalry.

"Well," he said to no one in particular, "this is a pretty pass."

In the sky, the stars – sharp as needles – were going out. Not all of them at once and, indeed, not even all of them at all, but against the Stygian black of space, stars winked out in patches here and there and, as Sir Donovan watched, he received the impression that these areas of darkness were moving. The thing in the lane hooted a complex cry of clashing, discordant crescendos and diminuendos. Sir Donovan did not speak fluent abomination, but it seemed upset.

"I suppose that you're right," he said to Grant, "but never

let it be said that Donovan Clay did not face death with his fists up." He went back to the switch cupboard where the open box of pistol ammunition sat where he had left it.

"Your revolver's useless against them, Clay," said Grant. He tried to laugh – clearly, the optimism of Clay's action amused him greatly – but the pain no doubt drained the humour from the moment.

"I dare say," said Sir Donovan. He studied the pistol for a moment – an artefact of the ingenuity of man and, like so many such artefacts, entirely inadequate for the task in hand – and then abandoned it by the ammunition on the shelf. "I dare say."

The ceiling vanished, torn away along with the room above it, a corner of the attic, the roof, and a chimney stack. The timbre of the crash that followed indicated that the discarded segment of house had landed perhaps a hundred yards away.

Sir Donovan looked up into the countenance, if it may be dignified thus, of the Enemy. "Before you start," he said, his voice tired, "I must point out that I have no idea what has gone awry."

The monstrosity ululated and thrashed, the embodiment of fury. Sir Donovan pressed on.

"I cannot understand you when you carry on in such a fashion. Let us be calm, and decide upon our next move. We are not without assets, after all." He nodded at Miss Trent, noting that she was slumped in the great chair, exhausted but no longer in pain. The wrecking of the corner of the house had plainly damaged the electrical wiring. He could see a shattered gas pipe nearby, hissing uselessly as it vented coal gas into the air. "We have a Yithian."

This did not seem to appease the Enemy. Beyond it, another blasphemous form stalked heavily into sight in the lane.

Sir Donovan sighed through his nose and tried one last time. "I would remind you that I am your only human agent of note, that – by the offices of honour and capital – I am powerful among the peoples of Earth, and that the device is reparable, using this ..." he held up the module Grant had replaced and then ill-advisedly given to Sir Donovan in a show of hubris and bravura. "I merely need time to gather more suitable minds to give the device new energy and–"

The thing in the lane piped a tune of bitter failure and indicated the sky by its attention. The moving dark patches were growing larger. No, the humans present realised. They were growing *nearer*.

Sir Donovan, who had recently discovered a proclivity to realise the truth a shade too late, sighed once more. "Oh, shit," he said, disregarding the presence of a lady, of sorts.

Lying in pain and with his lifeblood leaking over his fingers, William Grant could not be sure that what he saw was real or illusion. Was the darkness growing thinner? Where those places of darkness blacker than space fading away? Behind each one, was there some dreadful moth fluttering down from the heavens? Deformed, clumsy insects beneath great grey and brown wings, but the body of each as large as a man?

The abomination in the garden turned its attention back to Sir Donovan, and its anger was as palpable as choking smoke. Sir Donovan threw the cloth off the lightning gun he had stored in the dining room cupboard, hefted the weapon to his shoulder, and shot the Enemy clean through its largest and angriest eye.

The electrical discharge seemed to flicker through the whole corpus of the great monstrosity, for it exited in an attenuated crackle of blue fire, and a slab of foul, unnatural meat the size of a sideboard crashed into the garden to the cost of a bed of geraniums. Possessed of only one leg, it should not have been able to stagger, yet somehow it did so, seemingly mortally wounded, and shocked in all senses of the word. It fell back still further, and then collapsed, crushing a gap in the hedge and splintering the garden door in the process.

"You see?" said Sir Donovan to Grant. "Everything and everybody respects force. Now we may begin negotiations." He walked out into the desecrated night, but while his walk retained a suggestion of his usual swagger, it was only a suggestion. His words were bold and defiant, but his tone was tired and even defeated. It was not the voice of a man going to meet with his equals, but with the gallows. Despite which, he managed to put some fire into his voice when he bellowed to the watching creature, "Well, you devil? I can still give you the world. What has your godless, boneless, joyless lot got to offer me in return, eh?"

There was a horrid, wet slicing sound, and a gaping wound appeared in Sir Donovan's back and continued clean through him. It took away several vertebrae with it in a spray of meat, blood, and bone that must surely have included much of his heart. Grant knew he must have died instantly, and all he was seeing was the spasms of a fresh corpse, but Sir Donovan nevertheless seemed to look up and back behind him, as if raging at something that wasn't there. Then his face grew slack, and his head lolled forward.

Horribly, however, he did not fall. Instead, he was slowly hefted into the air, the lightning gun falling from his hands as he rose up ten then twenty feet. The third creature slowly faded into existence, one of its flagella running clean through the corpse. It held it up, and Grant was reminded of Sir Donovan's action when he had studied his useless pistol only a minute or so before. Then, like Sir Donovan, it discarded its burden, directing a serpentine wave along the flagellum that sent the body whirling off into the night.

The two surviving creatures turned to face the swarm of great malevolent insects that were descending. From one, then two, then dozens of them, violet fire spat in long, liquid strokes, striking the monsters and tearing at them.

"What are those things in the sky?" said Grant. Summoning his last dregs of strength, he climbed to his feet and addressed himself once more to freeing Miss Trent from the chair.

"Mathias's people. They have come a very long way indeed to save him. I do not know how they will take the news of his death." There was something in her voice that made Grant pause for a moment. It could have been anything. It could have been emotion.

The night was lit with the sickening pale fire of the insects' weapons. The enemy of the Great Race of Yith were howling and piping, and the air above was in torment with their efforts to defend themselves, but they faced a foe that knew them of old and that was disinclined towards mercy. Grant ignored it all. His world consisted of the problem of undoing the chair's restraints and this he focussed on at the cost of all else, because to see the war in the air was to consider it, and to consider it was to court madness.

The straps were slick with his own blood, and he almost wept with frustration. Would he bleed to death before he could perform this one simple task? It was all too much, and in concerning himself so, he was able to ignore the crash of one great falling body, and then one more. The violet fire ceased to illuminate the night and the only sound was his laboured breathing, the slowing heartbeat in his ears, and the beat of great wings.

Something entered the room through the wrecked end, but he ignored it. Miss Cerulia Trent said something in a language that had surely never been intended to be spoken by anything as simple as a larynx, but he ignored that too, though the urgency in her voice was obvious, and he disregarded the short soft, whirring conversation that followed. He could not, however, ignore it when a wiry arm ending with a complex hand that bore too many phalanges, none of which were what he would identify as a finger, reached by him, and cut the straps as easily as a pair of secateurs deadheads a rose. Grant sat heavily on the floor and looked up at Miss Trent. It seemed absurd to look at Lizzie Whittle and wonder if he would ever see Lizzie Whittle again, or even see anyone ever again. He felt like he was fading away, growing thinner and more transparent with every second, until his heart would stop and he would have no more concerns again.

"Am I to die?" he asked.

She did not answer, but touched his side and, when she took her hand away, saw the blood staining it. Again, she spoke in the language of Mathias's people, and Grant had the impression of the room clearing of many new strangers. A minute later and he heard a heavier tread. He looked up to see Charlie Nine-Fingers being hurried at weapons point by the grey, brown, and green figures he studiously avoided looking directly upon.

Charlie was pale and sweating, but did not have to reach very far into his reserves to find sufficient wherewithal to comment, "You keep some fucking strange company, Bill Grant."

"He has been shot," said Miss Trent. "Please, help him."

"Has he now?" Charlie came to Grant and wheeled him around so he might more easily see the damage wrought by the bullet. Grant cried out when Charlie probed the wound with his finger. "Ah, shut up, you lead-swinging sod." Then to Miss Trent, "Lot of blood, I know, but it glanced off 'is ribs. Probably cracked one, so that's got to hurt, I expect. I knows a feller at the hospital in Whitechapel'll stitch 'im up a treat, give 'im a drop of physic, and have 'im home afore breakfast, no questions asked." He nodded at the attendant shapes. "That's if these kind folk'll let us go."

"We must go. They intend to sterilise this house and grounds out to a range of a hundred yards in all directions."

"Sterilise? You what?"

"They're going to blow the place up, Charlie," whispered Grant. "Any of your fellers who survived, get them together. We have to run for it."

"You? Run? I don't think so, do you?" Charlie hoisted him up as a child might lift a rag doll, and hefted him over his shoulder, ignoring his grunts of pain. "You're gonna bleed all over me, aren't you? You owe me a jacket, Bill, my lad. Come along, miss. Best not to upset the moths by dawdlin.'"

William Grant felt relieved as the pain became less sharp, but then felt perhaps this should concern him as, despite Charlie's expert diagnosis, he was actually dying. But as the pain faded, so did his consciousness along with it. He was only faintly aware of the jogging motion as he was carried at a dogtrot through the gate and onto the lane, and so towards Barking Town. He fell asleep, or possibly died a little, soon after that, but was reawakened by a sudden brilliant flash of the most intense white light that made no sound, although Charlie supplied the silence with some highly imaginative swearing. Then, as the sky darkened, so did Grant's mind until he was no longer aware of anything at all.

CHAPTER TWENTY-ONE

HAIL, AND FAREWELL

Detective Sergeant Bradley was not in the slightest part surprised to be summoned to the office of Detective Inspector Craddock. After all, he had been directly responsible for rousting a number of surprised citizens in the wilds east of Barking Town from their welcoming dinner tables and warm hearths on the vague grounds that there was some great disaster brewing. That the disaster had actually materialised and that a curious period of meteorological eccentricity and strange lights in the sky had culminated in a great white flash that excavated a shallow crater some two hundred yards or so in diameter, turning the soil to glass and festooning the area with fine white ash, and that this area centred on where the house of noted industrialist and entrepreneur Sir Donovan Clay had been, only served to mute the questions pertaining to Bradley's remarkable conduct for the space of a day.

During that day, he had written two reports. One explained that he had gone to speak with Sir Donovan pursuant to his enquiries into Sir Donovan's conduct with respect to experimenting with a novel new formulation for an explosive. He had explained previously to Sir Donovan that Barking was not ideal for such tests. A later interview with Sir Eberhard Jackson, the retired judge, made him believe that Sir Donovan was ill-advisedly attempting a very dangerous experiment at the house that very evening and, in a surplus of caution, he decided to evacuate the area. This caution, as subsequent events demonstrated, was well founded.

That report was in all respects the truth, or Bradley would not have put his signature upon it. But this he had only done after a long conversation with a man from the Home Office. Even so, it troubled him that the statement, while the truth, was not the whole truth and therefore neither was it nothing but the truth, for a lie of omission is a lie nonetheless.

He was a great deal more content with the second, longer report, which included everything without exception. He fully expected it to be nestling in a fireplace by that evening, but he had done his duty and faithfully recorded everything. It was all he could do, and he had to be content with that.

This report now sat on Craddock's desk. Craddock shoved the pot of tobacco towards Bradley. "Fill your pipe, lad. There's much to discuss."

"I'd rather not, sir." Bradley knew that he was about to be dismissed from the force. They would dress it up honourably, of course – the man from the Home Office had promised as much – and he would get a full pension despite his youth, he had no doubt. It would, naturally, be contingent of him remaining close-mouthed about the whole affair. As if anyone would ever believe him.

Craddock looked at him a little sourly, but then nodded and his expression softened. "You've done good work, Bradley. Better than the man on the street can ever know." He tapped the full report. "This could have gone very badly indeed," he added, thereby putting the Apocalypse in its place as "Very Bad".

Bradley glanced at the fireplace. "What will happen to that report, sir? If I may ask?"

"There's a whole filing office in Whitehall packed with reports much like this. Not many that stink so highly of Doomsday, perhaps, but plenty that might widen your eyes." Craddock tapped his temple. "Invidious for the sanity, however. Not what you'd call recreational reading."

Bradley felt reasonably sure Craddock meant "injurious", but it was close enough. "Shall I return to my duties, sir?"

Craddock was still gazing thoughtfully at the file and did not appear to have heard him. "You're a good man, Bradley," he said, but then added, "I shall be sorry to lose you," so perhaps he had been listening after all.

Bradley had been sure that this was coming, but it still chilled him to hear it. He drew a deep breath, exhaled his aspirations, and said, "I see, sir."

Pride and common sense dissuaded him from a single begging word. He loved his job, but he knew the decision had already been made in an office in Whitehall – or even

Westminster – and that there was not a single thing a lowly detective sergeant might say to change it. "I shall be sorry to go."

Craddock nodded. "Our loss, Norman. Very much our loss. And Manchester's gain."

Bradley blinked. "Sir?"

"It appears there is an opening for a detective inspector in the Manchester Police CID." He smiled slightly. "Don't you *want* to be promoted?"

"I do, sir, but... I should deserve it, and I don't think I *do* deserve it. Not yet."

"Your old governor disagrees, and so do I. You saved perhaps a hundred lives immediately and heaven knows how many in the long term by acting on your initiative. Consorting with the likes of Charlie Briggs is, I admit, a novel solution to any problem that I can imagine, but it turns out that it was the right one in these circumstances. Look," he leaned back in his chair, "we all want justice to be seen to be done, but how can we possibly do so in this case? Where would we start? For one thing, if the knowledge of these creatures got out, along with the knowledge that apparently subterranean Australia is stuffed to the gunwales with them, what would that mean for our country? The world? What if some new lunatic, borne along by overarching ambition, tries to contact them? We can hardly wall Australia off and declare it out of bounds." He took up his pipe from its tray and drew on it. "There were meetings to study the viability of such a course, but there are insurmountable problems, I understand. Turns out Australia's quite big."

Bradley could not help but smile. "I've heard that, too, sir."

"Besides, speaking of Mr Briggs, the records office is in a state of conniption. Apparently his file has gone missing. Now, if it were but a slim cover, that might be understandable, but it's reputedly large enough to burden an African bull elephant. And, if that wasn't enough, those of his lieutenants have gone astray, too. How could such a catastrophe occur? The records clerks are abuzz, the hive upset. There will be questions asked. Serious and reaching questions. Questions a man inclined to honesty in all lights might wish to avoid being asked."

Craddock once more pushed the tobacco pot towards Bradley. This time he accepted.

As Bradley loaded his pipe, Craddock turned his chair to face the window and breathed out a cloud of smoke at the grubby old town beyond. "So… the old stamping ground. Manchester. Do you accept?"

Bradley went to the fire to light a spill and took a long, thoughtful moment to light his pipe as he considered. His options were few, and his mind was swift, so long before the tobacco was glowing uniformly in the bowl, he was able to give his answer.

The feller in Whitechapel did as he was bid, and made a fine job of treating Grant's wound. He did, however, point out that a good deal of blood had been lost and that Grant was to be treated with kid gloves for a week or so, and kept under close observation to watch for fever or infection.

There was indeed a bout of fever, but it was shallow and he slept through much of it, although his sleep was disturbed by his dreams and his nightmares. Miss Church stayed close through the dangerous days, but her expertise was not sorely tested, and some five days after the destruction of the house in Barking, he was well enough to leave his bed and slowly wander the house in Chiswick and its gardens.

The house was busier than it had been when he left Miss Church there the night of that desperate expedition. More adherents of what they all assured him was most certainly *not* the cult of the Secret Masters of the Time Before (they only called themselves that, and even had rituals and ceremonial clothing, but that was surely not the constitution of a cult. Grant, though reasonably sure that it was exactly that, kept his counsel) had arrived in the interim. They were all foreigners, the majority of the British chapter having died in the first assault. They were an interesting group, several of them either being the subject of a mental substitution or being someone close to a subject, with the balance made up of assorted occultists and scientists who had discovered the truth of the Great Race of Yith for themselves by other avenues.

One such scientist was a Doctor Sassan Rajavi, a Persian physician with an interest in the physics of electricity. He had startled the Yithians in their redoubt of the ancient past by developing a device that sent a signal backwards through time, although as he gamely admitted, he had no idea it did that, nor any reason to suspect it. Yithian agents were sent to investigate him and, deciding that he was likely to be sympathetic, contact had been made.

Doctor Rajavi had proved his trustworthiness on many occasions since, and so had been further entrusted with several elements of the smooth running of the cult, which is to say, the society. Apart from a signalling device – a more sophisticated version of the first machine he had built – he was also the guardian and operator of a machine vital to their operations: a beacon that allowed the Great Race of Yith to exactly locate the consciousnesses of their field agents, and thereby draw them back into their bodies in the past, transposing them with the mind originally displaced.

Grant had this explained to him twice, but still had to be sure he understood the doctor correctly by asking, "You mean, this is how I get Lizzie back?" It was, the doctor assured him, exactly the way Elizabeth Whittle would be restored to her own body in the present.

"Sometimes there are insufficient people available to offer explanations and comfort to the returned," explained Doctor Rajavi. "Our fortunes ebb and flow, as may be seen in the loss of most of the British group, with the notable exception of Miss Church. And, may I suggest, sir, yourself?"

"Oh, no," said Grant. "I was just carried along by it all."

"Ah, well, isn't that the truth for all of us? One hardly joins this group as one might a bridge club. We are brought into it by circumstances, not choice."

Grant shook his head. "I don't feel like a 'Secret Master' of anything."

Rajavi gave him a wry look. "We all of us despise that title. It was inherited from our predecessors. We would very much like to change it."

"Why don't you?"

Rajavi shrugged. "Well, we also inherited a large quantity of stationery bearing the name. When that is all used, we may reconsider."

He left to find Miss Church, leaving Grant feeling that the world of the unseen was so much more than one might imagine in most ways, yet rather smaller in others.

And so, finally, came the day when, after an exchange of signals, it was agreed that Miss Cerulia Trent would finally cease to be, and Miss Elizabeth Whittle would be returned.

As Doctor Rajavi busied himself in the next room preparing the machine, Miss Trent sat with Mr Grant drinking tea, for she had developed an appreciation of the drink, and – as the tea plant had not yet evolved back in her own time – this would be her last chance to enjoy a cup.

"Miss Church has done well with this pot," she observed quietly. "She has a tendency to allow the leaves to steep too long."

"Professional habit, I daresay," said Grant. "You can stand a spoon up in hospital tea."

They sipped in silence for several seconds.

"What was done with the man in the cellar?" asked Miss Trent suddenly.

"I understand he was driven out to Barking, and shown the crater. You know, there's quite the cottage industry for tourists out there now. Mr McMahon was told in very blunt terms that this is what is done to people like Sir Donovan Clay, and only the fact that he himself was our prisoner at the time saved him from joining his boss as fine, grey dust. Then he was accompanied to the docks, given a ticket to Australia, and told to stay away from the Great Sandy Desert when he got there. He needed no second bidding."

The silence returned for a minute or so.

"What will you do when Miss Whittle is returned?" said Miss Trent.

Grant considered. "Well, we were going to go on the continent for a bit. France, mainly. See what business we could find along the Mediterranean."

"Business?" Miss Trent sipped her tea, thinking. "Ah, yes. You are criminals."

Miss Trent said it without an ounce of deprecation, yet it displeased Grant to hear it. Charlie Briggs, now miraculously unburdened by a criminal record, had settled back into his usual business like a crocodile submerging into the Nile with nary a ripple, but Bill Grant was not Charlie Briggs. A life of peripatetic duplicity no longer felt appealing to him, only facile and unsatisfying. There had to be more to life than that.

"No," he heard himself say. "No more. We're done with that. We made our money from it. We should do something useful. Constructive, you know? Or else... well, what's it all for? What is anything for?"

Miss Trent reached over and gently touched him on the wrist. The gesture startled him, but not so much that he drew his hand away. "I shall remember you, William

Grant," she said, then withdrew her hand and returned to drinking her tea.

"I will remember you, too." Grant felt as if his mind was so full of thoughts that he could no longer discern one from another. There was much to be said, but he hardly knew how to say any of it. "Look, this is ridiculous. You and I have been through the gauntlet together and I don't even know your real name. I've *seen* it, I suppose, but I've never heard it."

"The human throat is not ideal for speaking in my native language."

"You managed it with those…" he tried to find a suitable description for Mathias's people, and could only manage, "with Mathias's people."

"That was not my language. It was theirs. In my own language, several elements of my name are both above and below the limits of human hearing and of the human throat. But, the transition from one to the other would be audible to you, and I shall attempt it for you."

She put down her cup and stood. Grant watched as she breathed slowly in and out several times, then closed her eyes, tilted back her head a little, and sang a note that started high, modulated lower in a strange looping of frequencies that seemed to propagate harmonics in its wake, and then grew deep, fading away with her breath. She stayed silent a moment, then opened her eyes and looked at him. "That is slower by far than when spoken in my own body, but the human larynx is not ideal for such usage."

"It's beautiful," said Grant, and Miss Trent smiled.

"I am very sorry." It was Doctor Rajavi at the door. "I do not mean to interrupt. But the machine, it is ready. Please, come with me."

Miss Trent and Grant followed him into the adjoining room where the machine waited on an occasional table, connected to the municipal mains via a complex nest of transformers and storage batteries intended to keep it functioning in the event of a supply failure or fluctuation. The machine itself seemed almost apologetically simple compared to the means to energise it; a rosewood box from which rose a collection of glass, crystal, and metal rods, the lattermost being of strange alloys over which the light slowly crawled in vital patterns.

"What will happen?" asked Grant.

"Very little, really. Nothing spectacular, I assure you," said the doctor. "One moment our Yithian friend will be here, the next, Miss Whittle will be back in full occupation of her body once more. It can be traumatic for the unprepared one. However, such knowledge of the far distant past, which might damage her stability of mind, shall be taken from her. It will be as if she has woken from a particularly peculiar dream, but she has the advantages that she knows why her physical form was borrowed, and that we will do all within our power to cushion the inevitable shock of the transference. Very importantly, she has a friendly face awaiting her, Mr Grant. Yours. You will be very important in helping her adjust. That cannot be overstated."

Grant nodded. "I understand." He watched as Miss Trent seated herself before the machine and placed her hands upon two metal plates mounted upon the wooden base. When she was content with the firmness of the contact between her skin and the metal, she nodded to Rajavi.

"I'm eager to see Lizzie back," said Grant suddenly to her, "but I'm sorry to see you go. We've been through some ructions you and me, haven't we, eh?" He fell silent for an embarrassed second, then added, "Anyway... safe travels, friend." Miss Trent looked at him, sudden and searchingly, and her gaze made him feel unsure. He shrugged hopelessly. "Sorry. I've heard your name, but I can't manage it."

"Are we friends, William Grant?"

He considered, then nodded in an awkward jerking action. "I think so. Better'n most I've had."

Rajavi twisted the switch.

As he had warned, the process was not spectacular. The glass rods and crystals glowed warmly for several seconds in bluish yellows that somehow did not mix their hues, all to the accompaniment of a low electrical hum. Then the glow and tone subsided together. Rajavi, who had been carefully watching the face of his pocket watch throughout, twisted the switch back to break the circuit at the prescribed moment. "There," he said. "A little underwhelming, I know, but the task is done."

"Lizzie?" Grant went to her side and crouched by her to look up into her lowered face. "Lizzie? Come on, girl. Don't make us wait for you. Lizzie?" Her eyes opened slowly and Grant saw confusion there, but that was only to be expected. "That's my Lizzie! There you are! You've been on quite the adventure, haven't you?"

She slowly took her hands from the plates and looked at their upturned palms. Then she looked him in the eye. "William Grant," she said slowly.

Grant's smile faded away. "Lizzie? Come on, Liz, you're frightening me, girl." He had spent much time imagining this moment, imagining the spark of humanity rekindling in her eyes, heralding the return of Miss Elizabeth Whittle to the year of our Lord, 1891. Now, though he looked with a needful desperation, he saw no such spark. "Lizzie?"

She shook her head. "No."

Glancing wide-eyed at her, Doctor Rajavi started going over the machine, checking every connection, every element. "It's impossible. Impossible!" he muttered as he worked. "I've done this a score of times! It has never failed!"

Grant ignored him. He felt as one feels when one wakes up, and finds oneself still in dreams. "What went wrong?" he asked her.

Her voice was quiet and, he thought, bore a note of fear. That note frightened him more than anything else he had felt since the first fateful night in the house of Sir Donovan Clay.

"I do not know," said Miss Cerulia Trent.

ACKNOWLEDGMENTS

I can honestly say that *Call of Cthulhu* is the RPG that I have probably played more than any other (its only real competitor being *Traveller*). I had read a little Lovecraft in a scattergun sort of way previously to my first game in 1983, mainly what had happened to be in anthologies, but playing *CoC* piqued my interest (the Keeper, new to the gig themselves, unleashed Nyarlathotep upon us in the first session in full red tentacle mode with predictably hilarious results) and I sought and read all of the Lovecraft canon over the next year or so. Lovecraft was a famously problematical character, although I have a sense that he was only a few therapy sessions away from being a much better man, or at least a less thunderously xenophobic one. We shall never know for sure, not unless I can source his "essential saltes" from a friendly graverobber. On consideration, I may know just the chap.

I digress. The point is that when Aconyte turned up on my doorstep at midnight during an unseasonable lightning storm and asked me if I'd like to write a *Call of*

Cthulhu novel, the answer was a conditional "Yes," the condition being whether my day job as narrative designer for Rebellion would permit me. Still, it was worth asking. Therefore, I am very grateful to the Kingsley brothers and to Rebellion for giving me the permission.

I have to say, Aconyte have been a great pleasure to work with, and I am indebted particularly to my editor, Gwendolyn Nix, for doing such a good job, and – on the occasions when I roll around screaming "Stet!" repeatedly – understanding and appreciating that I'm not just doing it to be noisome (although that's obviously part of it, too).

And, not least, I appreciate you, dear reader. I sincerely hope that you enjoyed the preceding.

JLH

March, 2024

ABOUT THE AUTHOR

JONATHAN L HOWARD is an acclaimed writer, video game designer, and BAFTA-nominated scriptwriter, well known for his darkly charming *Johannes Cabal the Necromancer* series, his Mythos-adjacent *Carter & Lovecraft* duology, and the YA science fiction *Russalka Chronicles*. He lives in the English West Country with his family.

jonathanlhoward.com
facebook.com/jonathan.howard.96199